TRAUMA

Why was the U.S. government secretly funding the most immense research project in history?

TRAUMA

Who was responsible for the strange disappearance of a group of gifted medical students years before?

TRAUMA

What was behind the keen interest shown in the project by the wealthiest, most brilliant and powerful men and women in the world?

TRAUMA

How could such famous names in the world of medicine as Dr. Preston March and Dr. Alan Fitzroy be involved in attempting to use both Dr. Alixandra Kendall's brain—and her body?

The horrifying truth will do more than hurt. It will keep on shocking long after you penetrate the ghastly, far-reaching, nightmarish depths of—

TRAUMA

Sensational Fiction from SIGNET

TRAUMA

ROBERT CRAIG

A SIGNET BOOK

NEW AMERICAN LIBRARY

PUBLISHER'S NOTE

This novel is a work of fiction. Names, characters, places, and incidents either are the product of the author's imagination or are used fictitiously, and any resemblance to actual persons, living or dead, events, or locales is entirely coincidental.

NAL BOOKS ARE AVAILABLE AT QUANTITY DISCOUNTS WHEN USED TO PROMOTE PRODUCTS OR SERVICES. FOR INFORMATION PLEASE WRITE TO PREMIUM MARKETING DIVISION, THE NEW AMERICAN LIBRARY, INC., 1633 BROADWAY, NEW YORK, NEW YORK 10019.

SIGNET TRADEMARK REG. U.S. PAT. OFF. AND FOREIGN COUNTRIES
REGISTERED TRADEMARK—MARCA REGISTRADA
HECHO EN CHICAGO, U.S.A.

SIGNET, SIGNET CLASSIC, MENTOR, PLUME, MERIDIAN AND NAL BOOKS are published by The New American Library, Inc., 1633 Broadway, New York, New York 10019

First Printing, February, 1984

1 2 3 4 5 6 7 8 9

PRINTED IN THE UNITED STATES OF AMERICA

──Prologue──

The sun's first light was just beginning to disperse an early-morning fog as Dr. Alixandra Kendall drove across the P Street bridge into the Georgetown section of Washington, D.C. The sudden vision of carefully maintained row houses poking through the receding mist was magical and Alix smiled to herself, momentarily forgetting why she was here. She needed desperately to forget the last ten hours, the last months, but she also needed to keep her anger stoked long enough to complete the ugly task begun last night. Alixandra Kendall was owed one final debt, and nothing was going to stop her from collecting it.

She eased the car into Twenty-fourth Street and tightened her grip on the steering wheel. The block was a short one, ending in a ninety-degree turn to the right onto O Street. Alix's reflexes were dulled from lack of sleep and she took the corner too wide, letting the car drift into the oncoming-traffic lane. But there was no oncoming traffic. There was only the mist evaporating as the April sun rose, and the fairy-tale streets of prestigious Georgetown lined with pristine homes and tiny, manicured front gardens. Georgetown bespoke money, success, and good living. And all Alix could think of was death.

Dr. Philip Greenspan's house was halfway up the block on the right, opposite the tennis courts. It was larger than the others and stood out more toward the sidewalk; entrance was gained through an ornate gate in a wrought-iron fence, then up several steps to the front door. In her mind Alix involuntarily began to imagine the next ten or so minutes. She'd leave the car, walk across the dewy sidewalk and up the front

5

steps to ring the bell. Then there'd be her voice edged with weariness and the surprised looks as she explained why she was there so early in the morning. Finally there'd be the inevitable invitation to come in. That was as far as she allowed herself to fantasize.

She parked in front of the Greenspans' house and sat for a minute staring into the small park opposite. She wondered if Philip and Nancy Greenspan played tennis there; if before breakfast they hustled to keep themselves young. Alix sneered at the thought; they might exercise, but they didn't have to. None of them did. And with this thought Alix's tiredness vanished. She felt as awake and as determined as she had last night when this all began. The Greenspans were the final score to be settled.

Alix rang the doorbell three times before it was answered. Philip Greenspan was still half-asleep when he opened the inner door. His eyes were puffy and his hair was wildly tousled. Although an overnight growth of beard darkened his cheeks and neck, his youthful good looks and outfit of pajamas, robe, and slippers made him look like an adolescent. But Dr. Philip Greenspan, mathematical genius, was no adolescent. Alix could vouch for that.

"What do you want?" Greenspan asked with the rude directness of someone roused from a deep sleep.

"Preston March sent me. We have to talk."

He looked Alix up and down while forcing his eyes to remain open. "March, huh? Leave it to him to get me out of bed at the crack of dawn. I guess you'd better come in." He pushed open the screen door and let her pass, then indicated the living room through a short entrance hall.

"Will you get your wife, please?" Alix's request was a demand.

"Why do you want her?"

"Preston insisted I talk to both you and Nancy," Alix said, knowing the weight March's name carried with people like the Greenspans.

He shook his head in mock disgust, then started back toward the staircase opposite the front door. Alix watched him closely. For someone twenty-five, Philip

Greenspan walked with the careful deliberation of someone twice that age. She wondered if Preston March, too, had noticed it.

As Greenspan reached the foot of the stairs, he hesitated, then smiled up at something Alix couldn't see. "We were just talking about you," he said softly.

"I'm flattered," Nancy Greenspan said as she descended into view. "But I'm not sure being the topic of any conversation is worth getting up so early."

Nancy Greenspan was a year younger than her husband. She had flawless skin that seemed pulled almost a little too tightly over her fine cheekbones; there wasn't the slightest sign she'd been asleep only minutes before. In fact, in her dainty pink peignoir and rose slippers, Nancy Greenspan looked like she'd been preparing for Alix's visit for days. She gave Philip a peck on the cheek and he escorted the two women into the living room.

"She has a message from Preston," Greenspan said to his wife, realizing he hadn't even asked his visitor's name. "It must be important to get you—and us—out of bed." He sat down next to his wife, opposite Alix.

"It's very important." Alix reached into her purse and wrapped her fingers around the familiar cold handle of the Colt Detective Special she'd become adept at using since last night. She took a deep breath, pulled the gun out, aimed it quickly, and fired.

The first shot penetrated Philip Greenspan's right eye, burrowed through his brain, and exited out the back of his skull, shattering a vase of daffodils behind him. His head lolled backward and his body arched forward. Alix fired twice again: the first bullet shattered Greenspan's larynx and spinal cord, and the second severed the superior vena cava of his heart, taking a piece of the right ventricle with it. He was dead long before his body fell to the floor.

Nancy Greenspan didn't scream. Other than pushing herself back up against the arm of the couch, she barely reacted at all. She examined her husband's body with cold calculation, then turned her attention to Alix. "In the back of my mind I always suspected something like this might happen. Who are you?"

"I'm no one," Alix said flatly.

Nancy Greenspan laughed loudly. "Of course it would be a 'no one.' The someones are all too busy making plans for the future." She sneered at Alix. "I'm not going to try to talk you out of this; you've obviously given your actions a great deal of thought. Well, I can't complain, really. I've had two chances at life, which is one more than most." She straightened the material of her dressing gown, then looked up at Alix. "Well, Miss No One, I guess you'd better finish it off."

Alix raised the gun, aimed, and pulled the trigger. The bullet caught Nancy Greenspan squarely between the eyes. Her head bobbed back, then dropped forward onto her chest. Dead, she remained seated as placidly as she had when alive. Alix left the house without looking back.

She drove out of Washington along M Street, taking one last look at the city she loved. A trickle of traffic was beginning to flow into the District from Virginia, and Alix wished she, too, were on her way in from the suburbs to work. But she was leaving. Forever. She was heading south, then west, and if they didn't find her, she'd probably live in California because it was warm and the life-style promised few pressures. Of course she'd have to change her name and her profession, but that would come in time.

An hour later, well into the lush Virginia countryside, Alix gave in to her exhaustion. She pulled off the highway onto a secondary road, then off the road entirely. All she wanted to do was sleep. She opened the windows enough to allow a light breeze smelling of spring growth to play through the car, locked the doors, and crawled into the backseat.

Everything that had happened since she'd left Boston to work for Dr. March at the Lafayette Institute in Washington seemed a dream. Even the people; most of all, the people. But none of that mattered now. Only survival mattered. She closed her eyes and said a silent prayer that when she awoke the memories would be gone. But in her heart Alix knew that if she lived to be a hundred, each day of her life would be measured out by how much of her time was spent in the past. It was the price she paid for being alive, and as she drifted off to sleep, she began to wonder if it was worth it.

—1—

Six Months Earlier

Sarah Williams fastened her mother's ivory-and-gold brooch to the lapel of her dressiest suit and stepped back from the mirror to survey the effect. The pin brought the navy-blue outfit to life, and Sarah grinned at herself. Ordinarily, jewelry—*and* clothing, for that matter—didn't interest her, but tonight it was important she look her best. Tonight Sarah had a date with Alan Fitzroy. Well, not exactly a date; an invitation to a small dinner party at his Georgetown house. But that was as good a beginning as any.

Sarah sailed into the bathroom and unearthed an ancient and almost unused bottle of cologne left over from college days. She sniffed it to make sure it hadn't gone bad, then dabbed a few drops on her wrists, throat, and behind her ears. And suddenly she felt more feminine than she had in months. Sarah's mother, dead for nearly two years now, would have been proud tonight; she had wanted her pretty daughter to have a good time while she was young and to leave the serious matters of life until later. But Sarah's only interest was medicine, and were it not for Alan's totally unexpected—and thrilling—invitation, Sarah would have spent the evening studying. Georgetown Med School hadn't earned its four-star reputation for excellence for nothing.

Sarah had met Alan Fitzroy accidentally one morning two weeks before in the hushed corridors of the Lafayette Institute while she was on a guided tour of the facility. Doing advanced medical research at Lafayette was her most cherished dream, and actually being inside had so enthralled her that she hadn't paid attention to where she was walking. In a nearly empty corridor she'd bumped into Fitzroy and practically knocked him over. If that weren't enough, recognizing him immediately as one of the most brilliant—and handsome—men on the Washington scene had rendered Sarah speechless. Had it not been for Fitzroy's infectious laughter and his devastating charm, the encounter might have proved disastrous. In fact, once he learned his "attacker" was a med student, Fitzroy's face lit up and he insisted on showing her the rest of Lafayette himself.

For that next hour Sarah was in heaven as Alan Fitzroy led her through the maze of corridors, laboratories, patient rooms, and lecture halls that made up Lafayette. She saw all of it and none of it. At home later that afternoon, all Sarah clearly remembered was the light touch of Alan's hand—twice on her arm, once on her shoulder—as he emphasized a point. She knew she was falling for him and she also knew what a waste of time that was; Alan Fitzroy was too busy and too important to indulge the fantasies of a starstruck med student. Then, several weeks later, just as she'd begun to put him out of her mind, the miracle happened: the invitation to dinner came in the mail.

Sarah scampered back into her bedroom and twirled around in front of the full-length mirror one last time. She looked good, but tonight nothing short of perfection would satisfy her. She wished her hair, which was brown and cut sensibly short, were platinum blond and long enough to swirl dramatically around her head. And her forehead seemed a little too wide and her nose a little too long. And her gray eyes looked just like mud! Why hadn't she been born ravishing *and* intelligent?

Sarah laughed at herself. She was a very attractive twenty-four-year-old woman. Everyone said so. Only, this evening she needed truly to believe it. She was head over heels in love with Alan Fitzroy. No, she intellectualized immediately, I'm *infatuated* with him. There's a great deal of difference. Being in love means I can't go to bed with him until he asks me to marry him; being infatuated means I don't have to wait.

She grabbed her coat from the closet and dashed outside into the cool early-September night.

Alan Fitzroy's house on R Street opposite Dumbarton Oaks was only a fifteen-minute walk from Sarah's Dupont Circle apartment. The house, with its stately brick facade counterpointed by black shutters and antique carriage lamps flanking the front door, stood on its own one and a half acres. Gardens bordered the house front and swept off into the darkness at the sides, filling the night with the fragrance of late-blooming roses. The circular drive was occupied by a single car—a Rolls Silver Shadow the color of freshly minted dimes.

Sarah strode up to the front door intimidated only by her feelings for Alan Fitzroy. She was acting like a schoolgirl. But I am a schoolgirl, she thought as she rang the bell, and I'll damn well act like one if I choose. This was one of the few times in her life she was allowing herself the luxury of just being a young woman instead of playing the demanding role of doctor-to-be, and the freedom was heady.

Fitzroy himself answered the door. In the brilliant back-lighting from the foyer he appeared only as a tall, dark figure of no outward importance. But Sarah knew who it was. She'd dreamed of him for weeks. And even though his face remained hidden in the shadows, she saw every detail of it in her mind. She smiled and said, "Good evening, Alan," so seductively that it scared her.

"Sarah Williams!" Fitzroy exclaimed as if she were his oldest friend returned after a prolonged absence. He reached out into the night and gently drew her into the house. "I'm so glad you could come. Let me take that." He easily slipped her coat from her shoulders and handed it to a butler who stood discreetly to one side. "Come in and meet the others."

Sarah smiled again and blushed and said nothing.
Fitzroy was elegant in an impeccable dinner jacket,
and for one brief but horrible minute she felt under-
dressed. But when she'd been ushered into the living
room (which was fully twice the size of her entire
apartment) she saw she was not alone in her in-
formality. Of the seven others in the room, three were
dressed like her and, she guessed correctly, were
students. Not only were they casually attired, but
they were at least forty years younger than the young-
est of the others.

Alan took her by the arm for a barrage of intro-
ductions. "Sarah Williams, this is Linda Strong, Jack
Finlay, Tim Donoghue," he acknowledged the other
guests. "They're in school too."

Sarah mumbled hello, noting that they looked as
uncomfortable with the grandeur of the setting as she
felt. Her eyes momentarily lingered on Linda Strong,
but once she'd evaluated the other woman's good points
and decided her own outnumbered them, Sarah relaxed.
Linda Strong was no competition for Alan Fitzroy's
affection.

"Here's our last guest," Alan was saying as he maneuvered Sarah toward a cluster of chairs where the
elderly guests sat. "This is Sarah Williams. She's in
medical school at Georgetown." He propelled her
forward, taking one step back himself.

"How do you do," Sarah said awkwardly as she
found herself under the scrutiny of eight staring eyes.
"It's very nice to be here." If Alan didn't rescue her,
she'd scream.

"She's beautiful, isn't she?" Alan stepped up to Sarah
and slid his arm around her waist. "Sarah, this is Max
Pomfrett, Antonia Watson, General Alistair"—he edged
her closer to the eldest of the four guests—"and this is
Gretel Heilbrunn."

"How do you do, my dear." Gretel Heilbrunn bowed
her head slightly, then extended her hand to take
Sarah's. "It's such a pleasure to meet you." The old
woman was dressed in a black evening dress long past
its prime. Her yellowed hair was piled high on her
head, and a small tiara was tucked discreetly into its

configuration. The fingers of her ancient hands were smothered with diamond rings in old-fashioned settings, and several strands of pearls adorned her sagging neck. Gretel Heilbrunn reflected a vanished elegance that was austere and cold. Perhaps she was a stray Hapsburg or a countess of the Austro-Hungarian Empire. But whatever she was, Gretel Heilbrunn was definitely taken with Sarah Williams.

"Come and sit down by an old woman," she urged softly.

"There'll be time for that later," Alan said immediately.

"I would prefer, Alan, to speak to Miss Williams now, while I have the chance." Gretel's eyes grew colder and her mouth froze into an insincere smile.

"It's all right, Alan," Sarah said to be helpful. "I don't mind."

"Well, I do," he snapped back, dropping the congenial facade. Then, seeing the surprise on Sarah's face, he immediately softened his tone. "Dinner will be served shortly. We can all get acquainted then. Now, let me get you a drink."

"Just a ginger ale, please." Alcohol made Sarah's head feel fuzzy, and tonight she needed to keep her wits about her.

"Sarah, this is a party," Alan chided. "You must have champagne. I insist. Just one glass?" He snapped his fingers and the butler appeared with a silver tray laden with full champagne glasses. "I want to propose a toast," Alan announced.

Everyone fell silent. The only sounds were the hushed tread of the butler on the thick carpeting and the clink of crystal against crystal. Sarah stole another look at Gretel Heilbrunn. The old woman was staring back at her, appraising Sarah as if she were something about to be purchased. Gretel Heilbrunn. Where had she heard that name before?

"Everyone have a glass?" Alan surveyed the room. "Good. Now, a toast: To the future. To life . . . everlasting." He raised his glass in a salute, then brought its rim back to his lips and drank. The others followed suit.

Sarah tasted her champagne and wrinkled up her nose. It tasted sour to her, and once again, as she always did when she drank champagne, she wondered why people made such a fuss about it. It was really just grape juice gone bad. But Alan wanted her to have it. She watched him now. Alan Fitzroy was so handsome, so proper. And proving to be an enigma. One minute he could be charming and lovely like when he'd taken her on the tour of Lafayette, and the next he could be abrupt and unpleasant, like when he'd refused to let her talk to Gretel Heilbrunn.

Gretel Heilbrunn.

Of course. The gates of Sarah's memory suddenly opened. That old woman, that ancient dowager, was the most famous woman scientist alive today. Before World War II she'd worked in Germany perfecting rocket propulsion. When the war came, she fled to the United States and continued her research. Had it not been for that German connection (it was felt that her work was in part responsible for the blitzing of London), Mrs. Heilbrunn would certainly have won a Nobel Prize. For over forty years she'd been an integral part of the U.S. space program and only recently had been forced to retire because of ill health.

The champagne was making Sarah feel drowsy. She looked around the room to keep herself alert. Alan was talking to the students, and the others seemed to be whispering among themselves. What were their names? Max Pomfrett—*the* Max Pomfrett, the brilliant mathematician? And Antonia Watson—the economic strategist, adviser to five presidents? General Alistair—George Alistair, once head of the joint chiefs of staff? Was it really possible that little Sarah Williams from Fall River, Massachusetts, was about to break bread with four of the greatest minds the twentieth century had produced?

The idea made Sarah laugh out loud. Or maybe it was the champagne. In any case, everyone stopped talking and stared at her. "I'm sorry, but this is all so silly. Imagine me in a roomful of such famous people." No one said a word, and she grew more and more uncomfortable. "I'm not used to drinking, you see. And I'm also not used to hobnobbing with great minds."

Gretel Heilbrunn was the only one to respond. "I quite understand your discomfort. My friends and I are not used to 'hobnobbing' with such young, vital people, either."

Linda Strong was the first to drop her champagne glass. It tumbled from her hand and fell to the carpet, leaving a wide, dark stain. Linda stared down at it in disbelief; then her eyes fluttered and closed. She fell into Alan's arms and he quickly placed her in a high-backed chair. Jack Finlay and Tim Donoghue started toward Linda in unison, but they dropped their glasses and pitched forward too, into the arms of Fitzroy and the butler.

"This isn't supposed to be happening," Sarah said thickly. "Must be the champagne."

"Of course it's the champagne." Alan came up alongside her. "Let me take your glass." He lifted it effortlessly from her hand. "Come and sit down."

"No, thank you. I'd better go home." Sarah started toward the front door, but her legs buckled and she fell to the floor.

"For God's sake, don't let her injure herself," Gretel Heilbrunn shouted.

Everything was getting soft and hazy. Sarah smelled the wool of the carpet and decided she'd just lie there a minute and rest. It was so comfortable, so peaceful. In a while she'd get up and have dinner with Alan and the others. And maybe later, if she were lucky, he'd take her home. But right now she needed sleep. She closed her eyes and let the waves of velvety darkness rise from her feet to her waist and up until they finally closed over her head. There was nothing to worry about. Ever.

—2—

"Ladies and gentlemen, we are now making our final approach into Washington's National Airport. Please return your seats to the upright position and fasten your seat belts. Also please observe the no-smoking signs and extinguish all smoking materials. Thank you."

Alix Kendall heard the stewardess's disembodied voice over the 727's speaker system, but the words meant nothing to her; her mind was too far in the past to be brought back to today by something as insignificant as landing instructions. She'd drifted back ten years to when she was twenty-two. That year Alix was in her first year of med school at Georgetown. She was away from her parents in Chicago for the first time and she felt the world was hers for the asking. Ten years ago Washington was an exciting place, a new world, a city with a rich history and an exciting life-style that was as different from Chicago as the grind of premed was from the thrill of a real hospital. She'd taken to the city like it was an older, experienced, and infinitely tender lover.

If only that brief happiness were all Alix remembered of Washington . . . but it wasn't.

The plane banked sharply left then; as it righted itself, the captain cut the engines to bring the craft down to landing speed. For a moment Alix felt weightless and, worse, vulnerable. To counter this she immediately pulled herself forward in her seat and began massaging the stiff knot of muscles in her neck, hoping to release the tension. It was no use. Today it wasn't the flight that frightened her, it was the thought of landing. She bit her lower lip and concentrated on

the pain, thinking it might keep her mind in the
present, but it was no good. Alix had sipped of the
past, and now she would have to drink fully of it.

Ten years before, she'd loved Washington with a
passion because Richard was there. Richard Hailey
had been her whole life, and if the accident hadn't
happened, they surely would have married, had
children, and remained in the District to pursue
their separate medical careers. But the accident *had*
happened. And Washington had become a tomb from
which she fled, promising herself never to return. Yet,
here she was again, high over the city, the magnifi-
cent view distorted by her tears. She was back because she'd allowed Dr. Preston March to make her
see she was wasting her life hiding in the labyrinth of
the Massachusetts Technological Hospital.

Preston March was a famous man. He'd had his
portrait on the cover of *Time* magazine, he'd been
interviewed on television numerous times, and he was
the author of a series of science books for the layman
that had become international best-sellers. His gift—
apart from his medical brilliance, particularly in the
field of the study of aging—was his unfailing ability
to make anything comprehensible to the average mind,
even the vast intricacies of the human body. In person
March had a way of talking that immediately put the
listener at ease, as if this famous man's only goal in
life at that moment was to make himself understood
no matter how much time it took. In print, one could
almost hear his voice reading the prose, and the effect
was the same.

March had contacted Alix after reading a series of
articles she'd written for *The New England Journal of
Medicine* in which she'd outlined her theories on the
function of the thymus gland in aging. Because Alix
had little time for research, the articles were based
partially on her own experiments, partially on the
vast amount of reading she did on the subject, and
largely on hypothesis. They had caught March's eye
because her dedication to the subject and her expertise were obvious and, as he later explained to her, he
too was very interested in this particular field of

medicine. In fact, he believed the study of aging was the key to the future of mankind.

"It's not like we're trying to turn everyone in the world into a modern Methuselah," he said with a chuckle over the ebullience of the diners at Boston's Durgan Park restaurant; he'd actually flown up from Washington to see her. "But if we scientists never tried to attain the unattainable, the world economy would still be based on the speed of a horse-drawn cart!"

Alix just smiled at the thought. Preston March was seductively charming, but Alix wanted—needed—to remember that this dinner was not merely a social event. Although March assiduously avoided the subject of her research, he hadn't come all this distance just for a hearty slice of the restaurant's justly famous roast beef. She'd already told him earlier in the week when he first called that she wasn't interested in leaving Mass Tech to work for him at the Lafayette Institute, of which he was director, but he said he wanted to meet her nonetheless. What could Alix do but agree?

Preston March was in his early seventies but gave the impression of being a man ten years younger. It wasn't that his body didn't show signs of age—he had some difficulty moving about easily, in fact—but the intensity of his speech, the lofty flights of his intellect, were genuinely youthful. March most often spoke in a low-pitched machine-gun staccato that forced Alix to lean closer, creating an air of intimacy that unnerved her. March's blue eyes sparkled with enthusiasm when he discussed science, and often, in a wild gesticulation of his head, shocks of his white hair whirled over his forehead like a miniature snowstorm. Alix decided that Preston March was a brilliant and handsome man who knew it; and who also knew how to use this persona whenever he wanted something from someone—which was exactly why he'd invited her to Durgan Park that night.

"Now, tell me, Dr. Kendall, why exactly is it that you want to stay in the backwater of Boston when you could be in the mainstream in Washington with me at the Lafayette?"

March was so seemingly ingenuous that Alix laughed out loud at the question. "I'd hardly call Boston a backwater, particularly when comparing it to Washington, the original sleepy Southern town." She speared an oversized shrimp bloodied with cocktail sauce, lifted it from its bed of lettuce, and deftly bit it in two. "I'm happy in Boston, that's why. I'm happy with my work here."

"Your *work*!" he spit out. "Your work, as you put it, is being nothing more than a sawbones. When do you use that mind of yours? How much time do you have for research?" he pushed on mercilessly. "How many hours a week do you sandwich in between your rounds, teaching classes, the mundane hackwork that's passed off as modern medicine?"

His cynicism startled Alix. She hadn't really expected another Albert Schweitzer. Still. . . . "It's true, I don't get as much time to work on my own projects as I'd like to, but—"

"But what?" March interrupted, shaking his head. "Maybe you're just one of those people who, deep down, is afraid of success, real success. Is that it, Alix? Will you only allow yourself to go so far before you have to draw back?"

"That's nonsense," she quickly defended herself.

"Then prove it! I'm offering you a position with the Lafayette Institute. Do you realize what that means? Do you know how many scientists would give their left arm for that chance?" He shook his head again, and then, as suddenly as it had begun, the tantrum subsided. He smiled now and touched her arm. "What *am* I going on about? Here I sit having a wonderful dinner with a beautiful woman, and I'm ranting and raving like an old fool. Will you forgive me?"

"No harm done," she assured him, though she was still somewhat taken aback by his outburst. Obviously Preston March was the kind of man who was used to getting his own way, no matter who got hurt—or crushed—in the process.

"You mustn't let me badger you about working for

me. If you really don't want to, I'll accept that . . .
whether I understand it or not."

Alix smiled now, beginning to catch on to his ploy.
He was a sly one, all right. He had a way of making
her feel as if a refusal to work at the Lafayette were
not only groundless, no matter what arguments might
be used, but, if pursued, was a sure sign of incipient
madness. Maybe he was right. After all, exactly why
wasn't she willing at least to visit his precious Lafayette Institute? It was the most prestigious private
research center in the country—probably the world—
and with its director squarely behind her, Alix could
write her own ticket; that wasn't exactly something to
be ignored. Then what was it?

It was returning to Washington, of course, and the
fear of the past. But one day Alix would have to face
it; she couldn't go on grieving for her lost youth forever.
It was too romantic an idea, too much the stuff of
weepy eighteenth-century novels. In reality, pining
for her lost love had caused her nothing but pain.
Since Richard's death Alix had slowly become something of a spinster, despite her beauty and her desir-
ability to men. She was aware of her withdrawal from
the world into the protective cocoon of science, but it
had never seemed to affect her directly before, not like
it was now. Turning down Preston March's invitation
to inspect the Lafayette was one, two, a hundred steps
backward into the cold, dark past.

"All right, Preston, I'll come to Washington for a
weekend," she said suddenly, feeling the relief almost
immediately.

"Promise?"

March sounded so much like a little boy who'd finally gotten his way that she laughed. "I won't let you
down. Just give me a week or so. We'll talk."

March joined in her laughter and they finished dinner without again alluding to her work in Washington.

As the plane descended over the glistening Potomac
River toward its landing at National Airport, Alix
unconsciously gripped the arms of the seat. It was so
easy to say she'd fly down from Boston, so easy to call

the airline and make a reservation. But now that her
arrival was a reality, Alix was afraid of what she
might feel being back. She forced herself to pay attention to the endless vistas out the window, and as she
did, the clouds that seemed to have buoyed up the
aircraft since takeoff parted and Washington came
into view.

Most evident to Alix were the familiar monuments
duplicated on a million postcards sent by tourists to
thousands of hometowns every year. Alix traced a mental path from the Lincoln Memorial along the Mall to
the Washington Monument, then finally to Capitol
Hill. The richly ornate Capitol Building still gave her
an inordinate feeling of pride. All at once, from
nowhere, Alix remembered a wonderfully warm spring
day; she and Richard had walked from Memorial Bridge
to Capitol Hill, never letting go of each other's hands
for one minute. Richard again! Alix had loved him so
much, had cherished him in a way she could never do
again. And where had it gotten her?

"Excuse me, miss. You'll have to put your seat up."

Alix turned to the flight attendant with a start. "I
beg your pardon?"

"We're about to land ... your seat must be fully
upright." The attendant—a young, blond woman who
was cocktail-waitress-pretty—smiled indulgently at her
delinquent charge as she leaned forward and pushed
Alix's seat button. The chair immediately sprang
forward, pushing Alix into an upright position. "It's
just a precaution. You understand."

Yes, Alix understood. Precautions were something
you took when you suspected there might be danger.
When you thought you were safe, when it was difficult to imagine any harm coming to you or to those
you loved, you let your guard down. Like she'd done
ten years before. The last time Richard kissed Alix
good-bye (it was a peck on the cheek, really, because
she was in bed with the flu), there was no precautions,
no prescriptions of "Be careful" or "Watch your step."
It was just a routine good-bye. Richard Hailey was out
on a lark that day. He was one of four students who'd
been invited to take a tour of the ultramodern Lafay-

ette Institute Annex in the Virginia countryside at
Langley.

But the trip wasn't so routine after all. Late in the
afternoon Alix received the call that changed her life:
there had been an accident, a terrible accident; Richard's
car had been sideswiped by a bus. It had gone off the
road into a ravine. The car's gas tank had exploded.
Richard and his three friends were incinerated. The
bodies had been taken to the Lafayette Annex and
were autopsied there; the report stated that the four
young people had all received massive physical trau-
mas in the collision—they would have died even if it
weren't for the fire. So there was nothing to be done.
It was that simple. Richard was dead. And Alix was
alive. And all the precautions in the world couldn't
have changed that.

The plane landed with a shuddering lurch, and Alix
gasped audibly. She hadn't been in Washington even
a minute, and already she was inundated with the
memories she'd always tried so hard to master. Had it
not been for Preston March's promise not to pressure
her about taking the position at the Lafayette and her
own promise to herself to make at least one attempt to
start her life over yet again, Alix never would have
taken the trip to Washington. But somewhere deep
inside, Alix knew that this might be her last chance
to break out of the comfortable pattern of life in Boston,
the last chance to explore a new life before time and
her own fear locked her in forever.

Twenty minutes later, in a taxi racing along the
Virginia side of the Potomac toward her interview
with Dr. March at the Lafayette's headquarters on the
outskirts of Georgetown, Alix began to relax somewhat.
She couldn't—wouldn't—allow ancient history to interfere with this new life she was being offered. After all,
she was stronger than ever before in her life, she was
highly respected in her profession, and that made her
more self-confident. Washington was just a city. Like
Boston. Living here, if she decided to do so, would be
no different than living in Massachusetts; it was another beautiful city sprawling along a river with a

different name, that's all. Sure, there would be reminders of . . . the past . . . but making her stand here once and for all would be good for her. It would help exorcise her personal ghosts.

Even though it was faster to take Key Bridge into Georgetown, Alix instructed the cabbie to drive across Memorial Bridge, then down M Street. She would begin facing her fears squarely; confronting the Lincoln Memorial was as good a way as any to start. The taxi sailed easily along the highway through the scant midmorning traffic. Alix leaned back and nestled in her favorite coat—beige cashmere with an extravagant fox collar—and momentarily felt truly optimistic. For too many years she'd let the past define itself and, in doing so, had made Richard's death the focus of her life. Alix had read enough elementary psychology to know this was morbid, at best. But now, like someone who has been thrown from a horse and remounts immediately, Alix was ready to start over as if nothing had ever happened. True, ten years had passed, but it wasn't too late. After all, the past couldn't harm her.

The Lafayette Institute was on the District side of the Potomac, just beyond Key Bridge. Nestled in a heavily wooded and carefully landscaped area along the river, the Institute's buildings might have afforded a lovely view out over the Potomac and Georgetown, had its somber gray-tinted glass not kept natural light and scenery out, while at the same time keeping an artificial glare in. The main building was a stark five-story structure whose unbroken angularity was a mathematician's dream and an artist's nightmare.

The main building was connected to a smaller three-story duplicate by a glassed-in corridor; this was the patient wing, and other than the walkway, there was no entrance from the grounds—for security reasons. It was explained to Alix later that there had once been a front entrance, but during the turmoil of the late 1960's a group of agitators protesting covert and inhuman experimentation had broken in and barricaded themselves in the hallways. The charges, of course, were denied vehemently, but the attendant publicity was very negative, and from that day on, security at the Lafayette was extraordinary.

Alix stepped from the cab and took in a deep breath. A chill wind blew along the river and knifed through her coat; she looked at the twin Institute buildings and shivered. The umbilical corridor made the patient building totally dependent on the research building. Like mother and child, she thought as she paid the driver. Or more like people being so dependent on science, on medicine, was her second thought. And for one moment Alix realized that it wasn't the wind that had made her shiver, it was the buildings themselves and what they stood for—research, in the name of humanity to be sure, but in spite of humanity if need be; that was the Lafayette's reputation.

As Alix approached the Institute's front doors, they slid silently open, revealing a dark, cool lobby whose stainless-steel-paneled walls glistened with an icy brilliance. She stepped into the abyss almost gingerly and was immediately confronted by a stern-faced young guard who seemed to have come from nowhere. Alix explained her business, and after two phone calls, the guard was joined by another who took her suitcase and escorted her deeper into the building.

"Dr. March is expecting you; he's on five," the guard said as they turned a corner and entered a long, silent corridor which ended in a bank of elevators.

Alix smiled and nodded but said nothing. She was awed by the Lafayette and surprised by her reaction. In her career she'd been a stranger in hospitals before, in private institutions like this one—first as a student, then as an intern, and finally as a resident—but never before had she felt so uncomfortable, so totally alien. Except for herself and the solemn guard, the Institute's hallways were conspicuously empty. This surprised Alix only because she'd imagined she'd find the halls full of robots and automatons, sleek, efficient machines that did what had to be done without emotion, then moved on to the next project. And when she and the guard did pass an office filled with people—real people—her surprise was doubled, for they truly looked out of place.

By the time they'd entered the elevator, ridden to
five, and walked into Preston March's office, Alix was
nearly breathless from . . . What? Anxiety? Fear?
Maybe. Or maybe it was just plain excitement. She'd
been so cooped up at Mass Tech, so confined to her
own little world, that anything new was bound to
startle her. Alix hated to admit it, but she was beginning to see that she'd grown stale up in Massachusetts;
she'd forgotten how exhilarating it was to travel, how
very much alive it made her feel.

Like the rest of the Lafayette, Preston March's suite
of rooms was decorated with ultramodern furniture.
The blackness of the walls was offset by a pearl-gray
industrial carpeting which in turn complemented the
muted taupes of the furniture. Everything was subdued.
Everything said quiet, expensive good taste. Everything said that this office was a place where serious
work was done by serious people. It was not the kind
of room where laughter was often heard.

March's secretary, a hard, sharp-faced middle-aged
blond, buzzed him, then showed Alix into the inner
sanctum of the Lafayette Institute's director. Although
she knew the sun was shining brightly outside, Alix
was surprised to find the room grimly shadowed, the
light diffused into somber puddles that stained the
carpeting. But March himself made up for any lack of
cheerfulness. He was as chipper as ever, and as
Alix entered, he rose, smiling.

"Well, Dr. Kendall, how do you like the Lafayette so
far?" he asked, taking both her hands in his. "Is it
what you imagined?"

"It's far more than I imagined, Preston," she said
easily. "I can almost feel energy in the air."

March nodded sagely. "It's one of the reasons working at the Lafayette is so highly prized. By some. . . ."
His smile faded momentarily, as if he'd suddenly remembered that Alix was here, if not against her will,
then against her better judgment. But the smile returned again twice as big. "I've arranged for you to
stay close by, in Georgetown. We own several town
houses which are made available to select staff members and guests. You should like it there, and if you

do decide to give us a go, it'll be your permanent residence, gratis."

"Thank you," Alix said demurely, thinking: You sly devil. Tempt me with money, cushy jobs, town houses in Georgetown! What next?

"Now, before we get into any real serious discussions, why don't you come with me? I'd like you to meet some members of our Aging Sector." March rose rather unsteadily from his chair, then guided Alix out into the hallway and back to the bank of elevators.

They were whisked down two stories to the third floor, and as the door opened, Alix realized just how tight the security at the Lafayette was. Two guards stood directly in front of them, their hands hovering lightly over their holsters as if they were ready for any eventuality. When they recognized March, however, they touched their hats in an informal salute and returned to parade-rest positions.

"There's a great deal of highly classified information here," he said, explaining away the guards' readiness. "And we have had some unpleasantness in the past." He then explained about the protesters, not bothering to disguise his disgust for people of their ilk. "Imagine them accusing us of such work! Why, even if it were true, what business is it of theirs? The day the rabble leads this scientific world is the day the lights go out forever."

March touched Alix lightly on the back and guided her down a hallway. "This is a restricted part of the Institute, one that only the privileged have access to. This is where you'll work, of course"—he smiled—"if you decide to join us."

"And this section works in conjunction with the rest of the Institute?" Alix wasn't clear whether the Lafayette's research was homogeneous or whether it had splintered off into distinct fields.

"The Lafayette deals with aging, of course. We are attempting to solve the question of why man gets old; and conversely, how to stop it. All work that is done here has something to do with the aging process and the perpetuation of life. Each section is autonomous. You'll do your work, and the other sections, theirs."

"Sounds rather like a production line," Alix said tartly. Whether intended or not, the implication was that each section should mind its own business, and Alix didn't like being placed in anyone's "snoop" category.

"Oh, no, you miss the point: with no one person or group—save the few highly placed officials—knowing *all* about our work here, there is little chance of information leaks." When Alix looked unconvinced, he went on. "You haven't been in Washington long enough to know that it's a city of spies." He shook his head at the thought. "It wouldn't do at all to have our work spread all over the front pages of the Washington *Post*, now, would it?"

Before Alix had a chance to respond, they stopped in front of a pair of heavy steel doors. March inserted a plastic identification card into a waist-high slot, removed it, and when the doors opened, escorted Alix into a laboratory the tiled floors and walls of which were so white that the reflected light hurt Alix's eyes. At various points around the room, perhaps fifteen men and women in smocks worked intently; none of them looked up to see who had entered their domain. The far wall was covered floor-to-ceiling with metal shelves on which hundreds of jars sat, each containing a full or partial brain categorized by species, size, and weight. The sight was awesome, and Alix stopped for a moment, nonplussed.

"Most of them are monkey brains," March assured her. And even as he said the words, an inhuman shriek filled the lab. Alix involuntarily stepped backward, clutching March's arm. Now the others in the lab looked around, startled out of their deep concentration by the cries. Yet another scream filled the air, and something leaped into sight at the far end of the room. It bounced from one countertop to another, spilling various beakers and vials onto the floor in a cascade of broken glass and a rainbow of lost chemical solutions. Directly behind the creature, caroming down the aisles between the counters, was a red-faced young doctor who kept pushing at his glasses with his left hand in an attempt to keep them from falling off his nose; in his right hand he held a black box the size of a cigarette pack, which had an antenna protruding from one end.

Another screeching cry as the thing approached caused Alix to turn her attention from the running doctor toward the . . . rhesus monkey, she now realized, greatly relieved that it wasn't the monster she'd somehow expected. The monkey scampered low to the ground at an alarming speed, now and again crashing into a nearby cupboard because of the difficulty it seemed to be having in keeping its balance. The crown of the rhesus' head had been shaved and a series of wires embedded into the skull terminated in a small box attached at the back of its neck.

When the rhesus saw Alix, it bared its teeth and charged forward as if all the demons of hell were chasing it. Alix was riveted to the spot. Time compressed around her and the few seconds she'd been following the monkey's erratic course seemed days. The monkey leaped up onto a nearby table, screeched one last time, then sprang forward, its teeth bared, directly for Alix's throat. She saw the flashing eyes, the terrible contorted visage arching through the air toward her, but she was unable to move out of its way.

Just before the monkey's body struck her full force, Alix saw, out of the corner of her eyes, the red-faced doctor raise his hand to point the black box in the monkey's direction. And as his arm extended toward the rhesus, its features magically relaxed, its eyes and mouth closed, and it fell to the ground unconscious—but not before hitting Alix in the shoulder.

She stumbled backward against Dr. March, who braced himself to steady her. His face went purple with anger. "Dr. Winner! Just what the hell is the meaning of this?" he shouted.

"Sorry, Dr. March," Winner said as he ground to a halt at the scene of the crime. "There was a short or something in the controls and I couldn't get Daisy calmed." He looked from March to the unconscious monkey, then to Alix. "She sometimes runs amok," he said to Alix, as if this weak explanation might ease her discomfort; it didn't.

March glared for a moment, then said, "Dr. Winner, *this* is Dr. Alix Kendall." The emphasis made it clear he'd discussed her with the other doctor. March now turned to Alix. "Dr. Winner likes toying with behavior modification induced by electrical stimuli—control of epilepsy, that sort of thing. And he's *supposed* to be in full control of his subjects . . ."

"It was an electrical failure, not a human one," Winner said with more than a touch of anger.

"*All* failure is human, doctor. Next time check the circuitry before you let your animals out of the cage." March glared again; then a "public-relations" smile eased its way across his lips. "How does this look to Dr. Kendall? Here I am trying to convince her to join our project, when she's attacked by your berserk monkey. It's not very much of an inducement to become one of us, you know."

Alix began laughing at the whole incident, realizing now that there was no real danger. How different this atmosphere was from the hospital back in Boston. She was used to working in relative peace and quiet, but rather than put her off, the charged atmosphere of the lab intrigued her, excited her. Being in such close proximity to important experiments—like the one on Daisy—stimulated her sense of adventure.

"Don't worry about me and Daisy," Alix said as Winner picked up the limp creature from the floor. "This little exhibit of 'science run wild' might be just what I needed."

March just looked at her curiously, then shrugged. "Well, whatever it takes . . . Now that you've seen the entertainment, I'd like to show you where the *real* work is done." He began to escort Alix toward another set of doors, then paused for a moment. "Coming, doctor?" he asked of Winner, in the manner of an adult to a naughty child.

Winner, cradling Daisy like a baby in his arms, followed Alix and March through another set of steel doors into the hushed inner sanctum of a much smaller laboratory. Unlike the outer lab, there were fewer people working here—three men and two women—and they all looked up when the doors opened.

"Ladies and gentlemen," March announced, once sure he had their attention, "I'd like you to meet Dr. Alix Kendall. I've told you about her." He smiled, then nodded to Alix.

Alix smiled awkwardly, embarrassed not only by being put on the spot but also by the thought that, like Dr. Winner, Preston had already discussed her with these strangers. What had he said? she wondered now, confronting five pairs of staring eyes.

After a moment of tense silence, one of the two women approached Alix and extended her hand. "I'm Lisa Barth. It's a pleasure to meet you."

As Alix smiled and shook her hand, March explained, "Lisa is one of our resident T-cell specialists." T-cells were one of the important products of antibodies whose disappearance in later years had been linked to susceptibility to disease in older patients. Many thought that to unlock the mystery of T-cell production was to unlock the secrets of the aging process and, in turn, open the door to "the fountain of youth."

"Lisa and I should have a lot in common," Alix said, voicing her own interest in the subject, ". . . if we have the chance to talk further." March had put her on the spot, and she didn't like it. He—everyone, in fact— was acting as if she were already a bona fide member of the Lafayette instead of a guest. What if, after all this attention, she should decide to go back to Boston? She'd feel like a fool—but maybe that was the idea: pressure her into accepting.

"Preston, it's good to see you again," Lisa said, interrupting Alix's train of thought. "Your visits are the only time we dedicated scientists down here get the chance to relax." She winked at March, then turned back to Alix. "Let me introduce you to everyone, Dr. Kendall." She linked arms with Alix and ferried her around the room from one person to another.

Alix heard the names but forgot them as quickly as they were said. She also forgot just as quickly the specialties that were listed right along with them. While she was meeting people, Alix saw Dr. March draw Ted Winner aside for what looked like a very heated discussion. Several times one or the other of the two men turned in Alix's direction. Was it possible they were arguing over her? Because of the incident with Daisy? Alix knew March wanted her to work for him, but she was just beginning to see exactly *how* much he wanted that.

When the two women returned to March's side, Lisa suggested they take a coffee break, but Preston demurred. "Some other time, Lisa. There's more I want Alix to see. You know, she's not really convinced that working here at the Lafayette will be good for her."

Lisa pulled back and looked at Alix like she'd suddenly been dropped from another planet. "I'm sorry, Dr. Kendall," she apologized, "but . . . it's just hard to believe that anyone could have reservations about being a part of the Lafayette. As far as I'm concerned, my life didn't really begin until I walked through these doors. And I think the others would agree with me, too." The other doctors, almost as one entity, nodded in agreement. "The Lafayette's a researcher's paradise. You want something you requisition it, you get it—simple. You read about a piece of equipment, and it's yours. There are no drawbacks, no strings—nothing."

"No strings at all?" Alix asked impetuously, finding this degree of loyalty—and the promise of such riches—too good to be true.

Ted Winner answered the question for Lisa Barth. "No strings that can't be dealt with," he said flatly, rubbing the head of Daisy, who was now conscious and conspicuously docile.

March stepped forward now between Winner and Alix, looking at Winner as if he expected him to say something more, something . . . unflattering, perhaps. But there was nothing more. Obviously relieved, March thanked the members of the lab for their time and escorted Alix back the way they'd come. "Ted Winner's a first-rate scientist, but he's been working too hard," he said, as if answering some unasked questions. "If you *do* decide to join us, you'll do a lot to ease his workload."

"I'm sure I'd do the best I could," Alix said noncommittally. "I suppose one more pair of hands would help, if only a little."

March stopped her. "One more pair of hands? Alix, you misunderstand: I want you to be Ted Winner's personal assistant, second-in-command of the lab."

"I had no idea." She blushed with pleasure even as she felt the pressure to take the job grow heavier.

"We need you, Alix." March slipped his arm easily around her waist and gave her a little squeeze. "I thought you understood that."

"I'm just beginning to, Preston," she said as she eased out of his grasp.

As they waited for the elevator to take them back to the fifth floor, a man in a blue work uniform entered the hallway with a mop and bucket from what appeared to be a utility closet. He moved slowly toward them, his body bent low, his gait awkward and halting. He kept his eyes on the floor in front of him until he was within several feet of Alix and March. Then, as if sensing their presence for the first time, the man raised his head and stared at Alix.

Alix was shocked when she saw his face, but managed to hide her surprise. The left side of the workman's face was perfectly normal, handsome in fact, but the right side was pulled and twisted toward a central point in the middle of his nose. The disfigurement seemed to be caused by nerve damage—there was no physical trauma, no tissue damage, no scarring—just that awful pull of muscles that wrenched his face out of proportion and nearly closed his right eye completely. His mouth on the damaged side was drawn up into a half-sneer, and when he smiled, as he now did at Alix, the sneer was completed.

Dr. March had his back to the workman, but when he saw Alix staring, he turned and confronted the man. "Hawkins, you know the rules; no work up here during the day," he said angrily.

"I had to get my mop," Hawkins slurred, the words no more than a guttural explosion that discharged a rivulet of spittle down his shirtfront.

"That's no excuse. Now, get going," March commanded.

But Hawkins didn't move. In fact, since first seeing Alix, he hadn't taken his eyes off her. Even when responding to Dr. March, he'd watched her, even to the point of craning his head forward to get a closer look. The sneer/smile appeared on his lips again and his eyes glinted with barely hidden desire.

"Hawkins! If you don't leave this minute, I'll be forced to call a guard . . . and you know what that means."

The smile vanished from the workman's face. "I'm sorry, Dr. March," he said immediately. "I'll go now, I promise." Hawkins backed slowly away, reluctant, even in the face of this harsh threat, to let Alix out of his sight.

Try as she did, Alix too was unable to look away. There was something in the man's eyes that touched her, oddly enough; something trapped deep inside that she sensed needed to be freed, to be understood. Feeling this way was crazy, she knew. After all, the man was really just being plain rude by ogling her that way, yet it didn't matter. Alix had seen that same look many times in the eyes of the retarded and brain-damaged men and women she'd encountered during her medical career. There was a core of pain deep down inside that was reflected through the eyes. They are the windows of the soul, she thought, remembering now that she'd seen that look of sadness in her own eyes in a thousand mirrors during the hundreds of days since Richard's death.

The elevator doors opened and Dr. March escorted Alix inside. "Hawkins is a sad case. He's worked here for years. There was an accident—he got tangled up in some of the equipment and was nearly electrocuted. There was brain damage." March shook his head. "He tends to be passive, but occasionally he has to be reminded just exactly who's boss here. You understand."

"Of course," Alix said sadly. This should have explained March's threat about the guards, but it didn't. Something about the encounter left her unsatisfied; she sensed there was more going on than appeared.

"You don't have to worry about Hawkins. He lives

in the basement and is downstairs and outside until after hours."

They went back to March's office in silence. Alix was unable to forget the sadness in Hawkins' face. How ironic that such a pitiful creature should mirror exactly the way she felt so much of the time. And how sad to think that she had the opportunity to succeed, whereas Hawkins could only fail, and that she'd given up trying . . . until accepting this interview, anyway.

Back in his office, March ordered coffee for two. When they'd had a cup and filled the time with small talk about the joys of living in Washington with its proximity to the beautiful Maryland and Virginia countryside, March reiterated what he'd said earlier. "You're a brilliant doctor, Alix, and I'd like you on my team here at the Lafayette. And I guess I'd do just about anything in my power to get you to say yes."

"That's very flattering," Alix admitted, "but I'm not susceptible to flattery, particularly where my work is concerned."

"How commendable," March said with distinct iciness.

"You've been very good to me and I appreciate the offer, but you're asking me to change my whole way of life, and I'm not sure I'm willing to do that quite yet."

"Have it your own way." His voice had gone from cold to unfriendly.

Alix realized immediately that he'd expected her to jump at the chance to join him, without thought. He was angry now, that was for sure; and in a way, Alix couldn't blame him. He *had* been good to her—going up to Boston, and now, here in Washington, treating her like royalty—but business was business. "I'll need some time to consider all this, Preston," she said without apology.

"I can give you until the end of the weekend—Sunday—to make up your mind. No longer."

"I'll know by then," she said, rising. "And, Preston, no matter what I finally decide, I want you to know how much I've appreciated all you've done for me." Impetuously, Alix kissed him on the cheek.

The kiss thawed March out immediately. "*That* makes it all worth it." He smiled now and moved a little closer to her. "If you don't mind taking a compliment from an old-fashioned male chauvinist like me, you're a very beautiful woman. I can't imagine why some young man didn't marry you long ago." His eyes gleamed mischievously.

"It's my work . . . of course . . . you understand," Alix sputtered, unsure whether March's leering or the oblique reference to her dead fiancé was making her so uncomfortable.

"Well, you've seen the Lafayette; that's what's really important." March led her to the door. "Don't rush your decision, Alix. Take the full three days. And remember, your working here means more to me than you realize." His mind seemed to drift off for a moment. "If only there were some way to make you. . . ." He came back to the present and shrugged. "There's really no point saying anything more. Make a decision, and we'll have brunch on Sunday, either to celebrate or to commiserate."

After Alix left, March returned to his desk and thought about the interview. He wasn't totally convinced that emotionally Alix Kendall was right for the job of assisting Ted Winner. Of course he had great respect for her ability and her intelligence, but to work at the Lafayette—particularly on the project he had in mind for her eventually—she *had* to conform, do what she was told, be completely trustworthy. The last few hours with Dr. Kendall had proven to March that she had a very wide streak of independence, compounded by something close to impudence. Alix Kendall would never be as malleable as Ted Winner, but then, she probably wouldn't begin to fray around the psychic edges like Winner, either.

"Dammit!" March said out loud as he slammed his fist down onto the desktop. His rationalizations weren't working. Alix Kendall was the very best, and Preston March wasn't used to playing cat and mouse, particularly with a woman, no matter how sexy she was. Dr. Kendall had pushed him too hard, was a little too aloof, and now it was his turn to push back. He picked up the telephone and punched out a Boston phone number.

"It's Preston March in Washington. Is he there?" He waited thirty seconds before a familiar male voice answered. "Jason, I hate to exert pressure on you, but we want Alix Kendall down here very badly. It looks like she may turn us down. Do you think you might be able to give us a hand? It would be greatly appreciated."

Jason Pankhurst was a powerful man at the Massachusetts Technological Hospital. As chief of staff he could do as he pleased with his doctors, but had it been anyone but Preston March suggesting he interfere with someone's career at Mass Tech, Pankhurst would have seen red. But March was head of the Lafayette, and that meant money, power, prestige. And if he wanted Alix Kendall out of Mass Tech, there was no refusing him.

So, with no more than a moment's hesitation, Pankhurst said, "She'll be given notice on Monday."

"That's great, Jason. I owe you one. But make it a week from Monday. We don't want this to look suspicious, do we?" He lit a forbidden cigar and sucked on it luxuriously. "And next time you're in Washington, let's have dinner . . . I'll show you *around*," he added slyly. Knowing Pankhurst's weakness for the prettiest, most available women in any city, March guessed the innuendo wasn't lost on him.

March hung up feeling he'd accomplished exactly what he'd set out to do. If Alix did agree to come to the Lafayette—which he now doubted after her coolness earlier—then all was well and good. If not, then she'd be out of a job in Boston. There was no guarantee that that would force her back to Washington; still, it was a trump card worth playing. Now all he had to do was wait and leave the final decision up to Alix Kendall.

The Institute-owned apartment where Alix was staying for the weekend was a pretty three-story house on Twenty-sixth Street in Georgetown. Each of the floors was a separate apartment, and because Alix's was on the top floor, the staircase ended outside her door, allowing space for one extra, though small, room.

This room, used mainly as an entrance hall, led directly into a living room with a wood-burning fireplace. Down a short hallway was the bathroom and bedroom. In the opposite direction there was a kitchen large enough for a table and two chairs. There were windows in every room, and the apartment was flooded with sunlight. Whoever had decorated the place had done so with solid, good taste—contemporary, yet somehow traditionally comfortable.

All in all, Alix liked the apartment, and should she decide to stay—which she doubted—she imagined she could be very happy here.

Half an hour after unpacking, Alix sat on the couch opposite the fireplace and breathed a sigh of relief. So far so good, she thought; then she laughed at herself. God, I've only been in Washington five hours; what possibly could happen in that short a time? She'd put a framed photo of her parents—both dead—on the mantel and the picture of Richard on an end table. But seeing him now, here, back where they'd once been together, gave Alix an unfamiliar twinge of remorse—not for Richard, but for herself. After ten years she was still carrying the torch for a dead man. She'd become one of those sad women who allow the past to suck all the life out of the present.

Even Preston March had seen it. He must have. Why else would he so suddenly ask why she'd never married? And God knew there were enough men in Boston—at Mass Tech, in particular—who must have asked themselves the very same question. Even the few women friends to whom Alix had explained about Richard didn't understand. They, in fact, considered her attitude to be downright unhealthy. Yet she continued to live in the past. Why?

The question was so uncomfortable, Alix got up and began walking around the living room. In Boston her life as a quasi-widow seemed perfectly normal. But suddenly, here in lively Washington, such mourning seemed positively Victorian. She was back where it had all started, only to find that saving herself for all these years had been a terrible waste of time. Richard wasn't waiting here for her. He wouldn't applaud her years of chastity because she'd saved herself for him. Alix wasn't the brave wife of a nineteenth-century New England sea captain who patiently looked far out onto the horizon hoping to see a glimmer of the ship that would bring her man back to her; and Richard wasn't that captain. Richard was dead. And Alix suddenly felt terribly, terribly unfulfilled. And worse, cheated.

Impulsively she stole Richard's photograph from its place and quickly, without allowing herself time to consider what she was doing, hid it among her lingerie in the top bureau drawer. She immediately felt so guilty about the act that, moments later, she pulled on her coat and gloves and went quickly downstairs and out into the autumn street.

Twenty-sixth Street was awash with a sharp light that filtered down through the brilliant foliage. Alix shielded her eyes momentarily and took in a deep breath of cool air. Everything smelled so good, so crisp and fall-like. It was the same in Boston, although by now the leaves of many trees had already died and layered the sidewalks with a crunchy carpet of brown. But here, so much farther south, the leaves were flamboyantly colored, drawn in shades of yellow and red that, in the sun, burst from the scenery like the bold brush strokes of an impressionist painting.

The air was tinged with the wonderful smell of wood smoke from neighborhood fireplaces, and Alix hungrily breathed it in, desperate for the comfort of its familiarity. She'd lived a long time in New England, and autumn was the most wonderful time for her, presaging, as it did, Christmas and snowfalls and dreams of fantasy sleigh rides, cheerful decorations, and the smell of good things baking coming from the kitchen. In the short season of autumn, Alix always felt as if nothing bad could ever happen to her.

She walked across N Street toward Wisconsin Avenue, the main shopping street of Georgetown. She was more excited now than she'd been in years. How odd that the return to Washington had triggered an entire catalog of wonderful feelings, when she'd always believed it would pull her down into an inescap-

able depression. How wonderful that the thing she'd
feared the most had become the thing best for her!
Maybe, just maybe, despite her age and education,
Alix really didn't know exactly what was best for her
after all—like staying in Boston, for example.

By the time she reached Wisconsin Avenue, Alix
was fairly skipping with delight. She felt as if she'd
never really taken time to look at the sky before, or at
the trees, or at the way people dressed and acted.
Everything seemed so new that, in a way, Alix felt
she'd stumbled into an entirely different world, or
dimension, where every turn of the corner might provide an adventure. Here, amid the hustle and bustle
of Wisconsin Avenue as she pushed through the crowds
of shoppers and tourists, Alix felt safely alone, untouch-
able, actually happy.

So much had changed in Georgetown in ten years.
So many places she remembered were gone or were
remodeled beyond repair. Georgetown, once a black
slum, had gradually, over the years, been revitalized
by money and window-dressed by chic. The transformation showed in every shop, every real-estate office
offering choice, expensive apartments. While the change
was for the better, Alix wished it were a little more
subdued, a little more like ten years before, when one
could walk peacefully along window-shopping without
having to fight the crowds. Still, it was exciting! And
that made her blood race.

By the time she began thinking about returning
home, Alix was actually whistling to herself. She'd
bought food for dinner, a lovely bottle of Pouilly Fumé,
and a wedge of sinfully rich chocolate cake for dessert.
She was also burdened with a bouquet of fresh flowers
for the apartment and an expensive jar of potpourri
whose spicy smell had immediately seduced her. Alix
was feeling good about her life for the first time in a
very, very long time, and she was no longer completely convinced that she could walk away from Washington without regretting it.

So engrossed in her thoughts was Alix that she
crossed Wisconsin Avenue against the light and was
almost hit by a car whose driver was paying more

attention to his blond companion than he was to his driving. But when he did see Alix and narrowly missed hitting her, he blew the car horn loudly, then shouted obscenities at her, drawing the attention of many passersby. Alix, trembling from fear and, mostly, anger, stood on the corner of N Street feeling like a fool. She scanned the faces staring at her and smiled, hoping that once they saw she was all right, they'd mind their own business.

It was at that very moment that Alix saw him.

He stood on the opposite side of the street, his attention momentarily caught by the car's jarring horn and the ensuing confusion. Then he continued on his way, walking north. Alix was transfixed. Without thinking, she darted through the heavy traffic back across the street, following him as best she could, but it was difficult to keep track of him in the crowds. With the shoppers bumping into her and with the clumsiness of her parcels, just walking without falling was a difficult task. Alix was tempted to abandon her shopping to run ahead in search of the man, but reason got the better of her and she resisted the urge.

By the time she reached the corner of Wisconsin and R Street, the man was gone. Alix stared down the leaf-strewn street, shaking uncontrollably. R Street was empty. She was alone. Her eyes darted back and forth in a vain attempt to ascertain where he'd gone—or if he'd even been there. But he *had* been there. She *had* seen him. She had. *She had!*

Alix walked slowly back to her apartment. The day was ruined. Her shopping now seemed nothing more than wasteful self-indulgence. All at once her worst fears had come true. She'd always known it would be a mistake to return to Washington, yet she'd let Preston March talk her into it. And now she was paying the price.

At the corner of O Street Alix turned once more and looked mournfully back into the distance. The failing afternoon light tempered the city colors, but Alix failed to notice this beautiful nuance. She'd lost him. She'd lost him once before, and now she'd lost him again. It was crazy, she knew. But not more than twenty min-

utes ago she'd seen Richard Hailey in the Georgetown
Street.

All the way home Alix told herself to forget the
incident—Richard was *dead*—but as she let herself
into the small garden that flanked the apartment
building, she admitted she was fighting a losing bat-
tle with her intellect; she truly believed she'd just
seen Richard, not just someone who resembled him.
And that meant Alix couldn't flee Washington for the
security of Boston. Not yet, anyway. And perhaps
never.

Alix let herself into the apartment and quickly put
away the groceries. When she finished, she found herself standing in the middle of the kitchen, unable to
decide what to do next. "This is no good for me," she
said out loud as she forced herself to go into the living
room. She lit a fire in the fireplace, then snuggled up
into a warm ball on the couch to think.

She wanted to pretend that everything was all right,
that the day wasn't ruined after all. But everything
wasn't all right. She'd seen a dead man in the street
not more than half an hour before, a man who'd walked
out of her life one morning ten years before and had
never returned. The familiar melancholy at the thought
of Richard doubled and redoubled, and within moments Alix was sobbing gently. If Richard were still
alive, then it meant that he'd *willingly* been an accomplice in his own death, had forsaken his love for Alix in
search of a greater reward. But what?

Alix sniffled back the last sobs and stared into the
dancing flames. There had to be an answer. And that
answer lay in Washington, not in Boston. And she
decided that no matter how painful it was, no matter
how long it took, she would find Richard Hailey and
confront him. Ten years of her life were gone, and she
had to know why.

—3—

"And how are you getting along after two months, Alix? Have you finally learned your way around?" Preston March leaned far back in his office chair and smiled warmly at the Lafayette Institute's newest and prettiest member. He knew Alix had had a habit of getting lost during her first days, and it had become something of a joke between them.

"I only wish you'd given me a map, Preston." She laughed. "I feel like I've cheated you."

"Oh? And how is that?"

"During those first weeks, I think I spent more time finding my way around than I did working. After all, you aren't paying me to be confused."

March laughed. "I wouldn't worry too much about that, my dear. We'll get the work out of you ... one way or another."

"It still amazes me that a building that looks so simple and direct on the outside could be so complex on the inside."

"The structural complexity mirrors the complexity of our research. The building, by its design, is a maze." He gazed across the room at a framed rendering of the Lafayette done long before the first concrete was ever poured. "The buildings are like science itself, intricate, everything linked to everything else in one way or another."

"Of course," she agreed, "but next time you decide to plan a building, why not make it on a more human scale? For your employees' sake?" March's eyebrows furrowed, and Alix instantly recognized that she'd struck another sore subject. In the two months since starting at the Lafayette and becoming something of a protégée to March, Alix had become accustomed to his habit of taking umbrage at any intimation that science and anything connected with it was less than king. He never joked about work and took any slight to his calling personally. While she most often found this side of his personality to be nothing more than eccentric, there was a darker side to it that occasionally showed through—a side that she could only categorize as ruthlessness.

March spoke now in direct response to her suggestion that he "humanize" the Lafayette; his voice was ice cold. "My dear Dr. Kendall, the Lafayette Institute is a cathedral built to honor science, much as Chartres was built to honor God. Would you suggest that Chartres be on a human scale, too? Would you feel more comfortable if it had been only two stories tall and had had picture windows installed instead of stained glass?" He shook his head at the thought, not noticing the slight smile that had spread across Alix's face. "I wanted people to know the power—the majesty—of science, and that meant building this." His gesture, a sweep of the arm, encompassed everything within and without the building.

Alix nodded. She did see—see that March sometimes seemed absolutely possessed by the idea of science as savior. Still, she would have been more comfortable if the architects had been instructed to give some thought to making the staff feel at ease, rather than trying to impress visitors—and possible sources of money—with the cold, calculated austerity of everything but the visitors' lounge and administrative offices. As it now stood, she felt like she was working in a vacuum, at the mercy of her work instead of in control of it.

Well, she couldn't complain too loudly. She had chosen to accept March's offer to work at the Lafayette, and with that decision came bad things as well as good. Had she not seen Richard in Georgetown, Alix would probably have returned to Boston for good. Preston March's cajoling, his promises of money and prestige, all meant nothing. Richard Hailey did. And Alix thought of him now with a curious blend of fond-

ness and hate. She sometimes felt like a woman
scorned, but more often than not she now remembered
what it had felt like to be a woman loved. Seeing
Richard in the street had rekindled all the desire—
emotional and physical—she'd ever felt for him, and
she suddenly began to long for him, for a man's caresses
more than at any other time in the last ten years. And
that was the true reason Alix needed to find her ex-
fiancé again; to feel the warm, loving feelings, the
fiery sexual feelings she'd been denying herself in the
name of grief. And now more than ever, with the
terrible suspicion that Richard had chosen to walk out
on her for reasons only he knew, Alix needed to prove
to herself that she was still very much alive and still
very much a woman.

She gave March the good news that Sunday over
brunch.

"Your attitude on Friday said 'no,' " March reminded
her gently. "Or was I to have taken your distance as a
'definite maybe'?"

"It did mean no, but I've changed my mind. I
would very much like to work with you . . . but only
temporarily," she said hesitantly. Temporarily until
she found and confronted a certain Mr. Hailey. And
once that score was settled one way or another, then
she could pick up and return to Boston free of the
horrible past once and for all.

"What do you mean by temporary? You must realize that installing you will entail a certain expense
and that acclimating you to the place will take a
certain amount of time. . . ." March smiled indulgently
and pressed his fingers together in front of his lips.

"Six months should be a good trial period," Alix
said.

"A year," March shot back immediately. "Anything
less wouldn't be worth our while, no matter how much
I need you." Alix stared at him but said nothing. "And
there must be a contract, of course. I want you to
know that I am very pleased by your change of heart.
If I may ask: what made you reconsider the offer?"

Alix shrugged, but decided to tell her new boss as
much of the truth as she could without sounding like

a mental incompetent. "Your attack on my work—my professional life in Boston, that is—made me reconsider myself and what I wanted from Mass Tech. I was furious with you, of course, but then I realized that that was because you were right: somewhere along the line I'd stopped growing intellectually, emotionally. I'd found a safe niche in Boston, where the evils of the world couldn't get at me, where I could lead a life that was totally within my control." She smiled, but was embarrassed by these personal revelations she seemed unable to stop. "I have a small circle of friends, occasional dates, a nice apartment on Beacon Hill, and a very comfortable job. It should be satisfying . . . but it never has been. Through my research I discovered that there was an exciting world within reach if only I decided to take a few risks. You called my bluff."

March reached out and took Alix's hand in his. "My dear, I feel like an ogre. I never meant to be the cause of such personal . . . turmoil."

Alix was beginning to get attuned to Preston March's moods—his shy grandfatherly side, his austere director side, even the lecherous side which he revealed intermittently. And right now Alix didn't believe a word he was saying. She knew he would have done anything, created any havoc in her life to get his way, but she said, "Thank you for caring, Preston. You did me a favor, actually; my life needed a good shaking up."

Suddenly March was all business again. "Good. Then it's settled. Bring your notes with you from Boston. In fact, why not make copies of them and send them directly to me as soon as possible."

Alix thought a moment, then shook her head. "I'd just as soon not, Preston. It's not that I don't trust you or the Institute, it's just that—"

March raised his hand to silence her. "Don't explain. I know; working on a project is like bearing a child. You don't ever want to let it go. So bring your work with you and I'll personally go over it with you. Now, I really must be going. I've got a long day ahead of me tomorrow; I'm flying up to New York to do a Merv Griffin interview." He signaled the waiter for the check.

Though Alix felt good about her decision to join the Lafayette, she would have felt better were it not for one thing: the uneasiness she sometimes felt being with Preston March. When she'd refused to send her notes, she saw in his eyes the truth that he wasn't nearly as benevolent as he pretended. In fact, despite his gracious acceptance of her refusal, there'd been a momentary flash of anger that seemed to border on rage. And for that moment Alix had actually been afraid.

"We're very pleased with your work, Alix," March continued, interrupting her reminiscence. "You've blossomed here at the Lafayette, though I can't say I'm at all surprised. Given the time—and the money— most people do thrive working at something they love, particularly with no pressure on them to produce."

"I am very grateful, Preston," she agreed. There was definitely no pressure to produce—yet.

"Just one word of advice. Relax, slow down a bit. We're not going to throw you out on the street, you know," he said, alluding to her self-imposed work schedule of staying ten, sometimes twelve hours a day. She already had a reputation as a workaholic. He lit a cigar, then carefully blew the cloud of smoke away from Alix. "Is there something . . . wrong . . . you'd like to tell me about?" he asked suddenly.

"Wrong?"

"Personal problems, for example. Working so hard can show dedication or it might just be a way to avoid going home. Are you having boyfriend trouble?"

Why was it that when March brought up the subject of dating—men in general—Alix always felt he was talking about sweaty sex, not affection? "No, there's nothing wrong in that area," she equivocated, thinking: If you can call being haunted by a dead man nothing.

"Good, good." He sounded relieved. "We have big plans for you, Alix. *Big* plans. I'd hate to see them shelved for any reason. Now, tell me, how is the work going?"

Alix spent the next ten minutes giving March a brief rundown of her work, knowing as she did that he was briefed daily by Ted Winner—her immediate superior. Well, there were many things far worse than having the head of the Lafayette take a personal interest in her, she figured. Like being ignored completely, for one.

"It all sounds very promising, Alix. Keep up the good work and one day we'll be talking about a promotion."

Alix thanked him, then started for the door.

"One minute. . . ." He got up and joined her. "There *is* a little something I want you to do for me—for the Lafayette, actually. There's a fellow outside named Jack Campbell. He's a reporter from *The District Columbian*, here to do a human-interest story on some of the med students we take under our wing from time to time. I'd like you to take charge of him . . . if you would." March touched her arm lightly. "I promise he won't be any bother; answer his questions—if you can—and show him around."

"Of course," Alix agreed warily. "But I'm not sure being a guide is exactly my cup of tea."

"You'll do fine. Just be yourself, and he'll be charmed, I'm sure." He opened the door. "And he wants a tour of the facilities and a choice seat at one of your lectures, so I agreed. I want him to demythicize the Lafayette as much as possible. You know what bad press we've had lately," he grumbled.

Despite his open love affair with the media—as a personality, as Preston March the lovable scientist—March was also very aware and leery of publicity's power when it came to the image he wanted for the Lafayette Institute. Over the years the press on occasion had been less than kind, and just recently several articles in the Washington *Post* had vociferously criticized the Lafayette for its alleged ties with the CIA, the FBI, and just about every other clandestine operation in the country. The article portrayed March and his associates as robots working day and night on "high-level, top-secret experiments that would blow the roof off the government if their exact nature were ever revealed." The articles pictured the Lafayette as a politically tied factory that churned out everything from nerve gas to mind-control agents while pretending to deal with gerontology. In the wake of the reports, several congressmen had insisted on being shown around, but were unable to uncover anything subversive.

"Please explain to Mr. Campbell the exact—and harmless—nature of our work. After all, we're just trying to deal effectively with old age; that's no secret. And please try to make him believe that just because the Lafayette is constructed of black granite doesn't mean it's a center for black magic." March frowned at the idea. "I suspect that Campbell's 'human-interest' angle might just be a cover to get him inside so he can do some real damage."

They went outside in search of their Grand Inquisitor and found him seated in a molded armchair looking very bored. Jack Campbell was a man about Alix's age, and although he wore a jacket and tie, there was definitely a casual air about him. In fact, he looked like a college student who was waiting for his next class to begin. The moment he saw March he smiled, and when he saw Alix he rose to his feet and unconsciously straightened his tie. He strode across the room toward them.

"Dr. March, it's good to see you again," Campbell said easily, his eyes scanning Alix as he spoke.

"Jack, this is Dr. Alix Kendall. She'll be your official guide for the next few hours."

Campbell shook Alix's hand, holding it a moment too long. "I couldn't have asked for a prettier guide," he said smoothly.

Ordinarily such a corny remark would have angered Alix, but surprisingly enough she was flattered by his attention. Campbell stood just over six feet tall and was handsome in a way she knew many women would find irresistible. Well, why not her, too? Campbell *was* extremely good-looking. Since her experience in the Georgetown street, Alix found herself smiling back at handsome men, and twice she'd actually had dinner in a local restaurant known primarily as a singles pickup spot, all the while telling herself she was there because she enjoyed the mediocre food. Something was awakening in Alix that had been dormant for a long, long time. And it scared and excited her.

Alix finally released Campbell's hand and even stepped back a bit, hoping March hadn't noticed what, undeniably, was an introduction with a heavy sexual subtext. "It's nice to know male chauvinism isn't dead, Mr. Campbell," she said haughtily before immediately turning her attention back to March. "Well, Preston, you've set me a task with this one, haven't you?"

"Count me out of this, Dr. Kendall," March hooted. "I'll leave feminist politics to you and to Mr. Campbell. Now, if you'll both excuse me. . . ." He bowed slightly and headed back toward his office, pausing at the door long enough to say, "When you've finished, Mr. Campbell, drop in and see me, won't you?"

Campbell nooded but said nothing. When March was gone, he turned back to Alix. "I hope my chauvinism didn't *really* offend you, Dr. Kendall. It's just my bedside manner."

"I'll take your word for that, Mr. Campbell."

"Jack," he quickly amended.

"Whatever. Now, if you'll follow me . . ." Alix walked away so fast Campbell had to run to catch up with her.

Although Alix had never personally shown anyone around the Lafayette, she felt as if she'd been doing it for years. During her first weeks acclimating herself to the Institute's myriad halls and labs, she'd watched as groups of officials, doctors, even schoolchildren were shown through the Lafayette, marveling at the *Star Wars*-caliber medical technology that made the Institute one of a kind. And during those weeks, she also noted that these groups followed the same—and very specific—course, like mice being prodded through a maze. The men and women who were funneled through the Lafayette's efficient public-relations office might have believed they were seeing the inner workings of the Institute, but Alix knew differently; there was much, much more going on that they knew nothing about . . . that she knew nothing about.

This duplicity unnerved Alix, for she sensed that behind the bland smiles of her co-workers and the upper-echelon management in particular, there *was* something hidden, a communal goal that some were privy to and others were blissfully unaware of. It was nothing Alix could put her finger on, yet it was a constant undercurrent during her workday. Even Dr. March's asking her to escort this reporter carried with it the unspoken command to follow the standard tour. And almost without giving her consent, Alix was being drawn deeper into the Lafayette's inner circle. And she wasn't sure she liked it.

"We admit patients on a limited basis," Alix explained as they walked into the patient building toward the private rooms, their footsteps hushed by the gray-tiled floor. "It's not that we're discriminatory, but there *are* enough facilities in the country to deal with the prosaic cases. We're interested in special cases that, one way or the other, have to do with aging."

"For example?" Campbell asked quickly.

"For example the patient in this room." Alix nodded toward an open door.

Campbell looked in and saw an old man sitting reading in a chair by the window. Other than the fact that the man was very small, there seemed nothing unusual about him. "What's so special about him?"

Alix paused and looked Campbell straight in the eyes. "How old would you say he is?"

Campbell shrugged and looked again at the old man. "Seventy, seventy-two?"

"He's fourteen years old," Alix said. "He's got progeria, a disease that ages children in a few short years until they look like that." She sadly looked at the aged child. "If we can learn something about progeria, maybe we can curb its effects and, at the same time, learn about the aging process."

Campbell nodded his head, feeling a certain awe for the ravishing Dr. Kendall's obvious dedication. In fact, Jack Campbell was completely in awe of medicine, the kind of man who found a simple suture to be a scientific marvel. So here at the Lafayette, encountering equipment that existed nowhere else, dedication that was almost inhuman, and the beauty of Alix Kendall—

he felt as if he'd been swept up into a science-fiction movie.

"Everything seems to be linked to everything else, as if the very essence of these buildings is symbiotic," Campbell commented later as they walked further through the halls.

"Exactly," Alix agreed. "All the data recorded from each patient each minute are automatically relayed to the nurses' station and, at the same time, given to TIM."

"Tim who?"

Alix stopped, stared at Campbell a second, then laughed. "Of course, you wouldn't know. TIM is our computer. TIM stands for Terminal Information Matrix. Each division of the Lafayette is equipped with terminals that feed directly into the main computer. TIM was designed so that every project, whether it involves one, two, or ten workers, has its own input terminal. There's a standard keyboard setup for filing daily reports and technical data into TIM, but there's also a faster system that stores all data produced during the course of each day; each work counter has a specially designed pen that not only records on paper what we're working on—even doodles—but also feeds the information into TIM."

"TIM sounds very hungry," Campbell said sarcastically.

Alix ignored him. "And every word processor used to keep the daily logs is also hooked into the computer. So everything produced every day by every person at the Lafayette is fed into TIM."

"What about the bathrooms?" Campbell asked.

"I beg your pardon?" Alix couldn't have heard him correctly.

"It sounds to me like the only place this electronic snoop you call TIM doesn't go is into the bathrooms."

"That's not very funny, Mr. Campbell," Alix said uneasily. TIM had seemed a little intrusive at first, but now, like so many things at the Lafayette, Alix took it for granted. She was also beginning to see why Preston was so leery of reporters—they wanted to make everything seem sinister, even TIM.

Campbell, despite Dr. Kendall's blithe acceptance of the Lafayette's surveillance system, was growing disquieted as he realized that even here in the patient wing the last vestiges of privacy had been romoved in the search for medical knowledge—an intercom system linked each room to the nurses' station and then to TIM. It seemed that to be admitted to the Lafayette Institute was to become part of a grand experiment, the fluctuations and variables of which were always under close scrutiny. In this heartless monument to healing, medicine was king. And its rules were the only rules, its demands the only ones heeded. Human beings were playing pieces in an intellectual game of strategy bent on beating Death at all costs, even if it meant sacrificing a few lives along the way.

Campbell heard Dr. Kendall spouting Lafayette Institute hype, but he barely listened. Two things were on his mind: first, the psychic chill he was experiencing just by being here; second, the soft sway of Dr. Alix Kendall's hips. The Lafayette Institute might have been cold and heartless, but not the good doctor.

They passed through a cardiac-monitoring unit—where the rhythmic electronic pings of eight patients' beating hearts were amplified and visually translated onto television monitors—into the eerie quiet of the coma unit. Here, five elderly men and three women lay suspended somewhere between life and death, their vital functions maintained both chemically and mechanically.

"When we understand more about the effects aging has on the brain, then maybe all this can be avoided," Alix said. "It's such a waste to see people like that, yet there's nothing we can do." She clucked her tongue, and it made her observation sound like a moral judgment.

"You can't stand to be frustrated when you want something, can you?" Campbell observed, meaning the question personally.

Alix answered it professionally. "When the object of science is to serve man and to help improve his life, then anything that thwarts that goal must be eliminated."

"Are you married, Dr. Kendall?" Campbell asked, turning the conversation around one hundred and eighty degrees.

"No, but I hardly see how that matters."

"It just gives me another angle for the article, that's all. Remember, that's why I'm here—to do a human-interest story," he said slyly. Then he turned serious again. "All this medical paraphernalia is just great, but it lacks one thing."

Alix stopped now, expecting to see one of his smug expressions. Campbell looked dead serious. "And just what is it that's lacking?"

"Heart," he said simply.

Alix actually smiled at the answer. "And that's where we doctors come in," she replied automatically, protecting herself and her colleagues from Campbell's acid observation. He was right, of course. She too had felt it since the beginning of her work there. Still, it annoyed her that so possibly damning an observation should come from a guest of the Lafayette. On the other hand, Jack Campbell was a reporter, and making people angry was obviously part of his job. "Is that why you're a reporter, Mr. Campbell? Because you're all heart?"

He shook his head. "Most of the guys down at the paper would call me a misanthrope, as a matter of fact."

"Then why are you here? Why throw yourself into the middle of work that is, by its very concern with human life, going to annoy you?"

"Maybe I'm just waiting for someone to prove me wrong, that's all."

Now Alix laughed. "Well, maybe I can help you there. Any more questions about this section?"

"Do your medical students work here too?"

"Yes, but we don't have medical students per se. They're usually third-year students from various universities around the country who stay with us for up to three months. They get a chance to see the best modern medicine has to offer, and we get a chance to view the best of the U.S. crop of future doctors."

"And then some are invited back to work, is that it?"

"A few of the lucky ones," she said, moving down the hall. "Now, unless you have any more questions, I'd like to show you the *really* inhuman part of the Lafayette." She pushed through the far door to reenter the research facility. Unlike the patient wing, this part of the Institute seemed virtually uninhabited. The atmosphere that permeated the hallways was one of tranquillity, controlled energy.

When Campbell joked about the quiet, Alix explained that in this part of the facility the feverish activity was all cerebral. "The faster you work, the more mistakes you're liable to make . . . and in this line of work, mistakes can often be deadly."

"And just exactly what is the Lafayette's line of work?"

"Many things," Alix answered cautiously. Certainly Campbell had done his homework by reading the press kit the PR department had handed out. Was this where he began trying to dig up a juicy story guaranteed to sell newspapers? Preston had warned her to be careful, and now she saw that the warning was for a good reason: Campbell pushed just a little too hard.

"Many things such as . . ."

"The nerve gas, is that what you mean? Or perhaps you'd prefer to see the laser weapons?" As Alix spoke, her voice rose and she realized she was suddenly very angry with Jack Campbell. She'd felt he liked her, but now even that seemed nothing more than reporterly nuance, a way to pry information out of her. And oddly enough, she felt betrayed. And odder still, it hurt.

"Hey, hey," he said, totally caught off guard by her reaction. "What'd I say?"

"It's what you implied," Alix retorted, embarrassed now by her outburst. "Look, I know everyone in this city—probably in the whole country—thinks this place is a hotbed of subversive activity, but it's not. And I won't be a part in tarnishing its reputation."

Campbell listened to this declaration of loyalty, hating himself for thinking how beautiful Alix was when

she was angry, and hating himself even more for
trying to bluff her. "You're right, Alix, and I apologize.
But don't blame the newspaper. They sent me here to
do just what I told Preston March—a human interest
story. It was my own idea to look a little deeper."

"Why?"

"Because that's my real job, not this Sunday-supple-
ment stuff."

"Then why was it assigned to you?" The plot seemed
to be thickening.

Campbell actually blushed. "Because I blew my top
about something and called Flanagan, the city editor,
a few names he didn't take kindly to."

Alix thought a moment, then began to laugh. "And
this is your punishment—medical students at the
Lafayette Institute. How you must hate it!"

He shook his head. "I thought I would, but I don't."

"It's really not so bad here, is it?" she mused.

"My feelings have nothing to do with the *place*,
but they have everything to do with *you*."

Now it was Alix's turn to blush. "That's very
flattering. Thank you. Now, I have a class to teach,
and you have one to observe." And before Campbell
had the chance to say another word, she was halfway
down the hall.

Alix taught on the fourth floor in a small lecture
hall with sharply banked seating that fanned out from
the podium like a cross-section of an ancient coliseum.
When she and Campbell arrived, the room was already half-filled with eager students. Because these
young men and women knew they were among the
crème de la crème of the student world, and because
Alix's reputation was growing, her lectures—basically
rehashing facts, but the perfect opportunity to trot out
and show off the Institute's *avant garde* pathology
equipment—were always well-attended.

Alix sent Campbell to find a seat, noting that he
nodded to several students—those he'd probably arranged to interview for the article, she decided. One of
them, a pretty brunette, batted her eyes unashamedly
at him when he acknowledged her, and Alix felt a
momentary flash of . . . Jealousy? No! The idea was

preposterous. She'd just met Jack Campbell and she wasn't the kind of woman who went around throwing herself at every handsome man who crossed her path. Yet, there was no denying that she felt something for him—that same something that had been unlocked and unleashed upon seeing "Richard" in the street.

But enough of that! Alix Kendall was first and foremost a doctor. And here in front of these students she was in supreme command of her life. Jack Campbell was arrogant, and she didn't trust him. He probably thought she was a sexual pushover just because she was a woman. Well, she'd show him! Alix sought him out, caught his eyes, and smiled at him while at the same time she leaned forward over the worktable in front of her, grabbed an edge of the shroud that covered today's specimen, and whipped it aside, revealing the waxy, naked corpse of a middle-aged man.

To Alix this was nothing more than another body, something to work on, but she suspected that to Campbell it might be quite another story. The body's skin was sickly gray-yellow and she knew that the skin looked, from a distance, like slick plastic. She also knew that the open eyes were wholly reminiscent of a steamed trout's. The man's jaw, rigid with rigor mortis, was partially open and it looked like he'd taken one last chance to suck in a great breath of air before being exposed to the prying eyes of so many strangers. The body had already been partially autopsied and a nasty Y-shaped incision ran from his sternum to the pubic bone. The wound had been carelessly stiched up with heavy black thread, and his abdomen looked not unlike the hind end of a turkey trussed up for Thanksgiving.

Alix smiled directly at Campbell, who sat rigid and pallid in the distance. "Well, here we are. Today we'll be starting our preliminary investigation of the effects of aging on the brain, which is here," she said, cheerfully tapping the corpse's head. Several students laughed; Campbell did not. "But first we have to get at it, don't we?"

Alix reached under the end of the worktable and pulled a chromium ring into view. Mounted on the lower part of the ring was a small metal housing with an even smaller protuberance that resembled the tip of a ball-point pen. She adjusted the ring so that the corpse's head was about a third of the way through, then returned her attention to her students. "We used to have to to this by hand; now it's done by laser."

Alix flicked on a switch near her, at the same time bracing her right hand against the top of the corpse's head as a thin red beam shot from the apparatus and seared through the forehead and the bone underneath. There was no sound whatsoever except for the faint hum as the laser made a 360-degree revolution around the ring, at the same time neatly sawing through the cadaver's skull. Alix turned the instrument off and with one deft motion pulled free the upper half of the skull, exposing the gray convolutions of the brain's surface.

"Voilà!" she yelled triumphantly. "Just like opening a grapefruit!"

There was a loud *thud* from somewhere back in the auditorium, and when Alix looked up, she saw that Jack Campbell was no longer in evidence. That should hold him! she thought contentedly. Next time, let him pull his macho act on someone else! Two male students carried Campbell out to the couch in an office near the amphitheater and Alix continued her lecture in peace.

Forty-five minutes later Alix sat next to a very sheepish Jack Campbell and offered him a cup of coffee while trying desperately not to laugh.

"I feel like a fool," he admitted quietly after taking a sip of the hot coffee. "Guess I'm not as tough as I thought."

Now Alix did laugh. "Don't be too hard on yourself, Jack. Most people—even new doctors—have trouble with their first autopsy. It's that human side you were talking about," she added impishly.

He nodded his head. "Maybe I'm beginning to see why you doctors have to keep yourselves detached. I guess getting personally involved is setting yourself— and your patients—up for trouble."

"Exactly," Alix agreed. "Just remember that *outside*

the hospital environment doctors are just as human as everyone else."

"You included?"

"Me included." She laughed again.

"Then how about backing up that statement?"

Alix cocked her head as if she hadn't understood.

"How about dinner tonight?"

"I don't know—" she began to demur, but Campbell cut her off.

"Look, Dr. Kendall . . . Alix . . . you've seen the most vulnerable side of me, which is something most people can't say. So why not give me a fair shake? That is, let me get to know you better. I'd like that, really."

Alix thought for a moment. She could say she had to work late—it was her habit—but that would be just avoiding the invitation . . . and, more important, the desire she'd been experiencing since meeting him. Working ten, twelve hours a day was nothing more than a way of escaping her own boredom and fear (even Preston was aware of how much time she was spending at the Lafayette). Besides, Alix suspected that if she turned Jack Campbell down, she'd regret it later.

"Dinner would be nice, Jack. I'd like it too."

"Great! Give me your address and I'll pick you up about eight, how's that?" Alix smiled in answer. "You know, it's hard to believe that a corpse brought us together."

For a moment Alix thought of the reason she was in Washington and she frowned at the joke. "Let's just say the Lafayette brought us together, okay?"

"Sure." Campbell shrugged. "Now I've got to go. I'm meeting my latest guinea pig—if you'll excuse the expression. Sarah Williams, my first interviewee, was perfect, but she took a powder and hasn't been heard from since. Maybe you know what happened to her; she was listed as one of your students."

Alix thought a moment. The name Sarah Williams meant nothing. "No, I don't think I've met her. I have so many students."

"There are plenty of other students willing to talk to the media."

Alix pictured the brunette in the lecture hall and now laughed at herself for that moment of jealousy. It was no contest. After all, which one of them had the date with Jack Campbell tonight?

Campbell finished his coffee and Alix walked him to the main reception area. "See you tonight, then? About eight?"

"Of course," she said as politely as her excitement allowed.

They smiled at each other, and he left. Alix walked slowly back toward her lab, her mind drifting back over the past couple of hours with Campbell. It had been so many years since she'd really been interested in a man—physically, as well as intellectually—that her reactions quite fascinated her. It was for that reason that she bumped right into someone in the hall and was so startled she let out a little scream.

"Oh, I beg your pardon . . ." she began to apologize, until she saw that she'd collided with Hawkins, the maimed workman. Alix had seen him several times since that unpleasant first encounter when March had threatened to turn him over to the guards, but he was always off at a distance. She was still aware, however, that Hawkins stared at her, that he was fascinated by her for some reason. Although he didn't really frighten Alix, she looked up and down the hallway and found they were alone.

"Dr. Kendall," he began, reaching out for her, "I . . . I want to talk to you."

"I'm very busy, Hawkins," she said as brusquely as possible. "Perhaps some other time." She tried to push around him, but he blocked her path. "Hawkins, really, let me by."

But he stood steadfast, his lips quivering, the pull of his damaged muscles seemingly in a spasm. "You don't understand. You've got to leave here now. You've got to get away."

Alix stopped and stared at him. "What are you talking about?"

"The experiments. They hurt me. They hurt others. You've got to leave or you may disappear too." He reached out for her, and when she stepped back from him, he looked down at his hand as if it should be amputated for offending her.

"I don't know what you're talking about. Now, please . . ." She looked into his eyes and recognized the pain and loneliness that were so akin to what she'd known for so long.

"I wasn't always like this. I was someone else." He slurred his words. "Please . . ."

"What the hell is the meaning of this outrage?" Preston March's voice echoed down the hall. "Hawkins, come here." March had turned the corner, discovered the two of them, and now stood, hands on hips, legs wide apart, his face red with fury.

"Protect me," Hawkins whispered before turning and staggering away to the far end of the corridor.

Alix couldn't hear what March was saying, but that hardly mattered. His fury was obvious. At one point he raised his hand as if to strike the workman, but seeing Alix, he desisted. After a minute Hawkins slunk away and March strode down the hall. "Why were you talking to him?" he demanded.

"I . . ." Alix was caught too off guard to answer.

"You know he belongs downstairs away from the main corridors! What if someone important had come through and seen him? This place has a bad enough name as it is. In the future, Dr. Kendall, if Hawkins comes up to you, ignore him."

"In the future, Dr. March, if Hawkins comes up to me, I shall ignore him. As it was, I went up to him," she lied, not sure why she was covering for him.

"*You* went up to him?" He was amazed.

"I wanted to thank him for keeping my lab so neat, for doing such a good job at night when everyone else has gone home." Now that she'd found the right track, it was easy to follow. "Hawkins is a sad case, and I doubt if anyone here bothers to pay any attention to him." Her raised eyebrow made its point. "If you find it objectionable that I speak to him as if he were a human being, then there is nothing further I can say."

A line of tenseness flared along March's jawline, then relaxed almost immediately. "You're right, of course, my dear. I'm too hard on him. It's just guilt, I suppose. I've always felt that somehow I was responsible for his accident. You see, I hadn't properly put away some equipment I was using, and . . ." He shrugged.

"Why don't we just forget it, Preston," she suggested, not for a moment believing what he was saying. Hawkins, brain-damaged or not, was afraid . . . and he was afraid for Alix. And she wanted to find out just exactly why.

"Then please accept my apologies." He bowed slightly. "Now, where is Mr. Campbell?"

"He left."

"I'd asked him to stop by my office . . . Oh, well, I don't suppose it really matters. He'll be back, of course?" Alix nodded. "Then there's no hurry. How did it go?"

"There's nothing to worry about. Jack Campbell won't be giving away any of the Lafayette's secrets."

March's face darkened. "What do you mean?"

"I simply mean that there are no secrets to give away, are there?" She smiled.

"No, no. Of course not. You've done a good job, Alix. Thank you. We won't forget you for this." He touched her arm lightly and went on his way.

Alix shivered at the thought of his touch and at the memory of him almost striking Hawkins. March was afraid the workman had told her something, but he seemed convinced now of her lie. Still, she knew Preston well enough to know that he'd do everything in his power from now on to keep Hawkins away from her. And that meant that one day soon she'd have to seek out the workman herself and ask him just what he'd meant about "the experiments."

Jean-Louis was one of Washington's top restaurants, and as such, was almost impossible to get into at short notice. But Jack knew the owner, and a good table for two awaited them when they arrived at eight-thirty, even though Campbell hadn't called to make a reservation until nearly five. The restaurant was located in the Watergate complex on Virginia Avenue, and its superb cuisine managed to transcend the lingering smell of Nixonian politics.

Alix, sitting in the lush, warmly lighted dining room, felt she, too, had transcended the past. Helping her concentrate on her immediate surroundings and the reason she was here was a purée of broccoli soup that enchanted her and Jack Campbell, a handsome man who, since picking her up forty-five minutes before, had been the epitome of charm. In fact, so good was he at making Alix relax that, for the first time in recent memory, she felt like a truly desirable woman.

Indeed, the newness and the freshness of these feelings made her realize yet again just how much she'd holed herself up after Richard's death, had locked herself in a prison within her own heart and had then tossed away the key. She had dated men in Boston, but they tended to be cool intellectual types who were usually looking for a companion who might enjoy the philharmonic, or a movie, never anything more. They rarely tried to make physical contact with Alix, and when they did, it was invariably awkward and, finally, embarrassing. One date was usually enough. But being with Jack made Alix want to be touched intimately, to feel a man's hands and lips on her body. And, oddly enough, rather than frightening Alix, the feelings excited her.

"I said I usually deal more with hard news reporting," Jack was going on, "and maybe I can bring a little of that technique to what might otherwise be a puff piece on the Lafayette." He attacked a slice of pigeon pâté and grinned at her.

"I hope you have better luck than you did with your first stab at it. I mean, your ideal specimen got away, if I remember correctly."

"Sarah Williams?" He looked up thoughtfully. "She was a sweet kid, very studious and very earnest. But nice . . . you know, naive in an academic sort of way," Campbell said, wondering now if Alix Kendall had been like that in her schooldays. Alix was a beauty, and in his mind he pictured her during her stay in the groves of academe, shuttling between her books and her dates with a wide variety of very anxious young men. "Sarah and I had just begun to get to know each other when *poof!* she was gone, disappeared into thin air."

"Isn't that putting it a little melodramatically?"

Jack shook his head. "Not really. I called her apartment house, asked around, and no one knew what had happened to her. Even the administrator at Georgetown—where she was in premed—was mystified. It looks like Sarah just packed up her belongings and headed for the hills."

"I guess studying medicine can be too tough for some people," Alix said absently, feeling somehow dissatisfied with Campbell's explanation. Being selected by the Lafayette was too great an honor to toss away like that. Alix decided to check into it. "Did you call her parents to find out if she ever got to 'the hills'—home?"

Campbell shook his head. "Her parents are both dead—that much I did find out. I don't know if there's anyone else *to* call. Besides, why bother? I've already got a new guinea pig."

"Yes, I saw her. I'd be careful, too. That particular guinea pig looks like she might bite," Alix said mischievously; then she grew serious once again. "It does seem strange, though."

"Have I got you interested in this mystery now?" he asked slyly. "I was wondering how I'd ask you out again. Now I know: we'll discuss the case of the vanishing med student." He smiled and caught her eyes, and for a moment felt closer to her than he'd expected would happen in such a short time.

"You don't need excuses to see me again, Jack. Just ask," she said softly. But he was right; she was interested in Sarah. The student had "disappeared into thin air," to use Jack's words, and "disappear" was the same word Hawkins had used when he warned Alix to leave the Lafayette! But the whole thing seemed ridiculous. What possible connection could there be between a deformed maintenance man and a pretty young med student?

The subject of Sarah Williams was dropped in favor of lighter topics, and as the evening progressed, Alix fantasized more and more what it would be like to be in Jack Campbell's arms. Jack Campbell was a man's man. He was the kind of guy one got to know in minutes, and that bond either held for years or it didn't hold for five minutes. To know Campbell for an hour was to know everything about him. Jack drew from his past like an artist returns to the same set of colors, but always mixes and applies them in a new way. Jack Campbell's past was so much a part of his present that Alix began to wonder where one left off and the other began.

He treated others with a casual respect that was often mistaken for arrogance. But to be arrogant was to care less about those others than yourself, and that just wasn't Jack. Alix watched him as he told obvious favorite stories, the stories that brought him the most joy. Despite his "tough-reporter" persona, she began to see that the plight of many of the people he wrote about touched him personally. Jack Campbell was a rare thing—an honest, honorable, and loving man, and with each word he won Alix over a little more.

By the time they were ready to leave, Alix had already promised herself to invite him over for a nightcap—if he didn't ask himself first. Jack left Alix at the entrance of the restaurant momentarily to get their coats. Alix was feeling deliciously sensual and warmly excited. She'd had a wonderful dinner with a charming companion, and now there was the definite prospect of an even more intimate encounter. But before she had time to imagine any further, her attention was drawn to a nearby table, where a couple was just being seated. The woman was tall and sleekly beautiful, with an air of self-confidence that more than suggested arrogance. She knew her beauty was attracting attention and she bathed in it while pretending hardly to notice. The man with her was as handsome as she was beautiful. He stood tall and erect, his black hair slicked back in a new fashion that suggested an old style. He surveyed the other diners with cool disdain, and when he allowed the maître d' to take their drink orders, he treated him like a stable boy. Alix couldn't take her eyes off him, for here, not more than twenty feet from her, was the man she'd seen on Wisconsin Avenue—Richard Hailey.

"Ready to go?" Jack suddenly appeared with her coat.

The sound of his voice startled Alix, but she managed to maintain her calm appearance. "Yes, of course." She allowed Jack to help her with the coat, all the time fighting the urge to run back into the main dining room of the restaurant and confront the man. Then, as they stepped outside into the parking lot, her feelings overwhelmed her. "I've forgotten my scarf," she lied nimbly. "I'll be right back." She left Campbell at the entrance and quickly made her way across the crowded restaurant to the table where the stranger sat. She stood for a moment staring at him before he saw her. Then, when his eyes did meet hers, she waited for a smile of recognition, shock, something . . . but there was nothing.

After a moment's embarrassing silence the man said, "May I help you? Are you lost or something?" His voice was heavy with sarcasm.

"Excuse me . . . I . . . thought you were someone I once knew," she mumbled, already knowing this man couldn't be her Richard. His voice was all wrong, his mannerisms too. He was Richard's double, but that was all.

"Sorry, wrong man." He smiled indulgently at Alix, then immediately returned his attention to his dinner companion, who'd surveyed the scene with utter disdain.

"You see . . . I thought you were. . . But you couldn't be . . ." Alix fumbled for the right explanation, refusing to be dismissed. But when the man continued to ignore her presence, Alix returned to Campbell, deeply humiliated.

"Anything wrong?" he asked immediately. "You look upset."

"No, there's nothing," she lied, choking back her tears. "I'm just tired, I guess. Please take me home." All her dreams of a warm encounter were dashed.

She said good night to Campbell at the door and went immediately to bed, feeling lonelier than she'd ever felt before in her life.

—4—

During the course of the next weeks Alix became obsessed with the man she'd seen at the restaurant that night. She tried to put him out of her mind, but it was impossible. The rational part of her mind told her that she was being irrational—to believe a man who had died ten years before could just suddenly turn up again alive *was* crazy! But the emotional part of Alix told her over and over again that the man was Richard Hailey, despite some outward differences, despite the fact that he'd pretended not to recognize her. *How* he was still alive didn't matter; *that* he was still alive did!

When finally her work began to suffer, Alix took a few days off from the Lafayette. It was just after Christmas, and she whiled away the hours walking through the city, hoping to be cheered by the music and the bright holiday decorations that seemed to be everywhere. But nothing lifted the depressing cloak of sadness and grief that had fallen over her. Ever since that dinner with Jack Campbell, Alix had spent most of her free time with him and had found some measure of comfort in his arms, but even his loving attention, the caresses that drove her over and over again into a sexual frenzy, didn't touch the core of her pain. She felt that a part of her had died yet again that night at Jean-Louis. But unlike ten years ago, this time, coupled with the familiar sadness was a new determination to take charge of her life and to make some sense of it! And that meant finding out the identity of her Georgetown specter.

The afternoon of the second day off from work, Alix was walking home when she realized she'd walked too far along M Street. She'd meant to turn up Twenty-sixth Street, yet here she was at Wisconsin Avenue, just like she'd been the day before and the day before that and the day before that. Returning to the corner where she'd seen "Richard" was now part of the obsession which Alix seemed powerless to stop. She followed the route up Wisconsin to R Street, across R to Twenty-sixth, then finally down to N Street and home. She'd walked this route in the morning, in the afternoon, and even in late evening, hoping she might accidentally confront her personal phantom. It never happened.

Alix's head began to pound with a familiar dull pain, and she knew she'd once again pushed herself too hard. She headed straight home, wondering how it was possible that she, an intelligent woman, was actually chasing through the streets of Georgetown after someone who was dead. Why couldn't she just let go of the past and begin living life today? It wasn't as if her life was miserable: she had her work, which she loved; she had Jack Campbell, whom she had begun to care about; she had all the trappings of a nice, contented life. Yet here she was driving herself to distraction because she *thought* Richard was still out there waiting for her.

Once back inside the apartment, Alix built a fire to cheer herself up and made a cup of tea, kicked off her shoes, and settled deep into the couch. As the tea began to revive her, her headache eased and she drifted into a state somewhere between waking and sleeping. The face of the man she was pursuing appeared in front of her mind's eye and slowly changed, transforming until it was unmistakably Richard Hailey's—as she'd known it during her premed days. She remembered the way the two of them lay naked in the bed of her garret apartment. Richard always smiled when he looked at Alix, but grew serious when he touched her. He'd always told her there would never be anyone else in the world for him, and she'd believed it. His delicate hands—the hands of a future plastic surgeon—

skimmed over her body as if it were fragile china. And when they made love, nothing else in the world existed for Alix.

Alix's eyes opened with a start. She slammed her teacup down on the coffee table, spilling some of the amber liquid onto its top. What was the use of these maudlin memories? What was the use of pretending there was any hope? Richard Hailey was dead! He'd burned to death ten years before. Alix had gone to his funeral, had seen his casket being lowered into the moist spring earth. Believing anything else was sheer insanity!

Determined now to start getting a grip on her life as she'd promised herself, Alix jumped up from the couch, went to the bathroom, took a fast shower to freshen up, then caught a taxi to the Lafayette. It was still early enough in the day to get plenty of work done. Whatever delirium she'd suffered these past days because of seeing Richard's doppelganger in the Watergate restaurant was over. And as she swung happily through the glass doors of the Lafayette, feeling the coolness of its halls, Alix told herself that she'd never again let the past get such a hold on her. She even forgot her promise to look into the disappearance of Sarah Williams.

During the following weeks Alix renewed her dedication to her work. She became so preoccupied that she allowed herself to drift away from Jack Campbell— telling him the truth, that she was working—but never really felt that he was gone from her life. Alix worked herself like a dray horse at her projects, and also taught three classes a week. She was given two assistants whose meticulous attention to detail mirrored her own, but despite her care and planning, the experiments she'd begun after arriving from Boston turned out to be a miserable failure. She was very discouraged by this setback, but Preston March, always the optimist, told her not to worry.

"Failure," he said, "is the first step toward success." And when he reaffirmed the Lafayette's faith in Alix's ability, she felt better.

During the holiday season there was an added flurry

of activity at the Lafayette, but for all the hustle and
bustle, Alix observed that the ironclad structure of
the Institute was maintained. An outsider, confronted
by the torrent of projects at both of the Institute
buildings, would have been hopelessly confused—who
did what and where, who had authority and who didn't.
To Alix, now accustomed to the turmoil, this blurring
of the lines of responsibility was done on purpose—by
none other than Preston March himself. Everything
that happened at the Lafayette always found its beginnings with March.

It seemed that March was a conjurer nonpareil, an
administrator able to produce vast, flashy displays of
legerdemain while the real magic, the true sleight-of-
hand, happened offstage. But Alix wasn't fooled. She
had kept her eyes open and was able to segregate
superfluous activities from important ones, drones from
soldiers, figureheads from the truly important. And in
doing so, she began to get the uncomfortable feeling
that she—indeed the Lafayette itself—was a very small
part of something far greater, more far-reaching than
she or even Campbell had ever imagined. This feeling
was nothing she could substantiate with hard, cold
facts, but it was enough to make her more watchful,
more wary. And when she shook her head sometimes
and tried to convince herself that she was becoming as
paranoid as Jack, she'd once again hear Hawkins'
frightened voice babbling about "the experiments."

Alix hadn't seen Hawkins since that day. She had
never gone down to the lower, computer level to seek
him out and it wasn't odd that she hadn't seen him
during the day; after all, he was instructed not to
come upstairs during working hours. But often she
worked long into the night, and when he didn't appear,
Alix decided that Hawkins had been transferred out
to the Lafayette Annex in Langley, Virginia. It was
easier to believe that than to believe something had
happened to him.

The Annex was the highly classified sector of the
Lafayette. It was the mystery within the Institute, the
sector the newspapers so often attacked. It was not
open to visitors, yet Alix knew from personal observa-

tion that a phalanx of grim-faced, gray-suited men
shuttled back and forth from the main buildings to
the Annex at least once a week. She also knew that
Preston March treated these men with the respect due
only the highest dignitaries. She imagined these men
were government types only because they looked like
bureaucrats, but beyond that her imagination refused
to function.

But in the end Alix was too preoccupied with her
work to give much consideration to anything else. She
loved working for Ted Winner, but she also worried
about him. He was a sweet, nervous little man in his
early forties with a bland face dwarfed by thick horn-
rimmed glasses. Winner was driven by his work, which
might have accounted for his nervous state, but it
didn't explain the fact that he was obviously terrified
of Preston March. More than once when Winner was
summoned to March's office, Alix had seen him go
through a total transformation that left him trembling.
And more than once afterward she had smelled liquor
on his breath. Alix wanted to be a friend to Winner as
well as a colleague, but though he treated her with
nothing but the utmost respect, he always backed off
when her questions or the conversation became too
personal. It was obvious that Ted Winner was not
only a sweet little man but also a scared one.

Alix felt good about herself, but until Jack called
one rainy afternoon, she'd forgotten that with him she
felt even better.

"I never see you anymore, Alix," he complained
without bothering to say hello.

"That's ridiculous," Alix replied, knowing it was
true. "We're together all the time."

"And when was the last 'all the time'?" he challenged.

Alix thought a moment before answering, "Just a
couple of days ago, surely . . ."

"It was nearly two weeks ago, to be exact. We haven't
even talked in five days. Alix, if you're trying to tell
me something, why not just say it? I'm a big boy now.
I can take rejection without falling apart."

Jack was right. She'd tipped the balance too much in

the other direction; work was taking up all her time now. "I'm sorry. I do want to see you, but—"

"Then see me," he interrupted. "Tonight. And let's go out for a change. You're either locked away in that godforsaken black castle on the Potomac or, when I do see you, we stay in your apartment."

"I didn't know you objected so strenuously to being alone with me," Alix said dryly.

"Don't take umbrage, honey. I love being alone with you, but let's interject a little outside stimulus into our relationship. I sometimes get the feeling you're hiding from something . . . or someone."

Alix felt a jolt of apprehension. She hadn't meant to hide, but it looked like maybe that's exactly what she was doing—working long hours, staying at home, avoiding Jack. What was next? Leaving Washington again for another nice protective cocoon like Boston?

"You still there?" he queried.

"Of course . . ." She faltered. "Now where would you like to go?"

"The Kennedy Center. I've got orchestra seats for the tryout of a new play. We'll have a little supper after . . . *then* we can go back to your place and be as alone as you want."

"Dinner and the theater sounds divine. As for afterward . . . I don't know, Jack. I've got a long day ahead of me." She meant it as a tease, and Campbell obviously understood.

"We'll talk about afterward afterward. I'll pick you up at your place about seven-fifteen."

"See you then. And, Jack, thanks for reminding me there's a world outside the Lafayette."

"Think nothing of it. See you."

At five-forty-five Alix forced herself to desert her work. Since the failure of the Boston project, she'd been doing a study of the thymus gland, the originator—so it was thought—of the T-cell antibodies that protected the body from disease. As the aging process occurred, the thymus shrank until it was no longer functional. As this process of deterioration occurred, the absence of the T-cells and the concurrent rise of susceptibility to disease was always noted. Alix hoped that by studying the thymus she might learn to retard its "death" and at the same time assure the longevity of T-cell immunity, which, in turn, would make the aging body far less prone to fall victim to disease and, ultimately, death.

She pulled on her coat and hurried out of the lab, down the hallway to the elevators, where she rode up to the fifth floor. She was feeling so good about tonight's date that she decided to drop in on Preston March on her way out to say good night. She and Preston had established a very cordial relationship and had dinner once or twice a month as a matter of routine. Alix knew she'd been singled out for this honor, but it wasn't without its price. March always interrogated her not only about her own work but also about Ted Winner's. There was an air of urgency to his questioning that he was unable to disguise as anything else. But, given his age, his wish to succeed in the area of gerontology was understandable.

March's questions about Winner weren't quite so palatable. He always phrased his inquiries about Winner in terms of how he was "holding up," as if he expected the man to collapse one day. And it became evident that although Preston held Winner in high esteem professionally, his feeling about the man personally bordered on contempt. In fact, so intense was his dislike that Alix, when questioned about Winner, always felt as if she were betraying him, as if something she might say would push March over the edge and allow him to make the final decision to fire him. And replace him with Alix?

As she pushed into the reception area of March's office, Alix put these thoughts aside. She was there to say hello, not to judge. But neither March nor his secretary was in evidence. Alix decided to wait inside. Without March's commanding presence, the office seemed doubly gray and dull. Feeling slightly deflated by his absence, Alix walked past his desk to the window and stared out over the Potomac to the grim winter Virginia countryside opposite. How depressing this tinted glass makes everything look. How insular

it makes me feel, she thought morosely. Sometimes
Alix felt as if she were a hundred years old, as if she'd
already been through several lifetimes. But tonight
she'd promised herself to have fun with Jack Campbell,
and shaking off her gloomy mood was the first step
toward that end, so she turned to leave March's office
and collided with his briefcase, which lay on a small
table next to her. The case fell to the floor and its
contents spilled out around her feet.

The thick black folder caught Alix's eye immediately.
It looked like any one of the hundreds of lab reports
that were maintained throughout each section of the
Lafayette, but this was labeled "The Annex" and under that the simple but arresting word TRAUMA was
emblazoned on its front cover in gold. Alix picked it
up and opened it, knowing she shouldn't. She was
snooping, and to get caught was to get fired. Yet she
couldn't stop herself. And as her eyes scanned the
page, she wished she'd just cast it aside and gone on her
way.

The title page, too, was headed TRAUMA, with the
addition of "Third Run." Under that were four names,
each followed by a page number. *The first name on
that list was Sarah Williams!*

The moment Alix saw the name, her internal warning system screamed for her to return the folder to
March's briefcase and walk away, pretending never to
have seen it. But she couldn't. The same force that
had made her open the file made her flip through it,
and not only did she read the other three names, but
she committed them to memory, knowing that later
they would be useful. But useful for what? Alix had
forgotten all about Sarah Williams and her own earlier pledge to find out what had happened to her. But
now that the name stood before her eyes, her determination to investigate was renewed. She reexamined
the folder. TRAUMA. She'd never heard the word
used at the Lafayette outside its usual medical appli-
cation, but obviously there *was* a special meaning.
And these names were part of that, connecting it
directly to the Annex.

Someone entered the outer office. Alix quickly returned the TRAUMA dossier to its place and replaced the briefcase on the desk. She turned back to the window as, seconds later, someone entered, paused, and waited. Alix was tensed like a spring, but she pretended she hadn't heard anything; she forced herself to remain calmly by the window. Whoever had come into the room now moved forward.

"I hardly expected to find you in my office when I'm not here," March said dryly as he moved behind the desk toward Alix. "In fact, I don't like finding anyone here when I'm elsewhere." His voice was very low, still angry, but more controlled.

"I hope I haven't done something wrong, Preston." Alix used every ounce of strength she could muster to keep her voice even. She wanted to sound cheerful but not hysterical, apologetic but not guilty. It was a thin line to walk. "I just stopped by to say good night before I left . . . and Sally wasn't outside . . . so I came in."

"Next time, please stay outside," he said, taking a seat behind the desk, for the first time seeing the briefcase next to Alix's left hand. His eyes traveled from the case to Alix, then back again; her eyes followed his but gave no sign of recognition. Moments later it seemed that a crisis had passed. March smiled. "I must admit, though, that it does my old heart good to hear you say you wanted to say good night. Sometimes it's easy to forget the little niceties of life."

"Exactly my thought," she said quickly. "Well, now that I've done it, I'm off to the theater."

"Let's have dinner again soon," he said as she walked away. "I'm very fond of you, Alix."

She stopped and smiled. "And I'm fond of you, too, Preston." She left without another word.

After she'd gone, March sat silently for a few minutes digesting the little scene they'd just played out. Alix Kendall *was* the kind of woman who'd stop by to say good night, of that he had no doubt . . . but she was also the kind of woman who had an active imagination and a healthy—or unhealthy for her—curiosity. There was too much at stake for him not to take a few preliminary steps to find out just what she was up to.

If she'd seen the TRAUMA dossier, there was no telling what that might lead to. He wanted her to read it, but not just yet.

March picked up the briefcase and locked it, cursing himself for being so lax. I must be getting old, he thought ruefully. Well, one day soon we'll take care of that. He dialed an in-house telephone number. "It's Dr. March. Alix Kendall is just leaving the Institute. Have one of your men follow her tonight, then report back to me in the morning."

He hung up, thought a moment, then made a second call, this time to an outside number. "It's Preston. I think it's time to make a first move with Alix Kendall. She may have read a part of the TRAUMA dossier. Send her an invitation to the party, will you? Good."

If she were going to replace Ted Winner one day, Alix would have to be privy to a few things most members of the Lafayette were unaware of. Easing her into the Institute's inner circle was a beginning. And as TRAUMA was revealed to her bit by bit, either Alix's loyalty would be assured or she would be found unsuitable to continue. March truly hoped that she would decide to come over to their side. He liked Alix. And hated the thought of any harm coming to her.

The following Saturday, Alix spent the day at home cleaning and straightening up. Autumn was long gone and winter had set in with its rampages of cold winds and attacks of thick snow. Alix had read that Boston was submerged by a recent blizzard, and for a moment she reminisced about the hard New England winters. There was something nice, almost comforting about spending the winter months wrapped in heavy clothing, darting through snowdrifts and rivers of slush from one warmly heated place to another. Life in Boston— winter or summer—had always made Alix feel relatively peaceful. But life in Washington, despite Jack Campbell, was still tinged with too much sadness to be truly comfortable.

When Alix finished cleaning the windows, she stood back to admire her work. The sun sliced into the living room with all its brilliance. She wouldn't do the

windows again until spring, and because all during
the next weeks the house would be pelted with the
dirty rain and the soot of the city, this was her last
chance to see clearly. See clearly, she thought. When
was the last time I really saw clearly? For a moment
Alix remembered Jack sitting on the couch the night
they'd gone to the theater, the night she'd presented
him with the list of names from the TRAUMA dossier.
She'd wanted to be casual about it, but they both heard
the tenseness in her voice.

"And what's this supposed to be?" Jack asked as he
read the four names.

"I don't know, it's just something I found," Alix
equivocated. There was no use whetting Jack's appe-
tite for an exposé by explaining the real circumstances
under which she had "found" the names; it smacked
too much of the "mad-scientist" variety of cheap fiction.

"Sarah Williams is on top of the list. What's she
got to do with this?" Campbell was now definitely
interested.

Alix shook her head. "I told you, Jack, I don't know.
If you're not interested . . ." She reached out to take
the list from him, but he quickly put it in his pocket.

"Oh, no, you don't. I'll look into it, but I've got to
say you're acting very strangely." He'd let his arm
slip down around her shoulder as he readjusted himself next to her on the couch.

Alix only shrugged. She *didn't* know what the list
meant, but she did have a *feeling* that it was very
important. Sarah Williams' name had come up too
many times for it to be sheer coincidence. Involving
Campbell in this was a risky move, particularly since
he still believed the Lafayette Institute was involved
in something far more serious than medical research
on aging, but Alix had no choice. Jack was a reporter
with sources of information she couldn't even imagine;
she needed his expertise. What she didn't need,
however, was his prying. If he did turn up anything
concrete to incriminate March and his cohorts, Jack
certainly would want to expose them—placing Alix in
a very awkward position indeed. If he didn't, then
nothing was lost. But what were the chances of find-

ing nothing incriminating about the Lafayette? After her encounter with Hawkins, they seemed pretty slim.

"Let's talk about mysterious *after* you uncover one or more skeletons, okay?" Alix took Jack's hand, suddenly feeling like a traitor and wishing she had never opened the TRAUMA dossier. There was no way around the fact that she was being dishonest, and that made her uncomfortable. It was not a good way to begin a relationship.

"In that case, I've got a much better idea." Jack pulled her into his arms.

Alix allowed herself to be led into her bedroom without question. Jack's lovemaking freed her mind from all the doubts and fears she had about herself and her work. Campbell was boyishly direct in his sexuality, and boyishly clumsy when dealing with Alix physically. His macho swagger obviously had worked with some women—and with all men, probably—but in bed with her, that facade fell. And Alix loved him for it. After all, Jack Campbell was a newspaper reporter, a breed of man that had tough standards and archetypes to live up to. To the "guys" down at *The District Columbian*, Jack was the hard-boiled, hard-drinking misanthrope. But to Alix, holding him in her arms, he was the queasy kid who'd fainted during the autopsy, the gentle man who made love to her with a tender yet fiery passion that rose from an inner core of caring.

Alix's sexual encounters with Campbell burst the dam of repressed emotions that she'd kept locked in her heart since Richard's death. Whether it was Jack himself or the simple need for physical release, Alix didn't know, and she didn't care. All she knew was that when they became like one body, time momentarily stood still, the cold night air warmed, and the entire universe focused itself on the point where he'd become part of her. Jack built Alix's pleasure to a screaming high, and just when she thought it impossible to feel anything more, she exploded into a shower of ecstasy, an emotional electrical storm that shook her. And occasionally, when Jack's face blurred and became Richard Hailey's, it was only momentary and the demon of Alix's past seemed, finally, to have been exorcised.

That night, after not being together for two weeks, they lay in each other's arms after making love like they always did, but something had changed. They clung to each other like longtime lovers. The time apart seemed to have brought them far closer together than either had expected. Alix was confused. She'd given so much to Jack that night that even though they talked of things in general, the subtext was a new and vibrant love for each other.

And that scared Alix. She'd allowed herself to love once before, and it had been taken away from her. Would that happen again? What was the use of speculating? She could never be sure of anything except that right now she was warm and safe in Campbell's arms. And right now was all that mattered. She'd learned that ten years ago. Tomorrow might change everything, but to live in fear of the future was to kill today. And she'd already had enough taken away from her.

They decided to have dinner on Tuesday, and Jack promised that by then he'd have some background on the names from the TRAUMA dossier. His parting words expressed how happy he was that Alix had decided to move to Washington. Although she appreciated his sentiments, Alix still wasn't convinced that one day soon she wouldn't regret that decision, despite Campbell and the joy he brought her.

The jangling telephone brought Alix out of her reverie. She threw the cleaning cloth onto the coffee table and darted to the kitchen extension.

"May I speak with Dr. Alixandra Kendall?" an unknown male voice requested.

"This is she."

"Dr. Kendall, this is Alan Fitzroy's assistant. Mr. Fitzroy is having a small cocktail party Tuesday evening and would very much like you to attend. There will be an invitation in the mail, but it is late and he wanted to be sure you didn't make other plans."

"I don't know any Alan Fitzroy," Alix said, perplexed.

There was what sounded like an exasperated sigh

on the other end of the line. "Mr. Fitzroy is on the board of the Lafayette Institute and is also a close friend of Preston March. The party is a small gathering for some Lafayette staff. Mr. Fitzroy would like to meet you."

"Oh," Alix said, suddenly embarrassed. "Well, in that case, tell Mr. Fitzroy I accept."

"I'll do that," the man said tartly.

"Thank you," Alix sputtered before he hung up. Alan Fitzroy. Where had she heard that name before? Well, she'd find out on Tuesday. Tuesday! She and Jack had a date for Tuesday night. Now she'd have to cancel. He wouldn't like the idea of being stood up, but he couldn't object when he learned it was business, not pleasure.

She again picked up the phone and called Jack. "Tell me, Mr. Ace Reporter," she joked when he answered, "what do you know about Alan Fitzroy?"

Without hesitation Campbell said, "Alan Fitzroy is one of Washington's Boy Wonders. He's head of the Roth Corporation—the think tank—and he's in so thick with the President that you couldn't cut them apart with a hatchet. And his politics are so far right you couldn't get the John Birch Society to touch him with a ten-foot pole."

"What's he like? I mean, how old, what's he look like, you know." Alix pictured a white-haired old man, a contemporary of Preston March.

"Fitzroy doesn't like to have his picture taken, so I don't believe I've ever seen him, up close that is. But from his background sheet I know he's in his late thirties, handsome, and he's also got something of a reputation as a womanizer." Jack sighed. "Personally, I think the man's dangerous. He's got too much power for someone with the beliefs he holds."

"And he's on the board of the Lafayette Institute," Alix said, musing aloud.

"How did you know that?"

"His secretary just told me," she said.

"Alix, do you want to tell me what's going on, or do we play more Twenty Questions?" Campbell was obviously getting annoyed.

Alix explained the phone call and at the same time canceled her date for Tuesday. "It's business, Jack," she said as she finished.

There was a moment's pause; then Campbell said, "I don't like it, Alix. Alan Fitzroy plays with the big boys, the power brokers of Washington—the country, for that matter. There have been reports about him I don't like."

"What kind of reports?"

"That he and the Lafayette—"

Alix cut him off. "If you're going to start that business about the Institute again, I don't want to hear it. If you want to know, I think you're just jealous because I'm going to a party held by a notorious 'womanizer'—that was your word, wasn't it?"

"Go, Alix. Go and have a good time!" he said angrily.

"I will," she said just as angrily. "I appreciate the fact that you care enough about me to be jealous, but I don't appreciate the jealousy, not this early in the game."

"That's just it—it's not a game, not for me, anyway," he said softly. "But you're right, I am overstepping my bounds. Go to the party and have a good time . . . but be careful."

"Afraid he might woo me into his well-worn bed?" she joked, hoping to ease the tension.

"I'm afraid you may already have been wooed into something way over your head," he said seriously.

"Don't worry. I'm a big girl now. I can take care of myself." She hung up and finished the last of her cleaning, growing more excited about Fitzroy's party with each passing minute. There was no real reason to feel this way, yet she did. If Jack hadn't made Alan Fitzroy sound so mysterious, so handsome . . . and dangerous, Alix wouldn't have given the party a second thought. But he had, and now she could hardly wait for Tuesday night to come.

—5—

Alan Fitzroy's house was an enormous Federal-style mansion on R Street opposite Dumbarton Oaks. The house was set back from the street on a large piece of prime real estate, and tucked into a corner of the drive was a silver Rolls-Royce. Alix stepped from the taxi onto the gravel drive and pulled her cloth coat closer about her, wishing it were sable. She paid the driver, walked under the portico, and as if by magic, the front door opened and a liveried butler showed her into a wide, spacious foyer whose marble floors amplified the sounds of her footsteps and the echoes of laughter from a room to her right.

The foyer was cautiously decorated in Louis Seize, but an open door at the far end of the hallway revealed a library whose fixtures were the best Bauhaus. For a moment Alix was overwhelmed by the opulence of Fitzroy's house; then, from the adjoining room, she heard Ted Winner's hearty laughter and she felt immediately at home.

After a moment spent alone in the foyer, wondering where her host was, Alix drifted into the living room, which was crowded with people. She recognized many of them from the Lafayette—including several of the "bureaucrats" who shuttled to and fro at the Annex—and many were strangers. A passing waiter paused by her side, offering champagne. Alix took a glass, then pushed herself deeper into the room, looking for Ted Winner or another friendly face.

The room was lavishly decorated with a startling blend of antique and modern, all placed on the largest Oriental rug Alix had ever seen. Everywhere in the room there were vases of fresh flowers, an expense anytime, an extravagance in mid-winter. The walls were covered with fine paintings, many by artists whom Alix was able to recognize, despite her minimal art education. All in all, Fitzroy's living room was the most intimidating she'd ever been in. Alix wondered, as she looked around, what the man who lived amid such splendor was like.

"Alix?" someone said next to her, and she turned; it was Ted Winner, obviously drunk. "I had no idea you'd be here." He looked at her with amazement, then belted down a half-glass of wine.

"Alan Fitzroy's secretary called me over the weekend and invited me," she explained. "By the way, where is our host?"

Winner shrugged. "Probably upstairs solving some world problems . . . or creating some, more likely," he said darkly. Winner took her arm and led her to the enormous fireplace, where a log fire crackled. "I'm *very* surprised to see you here . . . and very happy, too, I might add."

"I'm a little surprised myself. I don't even know Mr. Fitzroy."

"Ah, but he knows you," Winner said with a lop-sided grin. He signaled a waiter, took another glass of champagne, and proceeded to drain it forthwith. "Mr. Fitzroy knows everything, even the secrets of life."

"What?" Alix asked absently. Winner was too drunk to take seriously. She'd hoped to find a kindred spirit; instead she'd found an inebriated one. As he talked on, Alix scanned the room, looking for someone to rescue her.

In a far corner a group of elderly people stood huddled around a young couple; she was pretty and demure, he was toothy smiles and all-American good looks. Alix didn't recognize either of them, but whoever they were, they had to be something special, for the men and women circling them beamed with something close to adoration.

Maybe it's their youth, Alix thought to herself as she surveyed the wizened faces of the men and women nearby. Maybe they're remembering the beginnings of their own lives as reflected in the faces of those . . .

newlyweds? Was that the reason so much attention was being paid them?

"What's the story with that couple?" Alix interrupted Winner, who had grabbed yet another glass of champagne from a passing waiter.

Winner followed her gaze, took a long pull from his glass, then smiled crookedly. "So you *haven't* been told about TRAUMA. I thought not." His voice was thick and slurred, but Alix was now beginning to listen.

"TRAUMA?" Alix asked as calmly as possible, despite her wildly beating heart. "Ted, what *are* you talking about?"

"That couple are Dr. and Mrs. Philip Greenspan— Nancy and Phil—just your ordinary suburban couple," he said mysteriously.

"Don't be so cryptic," Alix said impatiently, noting that two of the dour "bureaucrats" had taken notice of her and Winner—Ted in particular.

"It's the Greenspans' birthday, that's all," Winner said happily. "Imagine that nice couple having exactly the same birthday ... right down to the minute." He sipped his wine, seemingly angry at the thought. "And I helped make it the shortest gestation period in history. Me and Preston March, of course, father of us all," he said sarcastically.

This time when Winner looked back at the Greenspans he saw the two Lafayette officials talking and nodding in his direction. They conferred one last time; then one of them quickly went out into the foyer. Ted drained his drink.

"Ted, don't you think you've had enough to drink?" Alix insisted. "You're drunk enough as it—"

Winner suddenly took her by the arm and spoke quickly, earnestly. "I'm going to pretend to stumble in a moment. Help me up and take what I give you, but for God's sake, don't look at it, don't let them know you've got it." His eyes blazed with fear and he sounded remarkably sober. "The key to TIM is the word TRAUMA. Can you remember that? That's where it is."

"I don't under—" Alix began to say, but before she could finish, Winner "tripped" and fell against the fireplace. Alix reached out to help him, and as her hand clasped around his, he transferred something into her hand, something that felt like a credit card.

"Need some help?" A male voice came from behind her.

"I don't think so," Alix said, suddenly aware from the look on Winner's face that he believed he was in grave personal danger.

"Dr. Kendall, why don't you let us take care of this?"

"But . . ." Alix looked up for the first time and found herself staring into the eyes of the man she'd seen in the Georgetown street, the man in the Watergate restaurant—the man she had once been convinced was Richard Hailey.

The man nodded, then assisted Alix, while a tall heavyset man with dead eyes and an unfeeling smile lifted Winner to his feet and ushered him quickly from the room. Still clutching the card tightly in her fist, Alix tried to catch Ted's eyes, but he looked away as if he'd never seen her before.

"Champagne sometimes does that to people," the stranger said condescendingly. "Are you all right, Dr. Kendall?"

Alix took a deep breath, smiled, and looked him directly in the eyes. "I'm fine, thank you, but how do you know my name?"

"It's my job to know your name; I'm your host, Alan Fitzroy."

Alix had no idea how composed her face was, but inside she'd completely fallen apart. She was still shaken by the scene with Winner, and confronting this man wasn't helping any. Alan Fitzroy! The ghost she'd been chasing since moving to Washington had, in the end, found her. Fitzroy's resemblance to Richard was uncanny. Of course, ten years' difference in age showed—Richard's hair had been jet black, Fitzroy's had a touch of gray at the temples; Richard's skin was like a baby's, Fitzroy's face had tiny lines that radiated out from his eyes and mouth—but the basic facial structure was the same.

"Anything wrong?" Fitzroy asked after Alix had stared at him for some time.

"You're a very handsome man, that's all," she said unexpectedly.

"And you're very beautiful," Fitzroy said just as easily. He took her hand and kissed it. "Much more beautiful than that night in the restaurant." He still held her hand.

Alix panicked momentarily. She hadn't expected him to remember her, yet there was no reason why he wouldn't. "You must have thought I was crazy, coming up to you like that. You just reminded me so much of someone I hadn't seen in years."

"Now, why would anyone let you get away from him for years? For minutes, for that matter," he said with open flattery.

Alix blushed. "Forgive me for breaking in on your dinner like that."

"My pleasure. If I hadn't been with that congressman's wife—it was strictly business—I would have forgiven you right then and there."

Alix blushed and felt the warmth of his gaze burn into every part of her body. It was as if Alan Fitzroy's eyes had penetrated a dark vault in her soul and freed a spirit that had been held captive there for years. She shivered slightly as she realized that it was the feeling she'd always had in Richard's presence. It was a feeling so subtle, so sublime, that her fear of it leaving was actually greater than its loss moments later. This is what's been missing from my life, she thought. This is what died and was buried with Richard! She wanted Fitzroy never to let go of her, but he did moments later.

"Preston has told me a great deal about you, Alix. He has a great respect for you . . . and cares deeply about you."

Alix smiled as though she were in a dream. Nowhere in her life—not at home in Chicago with her parents, or at school, or during all the years in Boston—had Alix been taught how to talk to a ghost or to the semblance of one. And if that weren't complicated enough, Alix knew that she'd fallen in love with Alan

Fitzroy on sight. Just like that. No, that wasn't true, she'd always been in love with him, even though they'd never met, because Alix had stumbled onto a hidden door marked "The Past," had found its key, opened it, and fallen back through time. And, like Alice down the rabbit hole, Alix Kendall had entered a world where time—and death—were meaningless.

"Dr. Kendall, are you sure you're all right? Maybe Dr. Winner's accident upset you more than you'd realized." Fitzroy was quite serious as he touched her lightly on the arm.

The mention of Winner's name forced Alix back to reality. "You mentioned Preston before. Is he here?"

Fitzroy's face fell. "Preston is ill, and I'm afraid he won't be able to make it."

"Seriously ill?"

"He'll be all right. Don't worry, the Lafayette will see to that; we take care of our own, you know."

"That's nice to know." She smiled, remembering how nice it was to be taken care of. "You have a beautiful house, Mr. Fitzroy," she said after a moment's silence.

"Alan, please." He smiled warmly again and touched her lightly on the arm. "We can't be so formal, Alix. After all, we're almost colleagues."

"In a way," she said automatically. Alix was still spinning from his touch; it had sent shock waves through her entire body that settled now deep in the pit of her stomach, and lower. "Are these all friends of yours?" she asked, trying desperately to keep her mind off his proximity. She wanted to take his head between her hands and kiss him and never stop.

"Friends and colleagues. Some are from the Lafayette, others the Roth Corporation."

"The 'think tank.' "

Fitzroy grimaced. "God, how I hate that misnomer. It makes me think of a school of dismembered brains swimming around in an aquarium."

"But you do just sit around and think, don't you?" Alix's naiveté—a trick that had always worked with Richard—was very calculated and it brought instant results.

"We sit around thinking as much as you scientists sit around and play with test tubes," he replied jokingly. But her question seemed to have turned the tide of their conversation, for Alan said, "Now, why don't you let me introduce you to some of the people you *don't* see eight hours a day at the Lafayette." He took her by the hand and guided her into a large group of men and women, introduced her, and then left her to her own devices.

The moment he was gone, Alix slipped the plastic card Ted had given her into her purse, then turned her attention to socializing. She allowed herself to get lost in the chatter of the strangers, but after a while she sought out Fitzroy across the room. He was a practiced and polished host as he made his way from one group of guests to another, staying just long enough to make them comfortable, then moving on. Richard Hailey wasn't like that at all. Richard was all thumbs when it came to being social. In fact, Richard was really no more than a boy when he died; his life had only begun.

This was a new twist to her thinking about Richard. In her reveries of him, she now realized, she'd aged him right along with her, brought him up-to-date. That was the true fantasy. Alix was no longer a young woman; she was ten years older now than those days. Thirty-two. And in those intervening years she'd grown used to being with men and women her own age— men, not boys. Men like Alan Fitzroy.

Forty-five minutes later Alix was ready to go home. She'd made several circuits of the room, talked to the people from the Lafayette she knew and to a score more she didn't, who all belonged to the Roth Corporation. Everyone was pleasant enough, but Alix detected an underlying tension she couldn't quite categorize. It wasn't anxiety, exactly, or a tension about something people feared might happen, but rather a holding back of joy over something that had *already* happened. Feeling this made her feel like the odd man out. She had the distinct feeling that everyone in Fitzroy's house knew something she didn't, and the minute she left, they would break into song and a spate of wild dancing to celebrate. But what?

When Alix found Fitzroy, told him she was leaving, and requested he call her a cab, he insisted his chauffeur drive her to her apartment in the Rolls.

"But that's ridiculous," Alix complained, even though she was thrilled at the idea.

"Someone as beautiful as you should have only the best, always," he assured her as he led her to the foyer. "Will I see you again?"

"If you'd like to," she said, not for a moment giving away the intensity of her desire to be with him again.

"I would like to. I'll call later in the week to arrange something. Dinner, maybe? Just the two of us?" He looked at her, then back into the living room. "Parties can be very nice, but tonight, being a host was a chore—it meant I didn't get to spend nearly enough time with you."

"We'll have to remedy that," she said lightly, feeling a stab of her old passion deep inside.

Fitzroy helped her into her coat, and for a moment they stood in the doorway, the cold night air enveloping them as it stole into the house through the open door. They said nothing, did nothing but look at each other, smiling. But in their smiles were promises to be kept, secrets to be shared. And they both knew it.

They parted without another word. Once ensconced in the back of Fitzroy's Rolls, Alix waved at Alan as the car pulled out of the circular drive.

Back home, Alix relived every moment of the time she'd spent with Alan Fitzroy. She felt like a young girl again, in love for the first time. It was infantile, of course, but that hardly mattered. What did matter was that she was going to see Alan again. So tonight wasn't the end of anything; it was the beginning!

She changed for bed and as she put away her things, she remembered the scene with Ted Winner, his falling act, everything. Alix opened her purse and found the card he'd given her. She sat down on the edge of the bed and held it under the bedside light: it was his TIM card, the key to the computer. He'd said the key word was TRAUMA—and that linked Winner to Preston, to the dossier she'd found in his briefcase, to the list of names, and to the young couple at the party, the Philip Greenspans.

Suddenly Alix was scared. She'd always taken Jack Campbell's paranoia about the Institute with a grain of salt, but now it was beginning to look like he might be right, though he had no idea that there was mounting evidence to support his theory. How ironic that Alix, of all people, had been placed in the driver's seat: she could investigate further or close her eyes for now.

Alix shook her head. Things weren't turning out the way she'd expected they would. She didn't *want* to have this responsibility thrust on her. She wasn't cut out to play a cloak-and-dagger role, yet she'd been thrown into the middle of one and she wasn't sure she knew the right lines. Part of her wanted to make a clean breast of everything to Campbell and be done with it. But that would not only end her career at Lafayette, but also alienate Alan Fitzroy. In the end she decided to continue with her own investigation, hoping that she would uncover nothing and, at the same time, hoping that it would take a very long time—time enough to get to know Fitzroy much, much better.

She slipped Winner's TIM card back into her purse, vowing to give it back to him tomorrow. If TRAUMA were the key, then she'd be told about it in good time when she got her own TIM card. But right now Alix had other, more important things to think about, like how to begin getting closer to a certain person named Fitzroy.

The next day Alix needed desperately to lose herself in her work, but she failed miserably. No matter what she turned her mind to, it kept returning to Alan Fitzroy. Dammit! she thought. Why does he have to look so much like Richard? If he hadn't been a carbon copy of her ex-fiancé, Alix probably would have gone her way without giving him a second thought. But he *did* look like Richard, and like it or not, that mesmerized her. It even made her begin fantasizing having

an affair with him despite Jack Campbell. Campbell.
The thought of him now made Alix feel like the world's
greatest traitor.

Jack had been so nice to her, so loving, that surely
she owed him something. Loyalty, for instance. Friend-
ship, too. But Alix refused to believe she owed him so
much she couldn't lead a life independent of him. Her
anger flared at the thought of being in debt to him
then it immediately subsided. The scenario she was
writing for her and Jack had nothing to do with reality;
she hadn't even had a single date with Alan Fitzroy,
yet she was already picking arguments with Campbell to accommodate that possibility. And in doing so
she'd given Jack short shrift again. It wasn't fair to
him, or to her.

At lunchtime, Alix drifted out of the lab to the
fifth-floor dining room, where she was to meet Preston
for their weekly lunch. Ted Winner hadn't shown up
for work, and Alix had assumed that he was at home
nursing a monumental hangover, until she called him
and got no answer. Then she began to wonder where
he was. When he'd given her his TIM card, it was as if
he knew he'd never need it again because something
was going to happen to him. But what?

Alix opened the doors to the executive dining room
and was instantly cheered by the bright decor. She
quelled her fears about Winner. After all, she had
promised herself to take things as they came along
and not to look for trouble. And a promise was a
promise.

Preston was already waiting for her at his regular
table, and as she made her way toward him, nodding
at several acquaintances, Alix spotted the two gray-
suited men she'd seen at Fitzroy's party last night.
They watched her closely, silently, but she just pretended not to notice them.

"And how did you enjoy Alan's party last night?"
March asked after seating Alix. "Sorry I wasn't there,
but I was a little under the weather."

"It was very nice. His house is quite impressive."
She now remembered Alan, for the hundredth time,

standing in the doorway waving good-bye, and she smiled to herself.

"Alan's earned everything he has. For a young man, he's done more work than many people do in a lifetime. And he's taken quite a shine to you, if I may get personal . . . just for a moment." March's eyes twinkled mischievously.

"Really?" Alix was pleased Fitzroy liked her, but was surprised he'd confided in March. "I didn't know you two were on such friendly terms," she said, the slight edge to her voice noticeable to both of them.

"I've offended you. I'm sorry," March apologized immediately.

"It's just that I'm not used to having my personal life bandied about."

"It's harmless, really. In many ways I feel like a father to Alan. I take a very personal interest in his life."

A father to Alan, Alix thought. Last night Ted Winner called Preston "father to us all." It had sounded so silly . . . then. "I didn't know Alan had so much to do with the running of the Lafayette."

"I owe the man a great deal. It was Alan Fitzroy who arranged for the funding of the Lafayette in the first place, though he likes to keep that quiet." He seemed to drift away for a moment. "Without his help we'd now be sitting in an open field."

"Did he also fund the building of the Annex?" she asked impetuously. The subject of the seldom-mentioned building out in Langley, Virginia, was not one they'd spent a great deal of time discussing.

"The Annex, oddly enough, already existed when this building was funded. Why do you ask?"

"It's such an enigma, that's all. I hear it mentioned now and again, but I have no idea what goes on there."

March nodded knowingly. "Most people don't. You see, that part of the Lafayette *is* heavily government-funded, and as such, remains only a distant cousin to us."

That explains the why of the Annex, she thought. But how about the what of it—what goes on there?

But now was not the time to begin pushing Preston, not after the little contretemps about his gossiping with Alan Fitzroy. "Will I ever get to visit the Annex? I see those men going out there . . ." She nodded towards the two strangers.

March's eyebrows raised almost imperceptibly at the mention of the "government" men. He studied Alix for a moment, once again amazed by her perceptiveness. Well, why not? She was a damned fine scientist; observation was a way of life for her. "You'll see the Annex soon enough, my dear. But don't rush things. There'll be time enough for that."

An hour later March looked at his watch and shook his head. "If we scientists could only arrange for a thirty-hour day, I'd be happy. I've a meeting shortly and must go."

He offered to walk Alix back to the lab, but she turned him down, explaining that she wanted to check further on Ted Winner's whereabouts.

"Ted won't be in today," March announced grimly. "I heard what happened last night."

"I'm sure it was just a case of nerves," Alix said lightly.

"Oh, no. This drinking of his has happened too often, much too often. Ted won't be back at the Lafayette at all."

"Oh, I'm sorry," Alix mumbled, remembering the fear in Winner's eyes as he'd forced the TIM card on her.

"Don't worry your pretty head about it. It's strictly an administrative consideration, my dear. Now if there's nothing else . . ."

March obviously was cutting her off without explanation. There was nothing she could do about that—not right now, at least.

"I'm just so sorry this happened. I liked Ted. And I'm going to miss him."

"We all will, but we must think of what's good for the Lafayette first. Besides, now that he's out, his job is open and I feel you're just the person to take over. What do you think?"

"I'm flattered," she said hesitantly after a moment. "I consider it a great honor."

March touched her lightly on the arm. "Then consider it a *fait accompli*. We'll discuss the details soon, but in the meantime, just carry on as usual, as if nothing had happened."

Carry on as usual, Alix thought as she returned to the lab. What *is* usual, anyway? It was beginning to seem that what was usual for the Lafayette Institute would be considered extraordinary to the outside world. The Lafayette, after all, was a world unto itself. It was privately funded, generated its own projects, protected its own members with fierce loyalty. It was almost like a living organism. And like all organisms, like the very work Alix was studying, it was beginning to seem that it also had a very finely tuned protective system—one that was able to keep outside invaders away, able to weed out any troublesome cells from within. But Alix knew that organisms like this had a tendency to grow, to become more autonomous, to begin ingesting other organisms in what oftentimes became malignant, uncontrolled growth. At that point no rules applied except those that came from within, and no life was worthwhile unless it benefited the whole. Ted Winner hadn't fit into that pattern, and now he was gone. And Alix was about to take his place because she was loyal, trustworthy. And if she should ever start to show signs of independence—in whatever form—she suspected now that she, too, might just disappear.

Back in the lab, Alix was trying to shake off these ominous feelings as totally irrational when her phone rang. It was Jack Campbell. "You sound out of breath. Anything wrong?" he asked.

"I had to run for the phone, that's all," she lied to cover her anxiety.

"Then you must have sensed it was me," Jack joked. When there was no reply, he got right down to business. "I traced your list of names."

"Oh, God," Alix whispered. She'd forgotten all about that. Lisa and a couple of the others were in the lab, but they were too engrossed in work to pay attention.

Nevertheless, Alix said, "Let me call you right back. You at the office?"

"Yes, but—"

She hung up and walked quickly from the lab down the hall to a small snack bar lined with vending machines full of inedible sugar-saturated food. There was a pay phone tucked into the corner, which she used to call Jack back. As she punched out his number, she recognized that switching phones was an open admission to herself that she no longer fully trusted the Lafayette Institute. She felt guilty about being so devious, but on the other hand, she also knew she had to protect herself first.

"What was that all about?" Campbell asked when they were finally connected.

"Someone came into the lab, and I need to be able to talk freely," she lied. "Now, tell me everything."

"First, I want to know where you got those names."

Alix paused as her anger flared. Dammit! Why was he pulling this stunt now? "Jack, don't be childish. I'll tell you later."

"It's now or nothing," he insisted.

Alix might have made it an issue, but Campbell held all the trump cards. She'd tell him the truth— part of it anyway—and as she did, she realized more emphatically than ever that the purpose of the lying, like hiding Winner's TIM card, was to protect her interest in Alan Fitzroy. "All right, you win. I found those names in a file at the Lafayette."

"I figured as much. Those four names—those four people—all had the same fate, all like Sarah Williams. They're gone, vanished, *poof*, up in smoke."

Alix caught her breath, only to feel her heart beating in her throat. "Tell me exactly what you mean."

"We'd better get together about this," he insisted.

"Later. Please, Jack, just tell me what you found out. It's not fair to leave me hanging like this."

"All right. But remember, you asked for it." He paused and took a deep breath. "Sarah Williams, we know about. The second woman, Linda Strong, did the same kind of vanishing act—just upped and left school without as much as a fare-thee-well. A school administrator assumed there was family trouble, but I checked her file—she had no family. None of them had families, as a matter of fact."

"Where was she studying?"

"George Washington University."

"Studying what?"

"She was a medical student."

Just like Sarah Williams, Alix thought. "Go on, tell me more."

"Jack Finlay and Tim Donoghue's disappearances aren't quite so mysterious—they're both dead, killed in separate car accidents. Burned beyond recognition, it seems."

A rush of bile rose in Alix's throat. "Burned beyond recognition" were the exact words she'd heard over the phone ten years before, when Richard died. For just a moment Alix was so disoriented that the array of junk food around her blurred into a gelatinous hazy rainbow of nauseating colors, and she thought she might be sick. But, no. Not this time.

"Alix? You okay?"

"Yes, of course," she whispered. "It's just that . . . it all sounds so horrible."

"I know." After a short pause Jack attacked. "What does it all mean? What the hell's going on at the Lafayette, Alix?"

"What's this got to do with the Institute?" To defend the Lafayette in light of this evidence was ridiculous, but her response was automatic; she needed time to think, and that meant stalling any way she could.

"It has everything to do with the Lafayette," Campbell declared. "Both Finlay and Donoghue were med students, too. And all four of them had applied for admission to the Lafayette's intern program. Sarah Williams was a year ahead, so she had already been accepted. The others had gone so far as to have had several guided tours by your precious Preston March," Jack now said nastily. "You still want to tell me these disappearances have nothing to do with the place where you work?"

"You're being melodramatic," she snapped back. This was too much information to digest all at once. She needed time, time to sort it out, time to think of what she was going to do, time to find out exactly what TRAUMA was all about.

When Jack spoke again, his voice was low and cajoling. "Alix, I want you to tell me exactly where you got this list of names."

Now was a moment of truth. She could either tell him about the TRAUMA dossier and about Ted Winner's behavior last night and his subsequent "firing" —and open up the Lafayette and everyone concerned to investigation; or she could lie. Lie now and find out the truth for herself—sooner than she'd planned. To lie now to Campbell was to betray him and their relationship, but to tell the truth now was possibly to betray Alan Fitzroy.

Alix laughed lightly to dispel the tension. "You really had me going there for a moment."

"Had you going? What are you talking about?"

"All those disappearances and deaths—it sounded so much like a TV movie that I actually got caught up in the drama of it all." She laughed again, so convincingly that she almost believed it herself. "I went through my inactive files a few days ago; that's where I came across a card with those four names. I recognized Sarah Williams, of course, so I passed them all on to you. I thought it might be helpful."

"It was," he said immediately.

"It was if you *want* to believe there's some kind of a conspiracy involving those four. Come on, Jack, face it: you're a reporter looking for a 'hot' story, and you're prejudiced against the Lafayette."

"That's not true," he defended himself weakly.

"Have it your own way. All I can tell you is that you're going to waste a lot of time making a fool of yourself about this . . . if it goes any farther . . . and I, for one, am not going to help you do it."

There was a moment's silence. "It's all too similar to be coincidence."

"Maybe I can convince you I'm right . . . or at least take your mind off it for a while," she said seductively.

"Now, there's an idea," he said, his mood brightening immediately. "How about tonight? Dinner?"

"Not tonight, tomorrow. I'm tired and I just want to get home from work, take a long, leisurely bath, and go right to bed."

"Too much champagne and caviar at Alan Fitzroy's last night?" he asked, alluding for the first time to being stood up.

"That party, my dear, was more work than any eight hours in the lab," she again lied with alacrity. "Remind me to tell you . . ." The phone went dead for a few seconds; then they were reconnected. "Time's run out. I've got to get back to the lab anyway. See you tomorrow night about eight." She hung up before Campbell had a chance to say anything else.

By the time Alix got back to the lab, she was all but drowning in her own guilt. Two days ago she and Jack Campbell had been headed toward an easy, loving, fun relationship. They'd been open and honest with each other about everything. It seemed the perfect beginning to what might become a long-lasting liaison. Now it had all gone sour for her. After only one meeting with Alan Fitzroy, Alix was ready to dump Campbell and walk off into the sunset with a man she didn't even know. She'd already betrayed Jack with Alan in her heart; she'd betrayed him for real when she'd lied about the list of names from the TRAUMA dossier. And she was already beginning to think of ways to get out of any commitment she might have made—or implied—to Campbell. And all because of one night, one meeting, one man!

Alix returned to the lab promising herself to put all that aside for the moment. There was work to do. But moments after she started making notes, the phone rang. "May I speak with Dr. Alixandra Kendall?"

Alix couldn't believe it. It was Alan Fitzroy! She felt so weak in the knees she had to sit down.

"I hope you don't think I'm rushing things by calling the day after we met . . . but we are colleagues, of a sort . . . and this *could* be a business call."

"Is it?" she asked coyly.

"No. Definitely not." His voice was low and breathy and it made Alix feel weaker still. "I'd like to have dinner with you one night. Tomorrow?"

Alix sucked in her breath, wishing Jack's call had come fifteen minutes later. She momentarily toyed with the idea of canceling, but then felt so guilty about it that she immediately discarded it. "Sorry, I'm busy tomorrow."

"Oh, I see," he said, definitely disappointed. "And I'm booked through the rest of the week. How about a week from today?"

"Yes, I can make it," Alix replied without hesitation.

"Good. We'll talk before then. And once again, thanks for coming to the party, Alix." He hung up.

Well, she'd wondered what could happen next, and now she knew. It seemed she'd become the birdie in what might turn out to be a deadly game of badminton, with Jack Campbell and his quest for truth on one side of the net and Alan Fitzroy, chief fund-raiser and member of the board of directors of the Lafayette Institute—and all that that might mean—on the other. And unless she played it very carefully, no matter which side won, Alix was bound to lose.

—6—

"God, you're beautiful." Jack Campbell swept Alix into his arms the next evening and covered her face with kisses. She'd been inside his house only ten seconds, but Jack couldn't keep his hands off her. Alix Kendall was the type of woman he'd dreamed about, but a type he'd never met before. Most of the women he dated were mainly interested in pretty clothes, fancy dinners, and evenings out. But Alix seemed to eschew all these for medicine. In fact, Jack occasionally wished she were a little more relaxed about life. More than once he'd had the feeling that Alix's body was with him but her mind was elsewhere—probably back at the Lafayette. Nevertheless, she was *it* as far as he was concerned.

"It's so good to hold you," he whispered as he nuzzled her.

"Thank you, kind sir." Alix lightly accepted the compliment, at the same time easing away from his hold. "After a long, hard day at the lab, that's exactly what I need to hear."

"There's plenty more where that came from," he said, shutting the front door behind her while trying—and failing—to keep his eyes off her beautiful breasts. "So, it was another hard day at the secret lab, huh?" He took her coat and hung it up.

Alix's face clouded. Tonight, much as she hated to admit it, Campbell's joke played right into her own fears. "My days are all tough," she admitted, sidestepping the provocation.

"I guess that's just life in the big city," he said philosophically. "How about a drink?" Alix asked for a Campari and he poured two glasses. "Anything *in particular* going on at the Lafayette these days?"

All the way over, her guilt growing with each moment, Alix had once again debated about telling Jack of Ted Winner's "separation" from his job—his disappearance, actually. But now that she was here, now that she'd put her feelings for Campbell on "hold" for the moment, and annoyed by the prodding tone of his voice, she remained silent about Winner.

"There's nothing happening at work that would be of any interest to you," she said pointedly. "I've started a whole new battery of experiments I hope will show that cell life can be extended by transplants into younger, healthier specimens."

"Oh? And what will that prove?"

"That cells have the possibility of living far longer than we expect, that some chemical trigger begins the aging process which eventually allows the cells to die before their time."

Campbell nodded. "So one day we may all get to live to two hundred. Is that it?"

Alix shrugged. Jack's tone was definitely belligerent, and in her present mood she wasn't sure how long she could put up with it. "Maybe only one hundred and fifty."

"That's still too long," he shot back at her. "The world's a very crowded place already, my dear Dr. Kendall. The food supply's running out, fuel's falling by the wayside, there's mass poverty and starvation in the world, old people are scorned by the young and are victims of crime. Yet you want to prolong life? Why?"

Alix immediately saw red. "Because it's my sworn duty as a doctor to do everything I can to achieve that end."

"Even if it means prolonged misery? Is that it?"

Alix slammed her wineglass down. "Jack, I don't know what's bothering you, but don't take it out on me. I'm too tired to fight theoretical arguments."

Campbell seemed not to register her complaint. "I suppose you could prolong the life of *some* people, those who counted the most—artists, musicians, great thinkers. But then who'd choose who was to live and who wasn't?" He scratched his head. "It's a philosophical conundrum, isn't it? Because those who did the choosing would, in effect, be shaping the form of the future. And what if they made the wrong choices?"

Alix refused to respond. She'd hoped to sail through this evening without any trouble, but she saw now that Jack had something on his mind. This attack was nothing more than a smoke screen; the real problem would come out later . . . if she decided to stay. "Jack, please . . . I'm a little tired for all this deep thinking."

"They really push you, don't they?"

Alix shook her head and sipped her apéritif. Tonight every question sounded loaded. "No. I'm my own taskmaster, and I'm merciless." She expected him to laugh, but he turned more serious than ever.

"What exactly *are* you running from, Dr. Kendall?" He asked the question as if he'd framed it hours, days, before and was just waiting for the right opportunity to ask it. "I sometimes get the feeling that your hardworking-career-girl facade is covering up a deep sadness."

"I had no idea you were such a romantic." She

laughed wearily. "Is psyching out your friends part of being a reporter?"

"Being a reporter means watching ... seeing ... assessing situations and not always believing what you're told. And quite often I just don't believe the picture you paint of yourself."

Alix shrugged. "We all have something to be sad about, don't we? Isn't that part of being human?"

"I suppose so." Jack nodded. "But being human also involves sharing with other people."

"Other people like you?" she asked softly, sensing that he was about to spring the real problem on her.

He nodded again, then leaned forward and kissed her longingly on the mouth. "You've really gotten to me, Alix. God, I hate to admit it, but it's true." He shook his head in wonder. "Think I've got a chance? A real chance?"

"What are you talking about?" Alix asked, wondering if he could see her reticence about further involvement. "Is *your* sadness thinking that you're about to lose what you've already got?" She said the words to reassure him, to get herself off the hook, but as she said them, Alix thought of Alan Fitzroy, and hated herself for wanting him as much as she did.

"I guess my sadness is not being able to believe my own good luck in finding someone like you."

"Then, here's to luck." Alix raised her glass in a toast, but her mind once again had drifted back to Fitzroy and next week's date with him.

Despite the freezing night, Jack, in a show of bravado, cooked steaks on a grill propped up in the snow on the back porch. They ate by candlelight at a table nestled in the bay window at the back of the house while watching the onset of a storm that tossed a flurry of snow at them. There was wine with dinner, cordials after, and as the evening wore on, Jack got slightly drunk; not enough to be obnoxious, but enough for his mood to become noticeably more belligerent and, oddly enough, morose.

After dinner they returned to the living room. They sipped brandy—Jack, his second—and drank a heady Italian roast coffee whose sharp smell filled the house.

By now Campbell was silently glum and Alix was beginning to fear that she'd failed in her mission to act perfectly content with him and that he'd intuited that her feelings were wavering about him . . . about them.

"I've got an idea," she said after a while. "Why don't you let *me* play investigative reporter." She scrunched down on the couch next to him. "Something's bothering you, and I want to know all about it." She raised her eyebrows hopefully.

Campbell smiled for the first time since they'd left the dining table. "I wish telling you were that simple, or that it would make any difference." He sipped his brandy, then looked up at her. "You're right. Something has been bothering me for some time. . . . I think you should quit your job at the Lafayette."

"You must be joking," Alix said incredulously. When Jack remained silent, staring at her, she realized that he was very serious indeed. "Why would you say such a crazy thing? You know that working at the Institute is my whole life." The statement excluded Campbell. Well, he deserves it, she thought angrily.

"I'd say such a 'crazy' thing because I've never trusted that goddamn Institute from the word go, and now . . ." He finished the brandy, but not the sentence. "After I was assigned to do the piece on the med students, I did some investigating of the Lafayette on my own. Like almost everybody else, I knew the surface details, the PR stuff, the puff pieces. Needless to say, they didn't tell the whole story."

"And just what is the *whole* story?" Alix demanded.

"You sure you really want to know?"

Alix's anger flared. "Don't treat me like a child, Jack. Don't tell me you've found a bogeyman in the closet, but that you don't want me to see what he looks like."

"Hey, calm down." He slipped his arms around her, but she pulled back from him.

"Never mind the delaying tactics, Campbell. Tell me about the Lafayette."

"According to the PR handouts, the Lafayette Institute is a privately run research foundation funded by private money—supplied by Big Business, foundations, et cetera. There is also some government money, but it's supposed to be just a part of the annual federal grants for certain kinds of research." He poured himself another brandy, but now he seemed not to be drunk at all. "The truth of the matter is that much— probably most—of the Institute's money comes directly from the government. Now, when I say directly, I don't mean they have a televised ceremony in which they present a check. Oh, no, the money is laundered through other sources, in different states, as a matter of fact. Some of the companies through which it travels are known CIA front organizations." He looked at her in triumph, expecting a reaction of shock, at the least.

But when Alix thumped down her glass, she was far from shocked. "This is all beginning to sound like a cheap melodrama. Preston March himself told me yesterday that the Annex is government-funded and, as such, off limits."

"You knew that?" Campbell sounded dismayed.

"Yes, but I hardly see what difference it makes. Honestly, all you have to do is mention the CIA and you've got a controversy on your hands."

"Maybe it's for a good reason."

"Maybe, but what has all this got to do with me?"

Campbell looked at Alix as if he'd never seen her before, not clearly, anyway. He'd been worried about this confrontation all day, and now that it was here, he saw that he'd had good reason to worry. Alix had given up her whole life in Boston to move to Washington, and he was telling her to quit her job. Why? What good reasons could he give her for leaving the Lafayette? That it might be CIA-connected? She was obviously politically naive, or uncommitted, so that avenue was closed to him. There was nothing else but his feelings, hunches, intuitions, second-guessing. But feelings weren't facts. Not in tough, busy, secretive Washington. To succeed you had to lay down cold figures and facts. None of which he had, except for some ugly history he'd dug up about Preston March. And he wasn't sure he wanted to trot that out just yet.

"Well!" Alix prodded. "I'm waiting for the reasons why I should give up my livelihood."

"Do you know what you're really working on at the Lafayette? I mean *really* working on?"

"Of course. I'm working on a project I originated myself."

"What about everyone else?"

"What about them?"

"Do you know what they're working on?"

Alix sighed with exasperation. "Of course I do. We have a weekly meeting at which a representative from every department makes a report on findings. Besides, the information that's fed into the computer is printed out once a week, condensed, and circulated."

"That's here in Washington. What about out at the Annex?" Now he had her.

"I don't know exactly what they're working on, but I can't imagine it's anything too different from what I'm doing." She didn't believe it, and they both knew it.

"I gave you credit for more intelligence than that!"

"Don't you dare talk down to me," she snapped. "I didn't come over here to be told how I should lead my life, or to have my I.Q. tested—particularly not by some arrogant journalist." She made the profession sound like the next closest thing to pimping.

The snipe hurt, but it also made Campbell decide to tell Alix what he'd found out about March. Maybe he could challenge her confidence and make her listen that way. "This is not a personal attack, honey. I care about you, and I don't want you involved in anything that's bad for you, that's all."

"I'm doing just fine, thank you," she growled.

Jack shrugged. "Have it your own way. But while we're on the subject of the Annex, I want to tell you something else I dug up. Years ago Preston March and a group of men got a small grant from the government and were allowed to use a vacant Army communications center that had been erected out in Langley, Virginia, during the war. Their work might have gone unnoticed, but somehow an antivivisectionist group heard about them."

"You mean the people who object to the use of animals in medical research?" Alix wasn't totally unsympathetic to their cause.

"The very ones. Anyhow, they staged a raid on the place—it wasn't guarded then—and found a slaughterhouse, rumor has it."

"In any kind of research, there has to be a certain amount of experimentation on living creatures."

Campbell shook his head. "This was like a charnel house. It seems like March and the boys were trying out transplant surgery long before it became chic."

"Did they succeed?" Alix immediately thought of the fear she'd heard in Hawkins' voice as he warned her about "the experiments."

"Who knows? The antivivisectionists caused such an uproar that March was closed down, the animals carted away, and that was that." He took a sip of his brandy, looked at the glass, wrinkled his nose, and put it aside. "Enough of that. That might have been the end of the story, but it isn't, of course. The Lafayette Annex is built on the very same spot where his slaughterhouse was. Quite a coincidence, eh?"

Alix shook her head, hoping to slough off her unpleasant memories, but it was no good. "So you think Preston and these others just went underground for a while until they could build a respectable version of the Lafayette abattoir? As a cover for the work they're really doing?"

"Exactly!" Campbell was exhilarated that Alix had caught right on. "Now, tell me, have you ever seen any of these men before?" He dipped his hand into a nearby briefcase and pulled out a yellowed newspaper clipping. "It's as old as the hills and the photos are bad, but it's the best I can do."

Alix took the clipping from him and studied the faces of the five men. She recognized Preston March immediately; he was considerably younger, quite handsome, and his hair was very dark. She scanned the other faces, at first thinking she didn't recognize any of them. But after a third look, after making allowances for the aging process, Alix recognized three of the men—the "bureaucrats," the "government" men, who shuttled back and forth between the main building in the District and the Langley Annex!

"The *only* person I know in this photograph is Preston March." She handed back the photo to him. Alix was so caught up in the pattern of her lying that she now did it without considering the consequences and without remorse. Campbell took the clipping, looking very disappointed. "I'm sorry if I've blown some theory of yours."

He ignored that for a question. "I just want to get a bead on something; indulge me a minute, will you? What if you *did* discover that Preston March and his henchmen were working on something, let's say, something *immoral*; would you continue to work at the Lafayette? Does your scientific curiosity transcend your duty to, say, protect life?"

"You're talking nonsense," she snapped.

"Nonsense, no. Possibilities, yes," he rejoindered, fixing his eyes on her. "Now, answer: Would you continue working for the Lafayette Institute if it were involved in something immoral, whether you were directly connected with it or not?"

Alix sighed. "You know, Jack, I'm beginning to wonder why I don't just get up and leave. You're getting drunker by the minute . . . and more insulting by the second."

"Sorry about the drinking, but I've been worried about you all day. I really don't want to interfere—"

"Then don't," she interrupted. "Either you have something concrete to tell me and we drop the subject, or I go home."

He studied her momentarily, then played what he knew was his trump card. "This afternoon I was in Sarah Williams' apartment."

Alix felt like the wind had been knocked out of her. Hearing Sarah's name no longer surprised her. The missing woman was the common thread that wound its way through the entire fabric of Campbell's interest in the Lafayette. Sarah Williams had indirectly brought Alix and Jack together; she'd been the first name on the TRAUMA list, and now it seemed she was the core reason Jack was afraid and wanted Alix to leave her job. And now, hearing the name again, even in the safe quiet of his Foggy bottom house, Alix began to grow afraid—for herself, this time. It was as if some invisible path she'd been walking was beginning to become clear, as if the random pieces of some gigantic jigsaw puzzle she'd been collecting were aligning themselves. Once again Alix was given the choice: she could back out and stop Jack or she could continue to listen to him. But if she chose to make herself a part of all this, there would be no turning back . . . ever.

"How did you get into her apartment?" Alix asked, her decision made by the question. "*Why* did you go?"

"I went because you didn't want me to. The other day you wanted me to forget those four names; you tried so damn hard."

Alix shook her head ruefully. "I thought I'd succeeded."

"You only succeeded in making me more curious than ever. On a hunch, I got Sarah's address from the registrar at Georgetown and went over there. Of course, the rooms had been cleaned and someone else was living there, but ten dollars to the superintendent got me some information."

"What kind of information?" Alix asked breathlessly.

"Sarah Williams went out to a dinner party one night, and the next day she was gone."

"Are you sure?"

He nodded. "The super—a Mrs. DelGado—talked to her; Sarah said she had a date with a very handsome and very rich man. Mrs. DelGado figured that was only natural, because Sarah was 'as pretty as Marilyn Monroe,' to quote exactly. Anyway, after a couple of days without hearing a peep from Sarah's rooms, Mrs. D. used her passkey to get in. . . . The place had been cleared out."

"Just like that?" Jack nodded. "Why didn't the super report the disappearance to the police?"

"Why bother? Like she said, students come and go; there was no sign of a struggle. Besides, the super had the month's rent, plus a security deposit of two months. She waited a couple more days, then rented the apartment out and pocketed Sarah's security, I'd imagine."

"There was no sign Sarah Williams had ever lived there? Nothing at all?"

Jack shook his head. "Someone cleaned the apartment professionally. They took everything but the paint on the walls. But they didn't know that two pieces of evidence weren't in the room." Jack opened the drawer of an end table by the couch and took out an expensive cream-colored envelope. He handed it to Alix. "I found this in the back of a yearbook Sarah left at Mrs. DelGado's the day of her disappearance."

Alix opened the envelope and removed a handwritten invitation to "a small dinner party" at Alan Fitzroy's house on R Street. She read it twice, wanting it not to be true. She'd just found Alan Fitzroy, and he *couldn't* be a part of this—whatever *this* was. She replaced the card in the envelope, trying not to blame Jack for doing this to her. "What is that supposed to mean?"

"Just that the highfalutin Mr. Alan Fitzroy is up to his pretty neck in something which includes the disappearance of Sarah Williams, that's what," he said hotly. "I bet he didn't tell you *that* the other night at his cocktail party, did he?"

The blood rushed to Alix's head, and for a moment it was difficult to catch her breath. "Is that what this is all about? Jealousy? Some petty jealousy of yours? Because if it is . . ."

"Give me a break, Alix. If you want to go off with Fitzroy, there's not much I can do about it, is there? I just happen to care enough about you to forewarn you, which is more than anyone did for Sarah Williams. She went to dinner at his house one night and was never seen again. Her name was on a list that originated at the Lafayette, and you know as well as I do that everything that happens at the Lafayette is scrutinized by Fitzroy. I'm not saying he personally supervised her removal—or whatever happened to her—but I'd be willing to bet a year's salary that he knew about it beforehand."

A picture of Ted Winner being escorted from the living room for a fast trip to oblivion flashed through Alix's mind. Was that what happened to Sarah, too? And to the others? Maybe, but until it was proved

beyond a shadow of a doubt, Alix refused to believe
that Alan was directly involved.

"This invitation means nothing," she said, tossing it
back to him. "What's the other clue you were talking
about?"

He reopened the table drawer and removed a large
package, which he handed to Alix. "Sarah was showing this to Mrs. DelGado one day and forgot to take it
back to her room. But when she upped and left, she
also forgot to take it, and that doesn't make much
sense."

Alix opened the package and found Sarah Williams'
Georgetown yearbook.

"Yearbooks are a personal thing. You don't just
leave them behind," Jack added triumphantly.

"Unless you've already forgotten them in your
landlady's room." She shrugged her shoulders. "So,
what's the point of this?"

"There's a photograph of Sarah Williams on page
twenty-nine. She was complaining to Mrs. DelGado
about what a lousy job the photographer did."

Alix flipped open the heavy book and quickly found
the right page. She was confronted by two group
photographs, each of which contained the smiling faces
of at least forty young men and women.

"This is Sarah." Jack pointed to a blond woman
with an expressionless face.

Alix looked once, twice, at the photo. She adjusted
the book under the lamp to erase the glare off the
glossy pages. She *had* to be mistaken. It just couldn't
be! But no matter how hard she looked, what ploy she
used to change the angle of the photo, there was no
denying the fact that the small photo of Sarah Williams was also a photograph of the woman at Alan
Fitzroy's party who called herself Mrs. Philip Greenspan. The hair was styled differently and had been
dyed black, there was more makeup and flash, but
underneath it all, it was still Sarah Williams. A wave
of fear washed over Alix, and the book slipped from
her fingers.

"Alix, are you all right?" Jack's voice shattered the
dead silence of the room.

"All right?" She repeated his words as if they were Chinese. She'd been all right until she'd met Jack Campbell and all this started. Now, nothing was right.

"You went white." He handed her his unfinished brandy. "You recognized her, didn't you?" Alix said nothing. "When you looked at that picture, it was as if you'd seen a ghost." He picked up the yearbook and studied the photograph as if it might give him some clue to Alix's reaction. "This is important!" he finally said, his patience at an end.

"I did know Sarah Williams, after all," she lied yet again, but this time she felt she was doing something terribly, terribly wrong. "I had seen her in class once or twice. I just never put a face to the name before. To recognize her now and to think that something awful may have happened to her is a shock, that's all." Her answer was perfectly believable because Alix was beginning to lie like a pro.

"Are you sure that's all?" Jack watched her very carefully.

"No, I'm not sure," Alix replied angrily, "but she does look familiar . . . and *that's* scary. It's like listening dispassionately to an accident report on the radio until, at the very end, you realize it's your best friend who's been killed."

"Are you sure you saw Sarah in the classroom? Maybe it was somewhere else—"

Alix grabbed the yearbook from him and put it on the coffee table. "Don't put me through a third degree too. I got a creepy feeling when I saw her picture that's all. Nothing more, nothing less."

Jack relented immediately. "Okay, have your own way. But I'll tell you one thing: All of this *is* connected to the Lafayette Institute. *That's* the one theme running through this whole cockeyed symphony."

"Boy, and I thought reporters didn't have imaginations." Alix whistled. "And here you are putting together bits and pieces of information into an incredible fairy tale."

"If reporters didn't have imaginations, they'd eat up and believe all the lies everyone else in this country digests without question."

"Then I should thank you for saving me from my own gullibility." In her mind, she closed the subject. "Tell me, do I really look like the kind of woman who's prone to becoming a part of a conspiracy—intentionally or otherwise?"

At first Campbell wasn't sure if she were serious or not, but one look at the smile creeping across her lips gave him the answer. "You don't look like the kind of woman who falls for anything she doesn't want to fall for."

Alix smiled and moved a little closer to him on the couch, knowing that this was the one way guaranteed to close the subject of Sarah Williams. She felt more like a whore than she did Mata Hari, but there was a trail of too many lies that she had to hide now. Now that she'd decided to deal with this whole situation her own way, at her own pace.

Campbell scooped Alix into his arms and pulled her to him. Her hair cascaded forward and danced lightly over his face as he pulled her closer, hungrily seeking out her mouth. Alix's lips were so warm and moist, her tongue so sleekly enticing that he never wanted to stop kissing her, touching her, holding her. After a moment's hesitation, she relaxed and he slid his arms up and around her, completely encircling her.

Later, in the bedroom, he undressed her and watched silently as she slipped between the sheets, marveling at the way just the sight of her naked body excited him. He undressed and moved in next to her. The proximity of her, the warmth and smoothness of her skin, further excited him, and he pressed against her, communicating his urgency. Alix responded to his caresses like a cat luxuriating in the warmth of the sun. She stretched and cooed and rubbed against him. His hands played lightly over the soft contours of her body while his mouth still concentrated on her face, her lips, her eyes. He cupped a breast with his hand and harshly rubbed his trembling palm against her nipple until it stood firm, waiting for his kiss. His mouth followed a direct path down Alix's neck, across her breast, until the nipple, further swollen with the pleasure of his touch, was between his teeth. Alix's whole body exploded with desire, and she arched against him.

They made love fiercely, yet sweetly, urgently, yet with a languor that made each second a sweet minute. They could have been together for hours or weeks— they didn't know and it didn't matter. What did matter was that for that short time in bed they were one, and in Jack's mind all differences were over, all the earlier mistrust and anger were finished, nothing could come between them now . . . or harm them.

Alix kept her eyes closed, keeping her mind focused on his touch—on Jack Campbell's touch. She watched him, watched his hands as they roamed her body, studied the shapes of his fingers as they explored her, examined his body as it pressed against hers. This was Jack Campbell, no one else. All she had to do was watch him to know that. Yet, the minute she closed her eyes in a moment of passion, the floodgate of her imagination and memory were flung open and Jack Campbell was washed away in the torrent.

Jack became Richard, and Richard became Alan. Alix's mind catapulted back ten years to her garret bedroom, to the long hours she and Richard lay in each other's arms, their silences only preludes to more exhausting lovemaking. So vivid were these memories that Alix had to keep herself from calling out his name, the name so long unspoken. But once her mind took over and told her that Richard was dead and vanished, Alan Fitzroy appeared. And it was he who bent over her, bringing her closer and closer to fulfillment every moment. Alix wanted to open her eyes. She wanted to bring Jack Campbell back, but her desire for Alan, for Richard, was too strong.

And when she tipped over the edge into the swirling pit of physical ecstasy, Jack was far from her mind.

When they'd finally satisfied each other, and lay tightly wrapped in each other's arms, Alix felt a confusion so deep, yet somehow so sublime that she was afraid to open her eyes for fear she might have been catapulted into a time zone somewhere between past and present. In the course of the last hour she'd been passed through the arms of three different men. She was exhausted, a little scared, and more than a little satisfied. And she knew, even through the post-lovemaking ennui, that she'd been emotionally fulfilled only because she pretended Jack was Alan. But next time, only the real Alan Fitzroy would be good enough.

An hour later Jack kissed Alix good-bye at the front door, and, for the first time, said he loved her. She pressed herself against him but said nothing. Jack Campbell was a wonderful man, but he was no match for the past. No man was. Except perhaps Alan Fitzroy.

"I don't want to pressure you, Alix," Campbell ended the night, "but please consider what I said about you and the Lafayette, about looking for work somewhere else." He helped her on with her coat.

"I will, of course, but I don't guarantee anything. And please, let's not let this become the sole topic of our conversations. I'd hate that."

"It's a promise." He pulled her close and buttoned her coat for her. "But I'm not going to promise to give up on the rest of it."

"The rest of what?"

"The list you gave me. I now know something about Sarah Williams that, rather than wrapping things up, opens them up even further. I'm hoping the other three names will do the same."

Alix cursed herself for having given him the list in the first place. "Do whatever you want . . . just keep my name out of it."

"There's nothing to be afraid of—" he began, but she cut him off.

"You'd like nothing more than the chance to be a newspaperman/knight on a white charger coming to rescue me and the world from the evil at the Lafayette, but we're talking about *my* job, my livelihood. If you start nosing around dropping my name, I'm going to be out of a job. And I couldn't forgive you for that."

Rather than take the news somberly, Jack smiled. "If that did happen—which it won't—then we could get married. I make enough money to support two people; I own this house, it'd be great."

Campbell's earnestness touched Alix, but it was still no good. She was drifting away from him, not toward him. "That's very sweet"—she kissed him on the cheek—"but if I weren't working, you'd never have a minute's peace. I'm just not one of those women who can be content taking care of a house."

"Then I promise to keep your name out of this; I don't want to lose you."

"And I promise to keep my eyes open at the Institute . . . just in case. How's that? If I hear or see anything fishy, I'll let you know."

Campbell gave her one last kiss, then sent her on her way. Minutes later he poured himself a nightcap and opened the Georgetown yearbook to page twenty-nine. Although he was looking at the photograph of Sarah Williams, he was seeing the shocked look on Alix's face earlier. Maybe Alix had seen Sarah in class, maybe not. Even if she had, Alix was lying about her reaction. She was frightened of something. And as he finished his drink, Jack promised himself to find out what that something was.

As the taxi pulled up in front of Alix's apartment house, she made a decision she'd been contemplating ever since leaving Jack's. "Take me to the Lafayette Institute," she commanded the driver, and after a moment's hesitation, he nosed the car back out into the dark night.

Until this evening Alix's conscience had been under control, but Sarah Williams' Georgetown yearbook had proven too much for Alix's powers of rationalization. Sarah had disappeared, only to reappear as someone else, the very night Ted Winner disappeared. And both were directly tied up with TRAUMA. Not to do something about this now was to become an accomplice, and Alix had no intention of doing that.

Once at the Lafayette, Alix paid the driver and entered the building, stopping only long enough to show her identification to a night guard who didn't recognize the beautiful and popular Alixandra Kendall. Still, he smiled at her, not the least suspicious of this nocturnal visit. He knew that these Lafayette doctors were all a little crazy one way or another, and if this beautiful piece wanted to spend her evening at work instead of in bed, more power to her.

Alix took the elevator up to her floor just in case the guard was watching, but once out in the hallway, she quickly descended the back stairs to the basement, where TIM was housed. The basement level of the Lafayette was dug deep into the rocky shelf that fronted the Potomac River, and down here the walls were thick, heavily reinforced concrete covered with sheet metal more for aesthetic than scientific reasons. All the work that was done in here was mirrored and mirrored again on the opposite walls, producing an effect not unlike a fun house. But as Alix removed her I.D. card from the pocket of her lab smock, she was not having fun. She was terrified. As part of her promotion Alix had been given a new I.D. card that cleared her for Red Stripe—the Lafayette's highest security. She'd never been down here alone before. In the past, Preston had always guided her into this special section of the Lafayette, and he'd used his own card to get them inside. Now she was going to use her own card, and because she shouldn't have been down here, she feared that the electronic devices would know this and would give her away. Still, she sucked in her fear, slipped the I.D. card into the appropriate slot, and waited breathlessly for something disastrous to happen, for bells and alarms to go off, to expose her trespassing. But after a few seconds of excruciating tension, the card was ejected without incident and the doors to the room where TIM dwelt opened.

Alix walked cautiously into the anteroom, through which she could see the main computer room and TIM itself. Despite the thick walls, everything smelled damp, like a room underwater, one that was soaked through and on the verge of rotting. For a moment Alix's stomach turned. The computer room, for all its newness, smelled like decay, death. But now was not the time to get squeamish; she had work to do. So, taking in a deep breath, Alix stepped forward and the door to TIM opened.

It was colder in the computer room than outside,

and Alix shuddered involuntarily. She was in the middle of the large square room that housed TIM, bathed in the unearthly light cast down from recessed fixtures. TIM was built into one entire wall, and when operating, it was a mass of flashing lights, LED readouts, fluctuating controls, and whirring wheels of tape. Alix had worked with the best equipment and was used to high technology, but there was something about TIM that transcended simple machinery. TIM was the closest thing to duplicating the human brain that man had ever achieved.

Alix stepped forward gingerly a few steps at a time until she stood directly opposite TIM. There was a distant faint noise that permeated the room, coming from somewhere deep inside the computer itself; it sounded as if the computer were humming. Alix smiled uneasily at the thought, and to counteract its implications, reached out, gently touching the black metal with her fingertips. TIM was warm, and Alix withdrew her hand immediately. Because the room was so cold, she'd expected the machinery to be also. Touching the warmth scared her.

She quickly left the machine behind and found a seat at the main control panel, a maze of keys and buttons which meant little to her. How would she talk to the computer? TIM understood only a special highly sophisticated language, and Alix's knowledge of it was very limited. She'd done some elementary studies of computer language back in Boston, but had never encountered anything quite so complex as TIM.

She'd just reached into her pocket for Ted Winner's TIM card when a gruff male voice boomed out from behind her. "Just a minute, you!"

Alix froze and turned around so slowly that time seemed to have ground to a halt. Behind her stood another unfamiliar Institute guard. Alix smiled and tried to look at ease. "Good evening, officer," she said cheerfully. "And how are you tonight?"

He nodded his good health. "Can I help you with something?" He got straight down to business. "This part of the Institute shuts down promptly at eight."

"I'll be doing some work here shortly, and I was just

checking out my new quarters . . . and TIM, my new pal!"

"So you'll be working down here, will you?" he repeated with only a slight trace of sarcasm. "Then you must have the proper I.D. card."

Alix smiled but said nothing. Nor did the guard. After a few moments' awkward silence, she realized he wanted to see proof that what she'd said was true. Resisting the urge to create a scene, she slipped her hand into her pocket and felt . . . two cards—her I.D. card and Ted Winner's TIM key. To be caught down here without authorization was one thing; to be caught with someone else's computer card was quite another. Panic quickly overtook Alix, but she forced herself to remain calm, hoping luck wouldn't fail her now. She removed one card and handed it to the officer.

He stared at the card in his hand, then looked up at Alix. "What's the meaning of this?"

"What do you mean?" she asked, already knowing what had happened.

"This!" The guard shoved Ted Winner's TIM card in Alix's face. "Where'd you get this?"

"I . . ." She began to concoct a lie to pacify him but he was one jump ahead of her.

"Never mind the stories, you're coming with me." And without another word he grabbed Alix by the arm and roughly hauled her to her feet.

Minutes later Alix was under the watchful eyes of a second guard as her original captor talked quietly to Preston March on the security-office telephone. He nodded once, then twice, looked at Alix, then mumbled something into the phone and hung up. He looked at Alix with disgust. "I don't understand it, but Dr. March said to let you go."

Alix was tempted to invent an explanation, but why bother? Both she and the guard knew she'd been caught red-handed, and he obviously was a dedicated man who didn't like to see the law broken. Nothing Preston could say would be enough to pacify his outraged sense of justice. As far as the guard was concerned, Alix Kendall was little better than a common thief.

As she made her way to the front exit, the guard

yelled after her, "If it was up to me, you'd be outta here on your ass!"

Alix stiffened at the epithet but made no comment. Right now the wrath of the security guard paled beside her need to think of an explanation to satisfy Preston March when he confronted her.

"It was a serious breach of security, Alix," Preston accused her the next morning. "Do you have an explanation?"

"Curiosity," she answered weakly, cursing herself for not having been able to come up with an unassailable reason for her actions.

"Curiosity killed the cat," he shot back immediately.

"I'm sorry, Preston, it was foolish of me. Ted gave me the TIM card the night of Alan Fitzroy's party. He said something about a TRAUMA project and that the computer held the key to it."

"Well, of course TIM holds the key to TRAUMA, as it does to everything here at the Lafayette." March looked puzzled. "I wonder what Ted could have meant? Why all this melodrama?"

"Ever since Ted left so suddenly, I've felt uneasy about him, worried that something might have happened to him."

"And you thought that by prying into the TRAUMA file you might have a clue to his 'disappearance'?" March's voice dripped with sarcasm. "My dear, I didn't know you were such a romantic. Here . . ." He slipped a postcard across the desk toward her.

Alix looked first at the color photograph of Los Angeles, then turned the card over, immediately recognizing the handwriting as Ted Winner's. The short, cheerful message explained how much he liked his new job in California.

"He's quite happy and safe. I just wish I could say the same thing for you."

Alix felt her whole world begin to crumble. She'd fancied herself in the midst of a mystery, and now to realize that Ted *hadn't* been harmed, that his actions the night of the party might have been nothing more than alcoholic paranoia, made a mockery of all her fears. Was it possible there was as simple an explanation for everything else, too?

"I know what I did was wrong, Preston, and I promise I won't do it again," Alix pleaded, knowing she sounded like a schoolchild.

March watched her carefully. "You're a very able scientist, Alix, and I had high hopes for you, but for you to work here, I must feel able to trust you implicitly, and I'm not so sure I can do that now."

Tears sprang into Alix's eyes. March had been so good to her, and she'd repaid his kindness with betrayal. "Give me another chance. Please. I really want to stay here."

"Then do as you're told!" he yelled at her, startling her. "There's no room for snoops of any kind here, understand?" Alix nodded. "Good. I'll give you one more chance, but screw up, and you're through."

After Alix left meekly, March picked up the phone and dialed an oft-called number. When it was answered, he smiled. "She bought the postcard story hook, line, and sinker, but there's still the problem with TRAUMA. Once we see how she reacts to that, we'll know if she can be trusted fully. Giving her her own TIM card should set that in motion. I never knew any woman who could say no to her curiosity. Trust me: sooner or later Alix Kendall will go back to TIM, and when she does, we'll know whether she's going to become a full-fledged member of TRAUMA or whether she'll have an unfortunate 'accident.' " March began to laugh, and when he hung up five minutes later, he was still chuckling.

"To you, Alan," Alix toasted as she touched the rim of her glass to Fitzroy's. The champagne caught the light and fractured it into a thousand golden shards.

"To *you*," Alan immediately countered, taking a thoughtful sip of the wine; his eyes never left hers. "I've thought of you, Alix, often," he admitted softly.

"That's very flattering," she replied. Even though she was sure he'd said these very words to a legion of beautiful women, it didn't matter. Alix was totally captivated by him. "I've thought of you, too. I hope that doesn't sound too forward of me." She'd decided on their way to the restaurant to strike a delicate balance between coquetry and naiveté. But in the presence of Fitzroy she wasn't quite sure how she was doing.

"I thought all women these days were feminists of one sort or another. You know, never let the man know where he stands." He laughed.

"Some women act like that, but not all of them . . . not me. Personally, I believe the world is a better place because there are men in it."

Alan nodded but said nothing. From what he'd been told by Preston, Alix Kendall was a professional through and through: she was unparalleled in her field, but personally she was a bit of a cold fish. And that's what Fitzroy had expected at his cocktail party, and he'd been surprised, and captivated, by her warmth. Given that, he wished he'd chosen a more cheerful atmosphere for this date than the opulent but sedate propriety of Le Pavillon on K Street. Still, the food was first-rate and the atmosphere was intimate. Against the dark background of walls painted the deep color of a robust burgundy, Alix seemed to shimmer. Winning Alix's trust might not be such a difficult job after all, Fitzroy thought. *She's certainly a lot livelier than Sarah Williams was—and for my taste anyway, one hell of a lot prettier.*

"You're in the perfect position to be very generous with your feelings about men," Alan continued, never betraying the gravity of his private thoughts.

"Oh?" Alix looked up at him from perfect poached oysters and tilted her head questioningly. "And why am *I* so lucky?"

"Because *you're* one of a kind: you're a beautiful woman *and* a knowledgeable scientist. Therefore you don't have to compete in the job market and therefore you don't have to get angered by men."

Alix disagreed violently. "What you really mean, Alan, is that my *work* is judged objectively and fairly. When we come back to me as a woman, as the source of that same work, it's another story."

"I'd never thought of it that way before."

"And I'd never thought of it at all." Alix laughed and shook her head like a schoolgirl who'd just said something that made the whole class laugh. "I'm afraid I'm not the best example of the liberated woman. In fact, when I'm away from the Lafayette, you'd think I was a housewife. I wash, iron, clean—a whole raft of domestic things."

"I'd heard you never were away from the Lafayette long enough to do anything." The statement was a question.

"Who told you that? Preston?" Alan nodded. "He's such a dear. I was very flattered when he asked me down here from Boston."

"But you're the best in your field."

"Still . . ." She let the rest go unsaid, as if she were willing to deprecate her own worth in face of March's attention.

"But it's true. I told Preston how good you were long before he finally said he'd go to Boston," Alan confided.

Although Alix smiled and managed to look pleased, she was stunned. Had Alan Fitzroy suggested that March interview her? If so, then he had far more power than she—or even Jack Campbell—ever suspected. "Then I should thank you for my happiness," she said, never once betraying her true feelings.

"You misunderstand," Alan corrected immediately. "I only told Preston you existed; remember, the Roth Corporation keeps tabs on everything important that goes on in the world. As for hiring you, that was Preston's idea." Alan paused as a waiter cleared the dishes away, and when he left, the subject was changed.

For the rest of the evening Alix smiled and bubbled and laughed and was a good companion. But she couldn't forget Fitzroy's slip—that he'd been instrumental in having her hired—no matter how much he denied it. And that made Preston March a subordinate. If Alan chose who was to be hired—and fired, like Ted Winner—then he might just be the real power behind the Lafayette Institute. And that connected him directly with Sarah Williams' disappearance. Why did it always come back to that?

Two hours later, Fitzroy dropped Alix off at her

apartment and said good night with a chaste kiss. Before he left, he promised to call again soon. Alix went immediately to bed, but despite her exhaustion, she was unable to sleep. There were just too many questions she hadn't asked herself, too many half-truths she'd accepted without question. But now they all bubbled up from her subconscious and kept her mind racing without stop.

Foremost among these mental demons was the simple fact that Sarah Williams was now calling herself Nancy Greenspan. Despite the subtle differences in appearance, they *were* the same person. And further-more, this transformation had been coordinated by someone at the Lafayette. How else could Sarah/Nancy's appearance at Alan's party be explained? But how had such a complete transformation taken place? And why?

Alix was vaguely acquainted with the techniques of brainwashing; she knew they existed and worked—for short periods of time. But that kind of mind control was usually too fragile, too erratic to make a person become anything other than a compliant zombie. Of course, the addition of drug therapy might help. Pharmacological medicine was the brave new world. Chemists had made enormous strides in the past years by creating a whole new catalog of magic pills for every imaginable ailment. Surely the right combination of these *plus* suggestive techniques could force a change. But again, Alix doubted if such a maneuver could be made permanent. And there was always the problem of impaired action, slurred speech, and the usual lack of coordination that drugged people exhibited.

Alix sighed deeply and rubbed her eyes, now totally awake again. She was on the right track, but she was still lost in the woods. How do you achieve the continual suppression of the memory, the personality of one person, while overlaying it with a new—and completely functional—one? Alix slipped from bed, threw on a robe, and went into the kitchen, where she made a strong cup of black coffee. It looked like this one might be an all-nighter.

An hour later Alix was on her third cup of coffee

and no closer to an answer than before. There had to
be a way to take over a mind, to put control elsewhere
... Suddenly she had it! Not only did her answer
explain how the change was effected, but if she was
right, it also explained another part of the puzzle that
centered around the Lafayette. Alix shook her head in
wonder. The answer had been there all along, from
before she was hired by the Lafayette; she just hadn't
seen it.

It was the memory of her wild encounter with Daisy,
the crazed rhesus monkey, that put everything into
perspective. Ted Winner had been experimenting with
the implantation of electrodes into the brains of his
laboratory animals—for seizure control, so Preston had
explained it. It was one explanation, for sure, but Alix
doubted if it were the right one. There was another
explanation that was far more sinister.

Now the whole scene with Daisy that day replayed
itself: Alix's tour of the Lafayette, the moneky out of
control, the exasperated Ted Winner, the furious Preston March, the secret conversation that obviously had
something to do with Alix. Of course that *was* it! The
Lafayette, under the guise of working on the aging
process, was actually doing research into mind control,
turning one person into another. Alix imagined the
leader of an unfriendly country being abducted, the
implant being made, and the politician being returned
unharmed—but in someone else's control, docile, ready
to take commands. And no one would know—ever.
The idea was terrifying!

And that day Ted Winner had let the monkey escape and Alix had seen it. No wonder March was so
angry. If Alix hadn't taken the job at the Lafayette,
then what? She'd been a witness to something that
only a privileged few knew about. Thank God she had
taken the job! And shortly after that slip up, Winner
had begun to fall apart, had begun to drink too much.
And then, at the very party where the Lafayette was
unveiling—*that* was the unspoken celebration she'd
sensed—two of its latest experimental creations, the
Philip Greenspans, Ted had gotten so loaded he be-

came a threat and had to be dealt with immediately
. . . and permanently.

A screeching car broke the late-night silence, and
Alix gasped with fear. Right now she was more afraid
than she'd ever been in her life. She had uncovered a
scientific terror whose implications were so far-reaching
that she could barely contemplate them. She wanted
to believe that she was fantasizing, that none of this
was possible, but in her heart Alix knew it was all
true. What other explanation could there be? Still, the
idea of one person being turned into another was . . .

Alix froze. For a full minute she didn't move, didn't
dare, for fear the revelation she'd just had would vanish,
leaving her empty again. If Sarah Williams became
Nancy Greenspan, then surely it was possible that
Alan Fitzroy . . .

Alix closed her eyes, dislodging the tears that had
begun to collect. Alan looked so much like Richard
because he *was* Richard—Richard, who had gone off
on a jaunt and ended up "dead," out of her life forever.
He and his three friends. Another thought struck Alix,
and she began to tremble. With almost dreamlike
motions she maneuvered into the bedroom, opened the
bureau drawer, and removed her own Georgetown yearbook from under a stack of lingerie. She sat on the
bed, the book in her lap, not daring to open it. Yet,
she'd have to.

After a moment she took in a deep breath and
flipped through the book until she found the class
photographs. Alix had never met Randy Metcalf,
Richard's good friend who'd died with him that day.
She didn't have to, for Richard talked of him con-
stantly and she felt she knew him anyway. When the
accident happened, Alix was glad they'd never met;
mourning one person was difficult enough; mourning
two would have been impossible.

Alix found the picture she was looking for, searched
out Randy Metcalf's name in the caption, then traced
through the last row until she came to the picture
of . . . Hawkins!

Alix dropped the book on the floor, staring down at
it as if it were a snake coiled to attack. That poor

pitiful creature was Richard's friend! Distorted almost beyond recognition. He'd been a failure, a victim of the Lafayette's early experimentations. Of course, that was it. And that's why Hawkins had warned her, because he was afraid they might get her, or get her involved somehow.

Alix's mind flashed back to Richard, suddenly returned to her after ten years. But was he? Only his body had been returned; his mind was dormant, had been for ten years. The idea was macabre! What would it be like for him to wake up now, to discover that he was middle-aged, that Alix was a fully matured woman? Would he still love her? He'd said he'd never stop loving her, no matter what. And Alix had believed that. Of course he'd still love her. Even after ten years of darkness.

Alix retrieved the yearbook and put it back in its place. She had all the answers she needed for now. Richard was still alive! And each minute she spent with Alan Fitzroy wasn't wasted time, after all. After ten years she could once again hold her beloved Richard in her arms, feel him close to her, have him make love to her. Richard had been returned to her, and she'd never let him go again.

She went to sleep that night knowing that her new knowledge had put her in a potentially lethal position. But it didn't matter, because as soon as she had realized exactly who Alan Fitzroy really was, she was already locked in a life-and-death struggle to get him away from Preston March and the others at the Lafayette. She'd lost him once, but this time, if she had to lose him again, others would go with him, with her, for she'd pull the Lafayette down with her bare hands if necessary, and in doing so, create a scandal that would rock Washington for years to come!

— 7 —

During the next week, Alix kept to herself. She'd been
overloaded with information, with bad dreams and
memories. Winter clamped down on Washington with
full force, smothering the city was a heavy blanket of
wet snow; traffic ground to a halt, and everyone stayed
inside. Alix spent most of her time at work again. She
was happy with the progress she was making with her
experiments on the thymus gland, but wished the
process didn't take so long. All scientific experimentation, to be worthwhile and valid, had to be observed
carefully and fully annotated. To rush forward with
wild theses and conclusions was to open oneself up to
ridicule and failure, and worse, possibly to expose
people to danger.

More and more, as the depression brought about by
her unresolved emotional situation settled over her,
Alix began to feel that her life was worth living only
when she was in the laboratory. What had living in
the outside world ever brought her? Nothing but disappointment and pain. She'd started at the Lafayette as
a way of beginning a new life by facing the old fears,
and for a while it seemed she might succeed. But one
by one her accomplishments were being taken from
her. She was now convinced that the Lafayette was,
indeed, a far more complicated—and ominous—creation
than she'd at first imagined. And the question of
whether she really belonged there nagged her more
and more.

The Lafayette Institute. That black granite building that hunkered down along the Potomac. Everything in her world began and ended there: Sarah
Williams' transformation into someone called Nancy

126

Greenspan, Ted Winner's disappearance, the TRAUMA
dossier, even her introduction to and subsequent affair with Jack Campbell was inexorably linked to the
Institute. Alix's greatest fear now was that she'd discover that Richard's transformation was irreversible,
that she'd have to content herself with only his body
for the rest of her life. She knew that one day she'd
have to face TIM and the terrible truth, but not now.
Not just yet.

It was no wonder she'd become addicted to work.
Each time these thoughts and their implied consequences crowded her mind, Alix panicked. She was
being given too much input from too many sources.
Her heart was telling her to forget it all, but her brain
wanted—demanded—her to piece it all together, to
find the answer. And what then? Would *that* make
her life better? Or would it be the final piece of the
puzzle that, once fitted into place, would tear her
apart for good? Because not knowing was worse than
facing the truth, Alix decided she had to take some
action.

Preston March was her first, safest, target. He'd hired
her, had brought her to Washington, and had a strong
personal interest in her. Despite the vast differences
in their ages, he was obviously sexually attracted to
her, and she decided to use it—if she had to. But first
Alix set about wooing Preston in a very conventional
and safe father/daughter way. She once again began
stopping by his office each day "just to say hello" and
to tell him how her work was progressing. They both
knew he could plug into TIM—and did so—anytime
and get that information, but this courtesy only under-
scored Alix's interest in Preston March the man, not
the scientist.

When she was confident he'd begun to warm up to
her even more than before, Alix invited him out to
lunch, not in the executive dining room, but at an
expensive nearby restaurant in Georgetown. March
was enthusiastic about the idea and readily agreed.
After the lunch, after a full bottle of a silly little
German Mosel, they were both in expansive moods—

March's genuine, Alix's as calculated as it was aggressive.

"This was a wonderful idea, Alix," Preston confided after downing a second chocolate mousse. "I rarely leave the Lafayette during the day. I'd forgotten that the sun shines quite so brightly."

She smiled, then assumed a faraway look. "The sun has its place, of course. It does make everything look so *pretty*." She scanned the restaurant, which overlooked the ancient remains of the C&O Canal. The sunlight cascaded into the room, turning the walls of polished pine into slabs of amethyst. The room was warm and cozy, and Alix had to force herself to keep her voice cold and impersonal.

"You don't sound captivated by beauty," Preston said.

"I'm not, really. It's too irrelevant," she replied with a pout. "When I'm working, I don't like to be distracted. That's why I, for one, am glad the Lafayette's architects chose gray glass for the windows."

"My dear, you sound more like an old scientist than a pretty, vital young woman." He almost leered as he said these last words. "What happened to the Alix Kendall who wanted to make the Lafayette on a more human scale?"

"She grew up," Alix snapped. "Believing in people can only lead to disappointment. I've discovered down here in Washington that I really am more a scientist than a woman. You saw that in me in Boston, didn't you?"

March shrugged. "I saw something, maybe that *was* it. But surely everyone—even you—needs some sort of personal life away from the Lafayette."

"Some sort," she replied, "But I'm not sure exactly what. I find when I leave the Institute, something stays behind. It's as if a part of me is so attached to my work that to abandon it is to kill part of myself. Does that make any sense to you?" Unless Alix missed her guess, it made perfect sense to March. He was a workaholic, the kind of man who never for one minute didn't think of what project was coming next.

"It's the way I live my life, too," he answered eagerly.

"I find that I do get everything I need from my work. I have no family, few friends—by choice, I might add—and the little socializing I do is always work-related. Does that make any sense to *you*?" March felt he was being offered a rare chance to establish a personal relationship with the beautiful and very desirable Alix Kendall, and he was most eager to take it.

"It makes perfect sense. I don't know, Preston, maybe I'm just getting older, but I don't seem to have much time for the frivolities of life anymore. Even most men don't much interest me."

"But what about your reporter friend? What was his name again?"

"Jack Campbell," Alix answered smoothly. She'd never mentioned to anyone at the Lafayette that she was seeing Campbell socially. March—or Fitzroy—must have been doing some investigating. "Jack's become just a friend, someone sympathetic to talk to."

"I thought all women needed a 'real' relationship in their life to keep them going."

"All I need," Alix said vehemently, "is work . . . and more work. Preston, I can't tell you how much it's meant to me to be part of the Lafayette. Working in Boston was just scraping the surface, just skimming along at life, as you pointed out. Now I feel that I'm finally being fulfilled through work."

She finished her wine and put the glass down suddenly. "And because of that realization, my attitude toward everything is changing."

"What does that mean?"

"I'm beginning to feel that the world, this world"—she made a sweeping gesture that encompassed the restaurant, Georgetown, Washington, everything outside—"is only a mirage, an experiment to deal with. What *we're* doing, you and I and everyone at work, is what *really* counts."

"But we're doing our work *for* this world," March said, for the moment playing devil's advocate.

"In the end, maybe, but for me it's only the process that's really important. It's what I—we—can achieve for ourselves, for science, that keeps me going. And if we are true to ourselves as scientists and to our own

goals, then the products will help mankind . . . whether
mankind knows it or not . . . whether mankind ap-
proves or not." Alix hoped she sounded sufficiently
inflamed about her proposal of science as totalitarian
initiator.

"Then you don't care what people think of your
work?" March asked cautiously. "I thought most scientists were aware of the moral consequences of their
projects."

"*If* you fear public opinion, yes. If not . . ." She let
the sentence trail off, knowing that it sounded like an
admission of treason.

"That's a very dangerous attitude, Alix," March said
sternly. "If you were to follow it to its logical conclusion,
you could rationalize doing almost anything in the
name of science."

"Not *almost* anything, Preston, *anything!*" she
amended, cheered on by the rising color of his cheeks.
Her words obviously were touching him where he
lived.

"I had no idea you were so ruthless," he whispered.

"Is that what it is? All my life I've wondered what
name to call this feeling, the exhilaration that comes
when I'm working, with no thought other than how
the experiment will turn out. Now you tell me it's
ruthlessness."

March smiled at her but chose not to continue the
conversation. Since finding Alix alone in his office
with the TRAUMA dossier within reach, he'd kept his
eyes—and the eyes of the Lafayette—on her. He'd
checked her daily input into TIM and had had the
security staff watch her around the clock until he was
satisfied she was safe. He—they—had big plans for
Alix Kendall, and he needed to be assured that when
she was told about TRAUMA she'd stay loyal.

After this luncheon he was almost convinced that
she was ready to be moved into the second phase of
familiarizing her with TRAUMA. She'd already seen
Philip and Nancy Greenspan, so when their part in
this was revealed, it would have a real impact on
Alix—much more so than a written or oral report. The
business about Ted Winner had been unfortunate, but

not damaging apparently; Alix had accepted his leaving without further question. And what she'd just said about how she felt about work was unquestionably true: she *was* spending a great deal of time at the Lafayette. Her daily reports were copious proof that her growing reputation as a totally dedicated member of the team was well-deserved.

Alix Kendall was ripe to be included in the TRAUMA project. And aside from the slight—and apparently unimportant—entanglement with Jack Campbell, it looked like Alan Fitzroy's detailed report on Dr. Alixandra Kendall, presented before the Lafayette Institute's inner circle months before, describing her as a brilliant, dedicated loner, still held true.

"I can't say that I'm shocked by your attitudes toward science, Alix, because they mirror my own. To be bound by an outmoded morality is to limit yourself as a scientist. That's one of the reasons the Lafayette was founded. There is the opportunity at the Lafayette to expand your horizons, to push them to their limit, if you so desire. Our prime concern is aging, as you know, and we deal with that very effectively here in Washington. But the process is too slow. Out in Virginia we use accelerated techniques."

"Out at the Annex?" Alix's pulse quickened.

He nodded. "In Langley and around the world, for that matter. The Lafayette Institute is more than one place, it is a vast network of scientists whose research complements our own. They may not use the same name, but they are funded by many of the same sources we are. Their work, however, does use the umbrella title TRAUMA. In fact, what you are working on presently is of the utmost importance to the entire TRAUMA project. Why else do you think we'd go to all the expense and time to get you down here to Washington?"

"This comes as something of a shock. I thought I was working independently," Alix mumbled, aware now that she'd been dragged right into the middle of the very moral dilemma Campbell had posed to her earlier.

"No one at the Lafayette works independently,"

March confided. "But the time will come when you'll become privy to everything." He pushed his chair back, ready to leave.

"And when will that be?"

"I really can't tell you, my dear, because I really don't know. I hate to admit it, but it has more to do with intuition than it does with scientific predictability. But in the end, I trust my instincts completely, and when I feel the time is right to draw you into my confidence, I will."

"And if you decide the right time won't come?"

March shrugged. "It's never happened before. Now, we must get back to work. I'm sure you're as anxious to get on with it as I am."

They walked the distance to the Lafayette in silence. A sharp wind skittered over the Potomac toward them, and Alix pulled the fur collar of her coat closer around her neck and ears; she shivered nevertheless. But she wasn't trembling because of the cold; she was shivering at the memory of the coldness of March's words. He'd said his instinct about people had never failed him before. But Alix knew there was a first time for everything, and because he'd already begun to draw her closer by mentioning TRAUMA for the first time, she knew that if later he chose not to trust her completely, she wasn't just going to walk away from the Lafayette Institute without a care in the world.

No, she wasn't going to walk away from the Institute at all. Just like Ted Winner hadn't. Or Sarah Williams. Or the others.

Exactly a week after Alix had last seen Jack, he called and explained that he'd been sent out of town to the coalfields of Pennsylvania to do a story about the destructive qualities of strip mining. But now that he was back, he had something for her that couldn't wait, something he couldn't talk about over the phone. She'd be receiving a package by messenger later that afternoon, and she should call him after she'd opened it. No matter how she tried to prod him, Alix failed to make Campbell say more.

At four-thirty a messenger arrived with a plain

manila envelope. Alix took it to the ladies' room, the only place at the Lafayette where she really felt alone (remembering that Jack had once joked about exactly this). She opened the envelope and found three eight-by-ten photographs. The first two people—a man and a woman—were strangers, but the third she recognized immediately: it was Dr. Philip Greenspan.

But how did Jack get his picture? And who were the other two? As Alix was asking herself this, she turned one of the photos over. Jack had written the name of each person on the back of the photograph. The woman was Linda Strong. The unfamiliar man was Jack Finlay. Alix turned over the last photograph knowing she wouldn't see the name Philip Greenspan. It said Tim Donoghue. These were the remaining names on the TRAUMA list she'd given Campbell.

Dazed, Alix slipped the photographs back into the envelope and quickly left the ladies' room. On the way back to her lab she stopped at security just long enough to run the package and the photographs through the automatic paper shredder, watching to be sure that they were thoroughly mutilated. Campbell was crazy sending that here. He might just as well have sent her a lighted bundle of dynamite.

She tried to work, but she couldn't concentrate. Four young people were gone—two had "died," two had "disappeared." Four young people whose names made up the TRAUMA list. And Alix had seen two of them using different names—one of whom was supposed to be dead. Four young people had walked out one day, and when they came back, they were someone else. They'd been through the process, the change known as TRAUMA. Two of them were now back in the world; the others? Maybe the process had failed, misfired. Maybe they'd been reduced to pitiful creatures who had to be kept hidden . . . like poor Hawkins.

Alix was getting a migraine. She wished she could believe she was crazy, that things like this didn't really happen, not in the real world, not in the world she inhabited. But the Lafayette Institute wasn't the real world; it was the domain of men like Preston

March, power brokers like Alan Fitzroy, men to whom
human life was an expendable commodity.

And to make matters worse, Jack was obviously
still investigating the background of the four people
on the TRAUMA list. That was definitely dangerous
for both of them. If she hadn't been so rash, if she
hadn't given him the names, none of this would be
happening. But Alix hadn't known about Alan then.
Well, what was done was done, and all she could do
now was try not to compound the mistake. She'd have
to mislead Campbell whenever she had the chance.
How simple that sounded—mislead someone who loved
you and trusted you. Alix shook her head with disgust,
wishing she'd never heard of Preston March, the Lafayette Institute . . . any of it.

The next morning, as Alix entered the lobby of the
Lafayette to begin her workday as usual, Alan Fitzroy
appeared from the security guards' office. Alix smiled
and stepped toward him, ready to call him Richard,
ready to give him a kiss on the cheek and to entwine
her fingers in his. But when she saw the grave look on
his face, the fantasy disappeared. And in that moment,
Alix realized she'd have to be very careful when she
was with Fitzroy, for her natural inclination, now
that she knew who he was, was to be overly familiar
and proprietary; and that would give her away.

"I need to talk to you," he said, linking arms with
her and leading her toward the security guards' office.

"That's nice to hear. I thought you'd forgotten I
exist," Alix joked.

Fitzroy halted and looked at her, puzzled. "I don't
understand."

The joke had fallen flat, and Alix wished immediately she hadn't said anything. Alan had promised to
call her for another date but never had, and in the
elapsed time it had occurred to Alix that the elusive
Mr. Fitzroy just might *not* be interested in her as a
potential mate. And that had worried her, for Alan's
attraction to her was the key to their relationship and to
whatever might eventually be revealed about TRAUMA.

"I only meant that I missed seeing you," she said
lamely.

"And I missed you, too, but I've had other things to think about," he said without his usual gallantry. "We've got a problem . . . a real problem." He led her into the office and closed the door behind them. "Preston had a heart attack last night. It's pretty serious, I'm afraid. He wants to see you."

"What floor is he on?" she asked, assuming that the ailing man was hospitalized in the Lafayette's patient wing.

"His case is far too serious to be handled here. He's out in Langley. We're going there now."

Alan led her back to the front entrance as one of the black limousines Alix had seen come and go nearly every day since she'd begun work appeared and halted before them. A uniformed chauffeur got out, opened the door for them, and once they were settled, returned to his place and they started their trip before Alix even had time to consider the implications of going to the Annex. She wanted reassurance from Alan, or an explanation at least, but he was too engrossed in his own thoughts even to acknowledge that she was there. A curious mixture of fear and excitement filled her as they drove farther and farther from Washington and from safety. All she could think of was that in a very few minutes she'd see the Annex of the Lafayette Institute for the first time, the birthplace and home of the TRAUMA project.

Fifteen minutes later the car slowed, then turned off the main highway onto a side road that led through the beautifully wooded countryside. There were no signs anywhere, no warnings, no announcements, but at the end of the road a guardhouse sat ominously at one side of an imposing eight-foot-high electrified fence. The limo slowed, then stopped. A security guard, in a uniform unlike any Alix had seen at the Lafayette, his hand resting lightly on his holstered gun, interrogated the driver, while a second guard watched from inside the guardhouse. When he received the proper signal from his comrade, he opened the gate and the car passed inside.

Alix looked at Alan, hoping for an explanation for all the security, but he didn't respond. His eyes were still staring off into space, while his mind traveled hundreds of miles away. The car wound through the snow-covered countryside until it came to a second set of gates identical to the first. And after the same procedure had been followed, the car once again was allowed to pass inside, and ten minutes later the limousine stopped in front of the Lafayette Annex.

Alix peered out through the tinted glass, attempting to discern the building's size, but it was no use. Moments later the door opened suddenly and the interior of the car was filled with blinding sunlight.

"Miss?" A disembodied voice broke the silence and a hand appeared just inside the door.

Alix took the driver's hand and was helped out. She stood unsteadily outside the car, trying to adjust her eyes to the light, and for a moment she felt a rush of vertigo. She leaned lightly against the car to overcome it and realized that fear, not the sun, had caught her off balance—she was about to go into the Annex, and if she needed help, there would be no one to call, for no one knew she was here.

The Lafayette Annex was a long, low building that had been built into the side of a rolling hill. From the front the building appeared to be only one story, but at the back the Annex was actually four stories, and inside, with several basements and many subbasements, it was much more. In fact the lower floors of the complex were part of a bunker of reinforced concrete and steel. The ground-level building was constructed in the same style and of the same materials as its twin back in the District, and it evoked the same feelings of impersonality in Alix. One didn't look at any of the Lafayette buildings and think of happy times; one thought of raw science, pure mathematics, theoretical perfection—never human imperfection.

"Wait here, we'll be back shortly," Alan commanded the driver as he took Alix's arm and led her to the front door. "I'd hoped you could see the Annex under more pleasant circumstances. Maybe next time."

"Of course," she said, breathing a sigh of relief—if she'd be coming back, then she'd be leaving, returning to Washington, to her own life.

"We'd best hurry." Alan passed them through another security checkpoint, then walked ahead of Alix to a bank of elevators in the lobby. "As I said, Preston isn't very well."

"He's going to die, isn't he?" Alix said, feeling nothing as she did.

"No," Alan replied flatly, "but I want you to talk to him today. After today you won't be able to see him for several weeks, and there are a few things which must be straightened out."

The elevator opened, and as they stepped in, Alix was afraid all over again. There was something in the way Alan had assured her that Preston wouldn't die, something so cold and calculating in his tone of voice, that it chilled Alix. She looked at Alan and for the first time realized that he was a man without a heart, no better than a machine. And she realized that if that were true, he was capable of doing anything.

The elevator dropped down ten stories at such an alarming rate that Alix held Alan's arm for support. "Speed, in this case, is a precaution," Alan answered Alix's unasked question. "There's a small nuclear reactor close by, and in case of emergency, we must be able to reach the lowest levels as fast as possible. The subbasements are reinforced, protected from radiation."

"Reinforced?"

"In case of an attack," Alan said simply as the doors opened, revealing a long, sterile hallway.

Attack, thought Alix. Do the men who work here, who designed the Lafayette, expect the United States to be attacked? Or is Alan talking about a direct attack on the Annex because of TRAUMA and its political implications?

Twenty feet from the elevator was a steel doorway, and next to that a control panel similar to those used in the other Lafayette, but more complex, more secure. Alan pulled a silver card from his pocket, inserted it into the slot, and punched in his private code number. Once cleared, he then placed his hand on a black sensitivity plate, waited a moment while a computer checked his finger and palm prints, then removed it. Seconds later the silver card was ejected and the doors

slid quietly open. Alan took Alix by the hand and led
her inside.

Unlike the hallway, this area was alive with people.
A wide corridor ran off into the distance, and along it
were patient rooms. This subbasement looked like a
hospital, except there were two or three times the
customary staff working here, and all of them were
men. Alan hustled Alix through this section, down the
hallway toward another set of doors, where a guard
stood watch. Beyond this there was a wide-open space
with one nurses' station and one patient room—Preston
March's room. His room had wide glass walls through
which the two male nurses could observe him con-
tinuously. Various monitoring devices kept them ap-
prised of his condition every second.

"This is the most advanced setup of its kind," Alan
said proudly as he stopped at the nurses' station.
"In a conventional hospital the vital signs—pulse,
temperature, respiration—are all that are watched
with any regularity. Here, we have every bodily function under our thumb, even the electrolyte levels in
the blood. If anything changes that might affect his
health, if any level drops or rises, signaling the possible onset of another heart attack, it can be dealt with
instantly."

For a moment one of the nurses looked at Alix. He
stared at her coldly, then returned to his vigil. Alix
shivered mentally, feeling more like an outsider than
she would have dreamed possible.

"Let's see how Preston is." Alan nodded to a guard
who stood by the door and then advanced into the
room, Alix following.

Preston was propped up in bed and seemed to be
asleep. He was pale and drawn, his skin a pasty,
unhealthy color, and he seemed to be breathing with
great difficulty, even though an oxygen source had
been attached. March looked very old and very tired,
changed physically; it seemed he'd grown smaller, as
if his illness not only had sapped his strength but also
actually reduced his stature. Alix had seen enough
heart-attack victims to recognize that March was

gravely ill and would probably not recover, despite Fitzroy's unqualified optimism.

A vast network of wires sprang from various parts of his body, and Alix momentarily thought of a mechanical man, a puppet on a string that danced to the commands of an unseen hand. But whose hand is it? she wondered as she stepped closer to the bed.

March's eyes suddenly flickered open, and he smiled. "Alix, you're here." He reached out and took her hand in his. "I'm so glad to see you."

"How are you, Preston?" Alix asked, feeling greatly conflicted now. She hated to see anyone suffer, yet she couldn't allow herself the dangerous luxury of feeling too compassionate. Preston March was a dangerous man, and she never wanted to forget that.

"I've felt better," he joked weakly. Then he turned his attention to Fitzroy. "Alan, would you leave us for a moment, please?"

Fitzroy nodded. "I'll be right outside," he said to no one in particular.

When he'd gone, March indicated a chair next to his bed, "Sit down, my dear. I need to talk to you."

Alix was totally mystified. Certainly there were others at the Lafayette who were closer to March, others who would be called to his bedside in such a time of emergency. Unless, of course, Alix's campaign of fanaticism at lunch had worked and he was about to open up TRAUMA to her. Or maybe he just wanted to say good-bye.

"You've been a great help at the Lafayette, a great asset," he began weakly. "I was right to hire you down from Boston, I knew it all along."

"Thank you, Preston," Alix whispered. "You've been a wonderful example to me."

He now laughed at her seriousness, and as a geyser of phlegm caught in his throat, he coughed and choked momentarily. The spasm subsided, and he went on. "You think this is a deathbed farewell, don't you? Well, it's not, so don't be *too* upset by all this." He waved his arm at the electrical equipment spread around him. "I want personally to give you a promotion, that's all. I want to welcome you to the TRAUMA sector of the Lafayette Institute."

"*That's* why I'm here?" Alix was incredulous. She was so sure he was going to die, yet he was so sure he wasn't. Why?

"Certainly that doesn't shock you. I told you at lunch how I've felt about your work from the start, and your recent work has only convinced me that I was right. I think you have a great future at the Lafayette. And as you know, we need someone to replace Ted Winner."

"Of course" was all Alix could say, so dumbfounded was she by the turn of events.

"You will have to learn the ins and outs of TRAUMA before that time comes—and decide if you wish to continue on, but that all can be accomplished after I get out."

Alix wanted to protest, but there was nothing she could say. How could she insist Preston was going to die when he said he wasn't? As for working on the TRAUMA project, she wasn't sure. From what she'd seen already—none of which Preston, or Alan for that matter, knew about—she would finally be forced to make a choice between her beliefs in humanity and her belief in science. Finally being confronted by TRAUMA, though frightening, was better than the fear of uncertainty—at least she'd know what she was dealing with.

"I'll be in surgery soon, and all this will be settled once and for all," March said with a little smile. "After all these years . . . it's such a relief." He reached out and took Alix's hand. "You're a beautiful woman, my dear. If I'd been younger, if I thought I'd had a chance with you, I might have given that Jack Campbell a run for his money." He winked; then his eyes closed.

The thought of making love to Preston March shocked Alix. She'd always felt that March basically considered her a daughter figure. To hear otherwise now, particularly in this setting, was grotesque. And as for the crack about Campbell, apparently her trying to mislead March about her relationship with the reporter hadn't been a success. And that worried Alix. If she was about to be let in on the truth of the TRAUMA project, then March, Fitzroy, and everyone else connected with the Lafayette would want her to be a good security risk. Having a reporter as a lover certainly didn't put her in that category.

March's eyes reopened, and when he spoke, his voice was dreamy, faraway. "That's all, my dear ... for now. Will you please tell Alan that I'd like to see him?"

Fitzroy was waiting just outside the room. Before going back in to March, he escorted Alix down the hallway to a small waiting area equipped with a coffee urn, cups, and several stacks of fresh Danish pastries.

"I won't be too long," he promised. "Have a cup of coffee and make yourself comfortable."

Fitzroy woke March as he walked into the room. "How'd it go, Preston?"

"She's on our side, or will be, I'm sure," he said confidently. "But to be sure, I think we should give her a preview of TRAUMA, ease her into it gently."

Fitzroy shook his head. "I don't like it. Alix Kendall's a very volatile young woman; I'm still not convinced she's emotionally equipped for the job."

"You were the one who suggested her," March whined.

"On the basis of her work, which is still excellent. She is the perfect replacement for Winner and would be able to continue his work implanting cells from the first run of TRAUMA into the subsequent donors, but—"

"There can't be any buts, Alan, there's no time left. This damned heart attack of mine has pushed us ahead by months. After the near-misses we had last time with Linda Strong and Tim Donoghue, I'd hoped we could make some more progress with counteracting the transplant rejection ... particularly since I'm the next guinea pig."

"Our success rate hasn't been that bad," Fitzroy argued.

March laughed cynically. "You can say that because you came out on top. Of a total of twelve attempts, only five have been unqualified successes, four have died, and three are . . . well, living as little better than vegetables."

"For Chrissakes, Preston, don't quote statistics at me. I'm only trying to make you feel good about the operation," Fitzroy snapped. He took a deep breath, hating the antiseptic smell of the room. He'd never gotten used to that smell, even though he'd once been right here for many, many weeks.

"All this is beside the point. We need Alix Kendall right now; there isn't time to find someone else. Besides, I think she can be molded to fit our needs, shown the way, if you know what I mean."

Alan was tempted to overrule March. After all, he had the final say about policy at the Lafayette, but what would be the point? There was no one to replace her, and the perpetuation of Winner's experiments was the important thing. "All right, I'll go with you about Alix, but we don't need the interference her boyfriend is causing. I think it's time we taught him—and her—a lesson they'll never forget."

March's eyes half-closed. "What are you getting at?"

"I think it's time we introduce Mr. Jack Campbell to the TRAUMA project," Fitzroy said flatly.

March considered the idea for a minute. They'd already selected a premed student for the next TRAUMA run, but he hadn't been appropriated yet. March thought about Campbell for a moment, remembering what he looked like, how he acted. Then he remembered that Jack Campbell was Alix's lover, and for a moment he pictured the two of them in bed together. What Fitzroy was suggesting was highly unorthodox, but on the other hand, it was greatly appealing—especially since Alix Kendall was one of its rewards.

"I think that might just push Alix right over the edge," March finally said, deciding to put the project ahead of his own personal appetites.

"It'll be the convincer, it will prove to her that TRAUMA and the Lafayette are greater than any one thing, any one person." His eyes gleamed with wild enthusiasm. "Campbell will be assigned to a special story, sent on hazardous duty somewhere; I'll see to that. I think one of these unstable South American countries would be ideal."

"You may be right," Preston finally agreed. He was getting very, very tired and his mind was unable to focus on the exact nature of what Fitzroy was contemplating.

"I *am* right. It will solve the problem of Campbell and at the same time bring Alix fully over to our side. We can't lose."

March shook his head. "I only wish I could be as sure of it as you are."

"Trust me."

March took in a deep breath and once again closed his eyes. He'd never been so tired in all his life. But that would soon be over. "One last thing: Has Alix used her TIM card yet? It would save us all a lot of trouble."

Fitzroy shook his head. "After the incident with the guard, she's probably afraid to try again."

"Damn! And everything's waiting for her?"

"TIM's been desensitized and recoded. All she has to do is insert her card and the TRAUMA overview will appear; she doesn't even have to know the numerical codes. She doesn't have to do *anything* right!"

"Then make it easy for her: see to it that she uses the goddamned card, will you, Alan? I want her to know everything before we talk to her . . . particularly, before we hit her with this Jack Campbell thing."

Alix finished a second cup of coffee and began pacing the room. Being inside the Annex made her nervous. From what she'd seen as she and Alan rushed down to Preston's room, there was a lot of activity here, much more than at the main building back in Washington, and she sensed that there was as much—if not more—going on on the other floors of the building. She peered out into the hallway, wondering if she should dare take a look around, but when she saw the guard at March's room take one step forward toward her, she immediately returned to the lounge. She had to do something! The suspense of not knowing what Fitzroy and March were discussing was killing her!

She stood in front of a mirror that was the only decoration in the room and began preening nervously. She fixed her hair, reapplied her lipstick, removed a smudge from under her right eye—all of it busywork, all of it maddeningly boring. But just as she finished and flicked her eyes upward to make sure she looked presentable for Alan, she saw someone walking down the hall. He walked partway beyond the lounge, saw Alix, then took a step back. She caught his eyes in the mirror and saw the same shock on her face that he saw: it was Hawkins.

Alix whirled around and was about to speak, when he coughed and stepped forward into the room, his kit of cleaning tools held before him, as if he'd intended to come in here all along. The gesture silenced Alix. He walked across the room past her and put his equipment down on the seat of a naugahyde-covered chair. Without looking at her, he removed a spray can of window cleaner and a clean rag and proceeded to begin cleaning the mirror.

Alix moved over near him and took a seat on the couch, positioning herself so that she could see the doorway to the room. "I need to talk to you. I know who you are."

Hawkins looked at her in the mirror but said nothing. His eyes were sadder than she'd seen before, and as hers met his, she saw a sheen of tears cover them. He quickly looked away.

"Did something happen because Preston March saw you talking to me?" Someone passed by in the hallway, and Alix turned away, as if she didn't notice the workman cleaning the mirror three feet away.

"Hawkins, I don't have much time. You've got to tell me what happened, tell me about the experiments!"

Hawkins suddenly stopped working. Now he turned on Alix and tried to say something, but only a guttural growl came out, a howl from the soul like a dying animal. He looked down at her, leaned forward, and opened his mouth, making the noise again.

Alix didn't know what he wanted. "Hawkins, I . . ." she began to say, but then she saw it and her words died on her lips. Someone had cut out Hawkins' tongue!

Alix closed her eyes involuntarily for a moment, and when she reopened them, Hawkins was back at work as if nothing had happened.

"Who did that to you?" Alix asked, barely able to speak herself. "Was it Preston March?" Hawkins nodded at the mirror. "Because he saw us talking together?" He nodded again. "What did he think you'd told me?" Hawkins didn't react. "Please, you've got to tell me, maybe I can do something!"

Hawkins watched her in the mirror; then he raised the can of window cleaner and, using it like a pen, wrote one word on the mirror. The foamy white cleaner was hardly the best medium for writing, but as the wobbly letters appeared, then began quickly to run down the mirror, their meaning was still clear. Hawkins had written the word TRAUMA.

"Ready to go, Alix?" Fitzroy's voice boomed into the room from behind them. With one sweep Hawkins erased the word and cleaned the mirror.

"How is he?" Alix asked nervously as she practically leaped from the couch.

"He's fine ... how are you?" Fitzroy looked from Alix to Hawkins, then back again.

"The coffee revived me, thank you." She purposely walked across the room on a path that hid Hawkins from view, but she had the feeling that Alan Fitzroy at that moment could look right through her. "Are we finished here?"

"For the time being." Fitzroy looked at Hawkins, his eyes narrowing. "I didn't think you'd be disturbed," he said, with reference to Hawkins.

"I wasn't, really," Alix was acutely uncomfortable. Because there was no safe way to play the scene, she opted for silence concerning Hawkins. "I'd like to say good-bye to Preston," she finally said to get Alan's mind off Hawkins.

"He's asleep. You'll see him later," he replied brusquely. He slid his arm around her waist and walked her to the door, stopping for a moment to look back at Hawkins, who stood watching them in the mirror. Then Alan led Alix out of the room, down the corridor to the elevators, and back to the waiting limousine.

* * *

Over the course of the next few days Alix was plagued by the distinct feeling that she'd been taken to the Annex for something far more important that a mere promotion. The entire sojourn had a contrived air to it—Alan meeting her so secretly at the Lafayette, whisking her off without a word to anyone, the new job offer made in the precincts of a subterranean hospital room, Preston being gravely ill . . .

Maybe that was it. Maybe Preston only wanted to show her just how sick he really was. The whole bedside interview seemed to have a teasing, playful side to it, if "playful" were the right word. Preston had talked like a dying man, had looked like a dying man, yet at the very moment when Alix was ready to believe she'd never see him again, he'd stunned her by convincing her that he *would* live. Not only live but also see her again in a few weeks and explain TRAUMA to her, surely an exhausting task in itself. Even the heartiest man who'd had a heart attack took many, many weeks to recover fully. And Preston March was hardly the type anyone would classify as hearty. Yet, he'd seemed so sure. . . .

And to make matters worse, Alix was barely able to work anymore. Campbell weeks before had planted a seed of real doubt in her mind about her work: what if she were working on something immoral, something she didn't know about, would she continue the work? Then it had been a hypothetical question; now it was a reality, and the answer wasn't quite as academic as she might have wished. She'd been told she was part of TRAUMA already, that her work was carrying on Ted Winner's. To March, who knew nothing of her own knowledge of the project, such an admission was probably meant to be enticing, tempting in fact, but to Alix it was proof that she was in way over her head.

She'd allowed herself to play both sides, Jack Campbell against Preston March and Alan Fitzroy. She was being fed information by Jack while being drawn further into March's confidence. She had information that both sides wanted, information that neither side knew she possessed. And all along, she kept working, getting herself deeper and deeper into this mire, believing that one day she could extricate herself ... and Richard. How much more, she often wondered, would she be willing to conceal, to lie about, to connive for, to bring her closer to Alan Fitzroy? At what point would her duty to herself and to others supersede what she now saw as her duty to herself? It was a hard question, a horrible question, one that for now she had no answer to.

By the time Alex decided to give up trying to work and go home, she'd wasted half the day. She packed up her equipment, made her final notations into TIM, and was on her way out the door when the phone rang; it was Jack.

"I need to talk to you," he said urgently.

"What's wrong?" Playing double agent seemed to be so precarious that she was always in danger of being exposed by one side to the other.

"I can't tell you over the phone. Will you come to my place tonight?"

It was good to hear his voice, but the urgency in it worried her. "I'd love to. About eight?"

"Good. See you then. I'll make something to eat." He hung up without another word.

Alix stood in the middle of the laboratory feeling like she'd just stepped off a rocket onto a strange new world. She'd heard fear in Jack's voice. That was something new for him. The danger that was all around her, the volatility of the knowledge she had, had never before touched anyone around her. Of course she'd thought about danger in abstract terms, but it always seemed like crime in the big city—it was something that happened to other people, not to her, not to Jack. Now with one phone call, all that seemed to have changed.

As Alix walked toward the Lafayette's main entrance, Dr. Bob Peters, a neurologist, stopped her with a smile and a well-worn joke between them. "What, not burning the midnight oil tonight? Are you sick or something?"

Alix managed a smile. "I'm actually giving myself a little time off for good behavior."

"And just when I was beginning to believe you were an android good old Preston had put in our midst to make us all feel guilty." He laughed. "The last person who was as dedicated as you was Ted Winner, and look where that got him."

Now Alix's ears perked up. "Just where *did* it get him?"

Peters shrugged. "Who knows for sure? Rumor has it that he moved out to the Coast to work on some hush-hush project for the government. That was a lucky break for you, I guess."

Alix's promotion was common knowledge by now. "Lucky, if I can stay a little more in control than Ted did," she said, hoping to elicit some information from Peters, who'd known Winner long before Alix took the job.

"Ted was driven, if you ask me. I've worked here for a long time, Alix, and I've seen people come and go, many of whom drove themselves right into the ground. But Ted Winner?" He shook his head. "He was like someone possessed."

Two doctors stopped momentarily to talk to Dr. Peters, and as they chatted about nothing in particular, Alix once again saw the contrasts that existed between workers at the Lafayette. At a certain low level of competency—such as these two researchers—work at the Lafayette was something to be done during the day, then forgotten at night. Maybe it did seem glamorous to the outside world, but to them it was nothing more than a job, working nine to five, just like being a stockbroker or an insurance agent.

Then there was the other world at the Lafayette, the world that Ted Winner had found himself in, the one Alix was inexorably being drawn into. This was a competitive world, one that dealt with higher science, with striving for goals undreamed of before by any man. It was a darker world, a more sinister world, a world in which some survived and some didn't. And Alix was beginning to feel more and more that Ted Winner had been one of the latter.

After the other doctors left, Alix walked Bob Peters to the front door. "Ted was a drinker, wasn't he?"

Peters shook his head. "Not always. I place the beginnings of his drinking around the time he was given his TIM card."

"Are you sure?"

"No, but that's how it seemed. TIM knows everything that goes on here—and out at the Annex—you know. Maybe Ted saw something he shouldn't have. God knows there's enough going on in the world to make anyone take a drink." He winked at Alix, then touched her lightly on the arm. "Well, don't work too hard, Alix, or you'll end up just like poor old Ted." He continued on down the corridor, leaving Alix alone.

Poor old Ted, Alix thought as she walked outside into the cold night air. He'd started off working for himself, working toward his personal goals. Then he'd been absorbed into the upper echelons of the Lafayette—and things started to go sour for him. Winner grew somber and started drinking. Alix remembered the night of Alan's party when Winner had been so dangerously drunk. He'd made those comments about the Greenspans and about Preston March—none of which Alix could now remember, dammit! To the outside world Ted Winner was a success—he'd been promoted, and been given a key to TIM ... and then things had really fallen apart for him.

What had Ted Winner found in the computer that had scared him so much that his life had turned around and he'd begun to drink? Had he found out the details of the TRAUMA project? Had he found out, like Alix was finding out, that he was part of something far larger and more sinister than he'd ever imagined? Alix didn't know any of the answers yet, but she was sure as hell going to find out soon. She now had her own TIM card and TRAUMA was the key.

Dr. Peters watched Alix walk out of sight through the gates of the Lafayette toward the main road and Georgetown in the distance. Once assured she was not returning, he picked up the phone and dialed the number he'd copied down earlier. Moments later a man answered. "It's Bob Peters. I just 'ran into' Alix Kendall and told her what you wanted me to." He paused and listened to the question. "Yes, I think she'll investigate TIM very soon. She's just as curious as anyone, and after the story I told her, I can't imagine she'd be able to stay away." He listened again, knowing from the pleased sound of the voice on the other end that he'd be properly rewarded for his help. It wasn't that he liked being a part of these inner-office politics, but Bob Peters knew on which side his bread was buttered. "Thank you," he continued. "Anytime you need me, just call. Good night, Mr. Fitzroy."

—8—

Alix saw immediately that Jack was upset. He looked tired and drawn, and the worry that lined his face made him seem years older than he was. In fact his handsome features appeared to have gone through an aging process overnight. There was a marked puffiness around his eyes, his skin tone was a little sallow, and the corners of his mouth drooped even when he braved a smile as he met Alix at the front door. "I'm glad you're here," he said, brightening somewhat. "Did you have any trouble getting here?"

"I walked," she said defiantly, wondering what kind of trouble he was talking about. "I needed the exercise."

"You sure that was wise?"

"I'm not sure of anything anymore," she admitted frankly.

Jack guided her to the couch in front of the front windows; the curtains, normally open, were closed tightly against observers in the street. "How about a drink?"

"Only if it's coffee."

"There's some left over from this morning. Game?" When Alix nodded, he disappeared into the kitchen and five minutes later returned with two coffee mugs. "Light with sugar, just as you like it." He clinked mugs with her. "Cheers."

Alix gingerly sipped the leftover coffee; the inky brew tasted like she imagined dirt would. Finally she had to break the silence. "May I make a personal comment? You look like hell. What have you been doing? Painting the town red?"

Jack shook his head. "I wish it were that simple." He sipped his coffee, grimaced at the taste, then put the mug down. "I'm being sent away."

"But you just got back from Pennsylvania."

Now Jack smiled. "This time I'm being sent a lot farther than Pittsburgh. The paper wants me in South America to report on a local revolution."

"When?" This trip was so sudden—too sudden.

"Tomorrow."

"That's impossible." Alix's world stopped spinning for a moment. Jack Campbell was her security in Washington, her hedge against getting swallowed up by the Lafayette. She needed him here, not in South America.

"Being sent away is unpleasant, yes; impossible, no. And quite frankly, I don't know what to make of it. That's why I was awake all night, and that's why I look like hell."

"And you agreed to go to South America, just like that?" Alix asked angrily. "For God's sake, it's dangerous down there."

"No more than here," he said ruefully. "I didn't want to worry you, but I think they're onto us." He put his coffee aside and poured himself a drink. "For the last week or so, I think someone's been following me."

"How can you be sure?"

"I can't but I've spotted the same car, the same man always around. And it's not just that, it's a feeling I have."

Alix's fear almost choked off her voice. She'd known the dangerous balancing game she was playing, but until now she'd never really believed that it might tip over against her or Jack. "Why would anyone be following you?" He looked at her sheepishly, and suddenly it all became clear. "You've been playing detective again, haven't you?"

He looked down at his feet, then up at her. "I told you weeks ago that I wasn't going to let this thing go."

"Oh, Jack, what have you done?" she asked, her voice tinged with despair. "Don't you know that they're playing for keeps?"

Now he looked at her curiously. "That's an odd thing for you to say, Alix. What have *you* been up to?"

"Nothing," she lied, "but the Lafayette is an important institution. If you start tampering with its reputation, there are some people who ... who may try to discredit you."

"Discredit?"

"If someone has been following you, it may be to pick up damaging information, something that will make you look bad, unreliable, if anything should come out in public."

"It sounds like you've done a lot of thinking about this."

She shook her head. "How could I? I didn't know you were pursuing any investigation. Just exactly *what* have you been up to?"

"Finding out a little bit more about the Lafayette and its directions."

It was the worst answer Jack could have given her. Campbell knew only that the Institute was linked to the disappearances of the four students; Alix knew how it was linked. She also knew that the Lafayette directors were ruthless and wouldn't let anyone get in their way. So here it was: Campbell was the victim of Alix's dishonesty, and now, as earlier with regard to her work, she began to feel condemned by her own complicity in the affair. "Why didn't you say something to me, Jack? Why?"

"Because, as I remember, you wanted me to drop the whole thing; why antagonize you?" He looked at her thoughtfully. "You're acting very strange about this, Alix. What's going on?"

"I don't know. I came over here to have dinner, only

to learn that you're going away . . ." She suddenly felt very tired and vulnerable. She did care for Jack. Maybe not the way he would have liked it, but it was more than she cared about most people.

"It's all settled," he said quietly. "I didn't want you to know earlier because I didn't want it to be hard on you."

Alix looked at him, looked at the little-boy earnestness of his protection, and tears sprang to her eyes. "I don't want you to go away. Please . . . ?"

He took her in his arms and kissed away her tears. "I have no choice."

"You could say no."

"I did, as a matter of fact." He smoothed her hair and lightly kissed her forehead.

"And?"

"And I was told that if I didn't take the assignment I was through."

"*They* arranged this," she declared as her determination to face March and the upcoming TRAUMA indoctrination began to waver.

"Who did what?"

"Preston March and his gang at the Lafayette. First you were being followed, now you're being sent away." She pulled back from him. "Jack, they know about you and me. They want me to head up a section of the TRAUMA project here in Washington."

Campbell shook his head. "I don't know what you're talking about, Alix."

My God, she thought, have I excluded him that much from my life? "None of that matters now, but you must believe me—if you go away, you'll never come back."

Campbell looked at her in disbelief. "Why is it that I have the feeling we've been through this scene before? Do you remember a while ago when I wanted you to quit your job and you accused me of being paranoid?"

"That was different," Alix said quickly. "There wasn't any proof then."

"And there is now?" He put down his glass and half-turned toward her. "What's going on, Alix? What are you hiding?"

"It's just a feeling . . ." She said lamely.

"Then it's no more valid than my feeling about you was. My job offer came from Mike Flanagan, not Preston March. Michael and I have known each other for fifteen years. The original reporter assigned to cover the revolution got drunk once too often and got himself fired. To tell the truth, I've been waiting to step into his shoes for years."

"So that's the real reason, is it?" she yelled at him, her fear turning to icy anger. "What we're really dealing with is your ambition."

"Bullshit!" He let her go and went to the bar, where he poured himself another drink. "I'm not a fool, Alix, if I thought there was any real danger, I wouldn't go, but as far as I can see, there isn't."

He was right: she had no concrete proof. Just an eerie feeling that Alan and Preston were behind all this. And if she told Campbell everything she suspected, it would hardly convince him to stay in Washington, but it would alienate him from her totally. And she didn't want that. It was totally selfish and unreasonable, but it was the way she felt.

"I'll ask you once again, Jack—will you stay here?"

He shook his head. "I have to go. What if I *did* stay? What would happen then? I'd be out of a job, you'd be working, and we'd end up hating each other. No, it's best this way." He brought his new drink back to the couch. "The real question is: What do you do while I'm away?"

"Me?" Alix stood up and walked across the room to the fireplace. "What I do doesn't really concern you anymore, does it?"

"Sounds like an ultimatum to me, am I right? I go to South America and our relationship is over. It reads like a bad play."

"Sorry I couldn't do better," she said angrily.

"Well, you'll have plenty of time to think of some new tricks while I'm away."

Alix turned on him angrily. "Why won't you believe me? The Lafayette is behind all this! They're up to their necks in this business with Sarah Williams and the others. And now they know you know, too. I don't

care who arranged for you to go away. Mike Flanagan
or no Mike Flanagan, friend or no friend, they want
you out of the way to assure my loyalty because they're
about to make me one of them." It was more than she
intended to say, but under the circumstances she felt
she owed Jack one last chance.

To Jack it sounded like Alix was talking gibberish.
It was obvious she believed what she was saying, but
it was too obtuse for him. He needed facts laid before
him, names, dates, reasons. Alix hadn't come up with
any of them. Hell, he and Mike Flanagan had been
pals for years. There was no one in the world with
enough money—or power—to make him turn on a
buddy. Jack *had* to take the job. He wanted to. It was
a field of reporting he'd always aspired to; besides,
there was a hefty hardship pay attached to the
assignment. He'd save that extra up, and by the time
he returned, there'd be quite a nest egg for him and
Alix. That was the reason he was taking the job, and
the real reason he'd never confide in her.

"I promise I'll be extra careful," he finally said,
knowing it would never be enough.

"Do what you want," she whispered. "Have it your
own way. Go off to South America and walk into some
goddamned rain forest and never be seen again. But
don't say I didn't warn you." There was now a hint of
acceptance in her voice. "If you're serious about this
harebrained scheme and tonight is your last night in
Washington, then I'm going to make it a memorable
one." The day Richard walked out for the last time,
she hadn't known it; tonight she did. "Are you already
packed?"

"I finished this afternoon," he admitted guiltily. "I've
got my shots, my passport and visas, enough blank
recording tape for my recorder to dictate *War and
Peace* and enough Lomotil to plug up all of Georgetown."

"What time do you leave?"

"I'm being picked up at six in the morning."

Alix looked at her watch. "It's eight-thirty. You'll
need an hour to shower and shave and eat before

going. So that gives us about nine and one-half hours
to say good-bye."

"What are you up to?" he asked coyly.

"Let's have dinner and then I'll show you. Since you
didn't let me know you were going away, I didn't have
the chance to get you a gift, but there's one I always
carry with me." She smiled, but it crumbled and she
put her arms around him. "I'll miss you, Jack," she
said, knowing now that it was true.

"I'll be back before you know it. Now, let's eat, I'm
starving."

After dinner, they did the dishes together, then
skipped coffee and dessert for Alix's promised gift. At
the bottom of the stairs she pulled him into her arms
and kissed him hard on the mouth, her tongue dancing over his. "You're giving up all this for some soggy
jungle? Maybe you *are* crazy, after all, and I'm better
off without you."

But as they walked upstairs, Alix felt a familiar
sinking feeling deep in the pit of her stomach. She
could joke for a thousand years and Jack could argue
that this assignment was really a stroke of good luck,
but Alix knew in her heart that behind this separation stood Preston March and, more important, Alan
Fitzroy. She was leading Campbell up the stairs like a
lamb to the slaughter, and there was nothing she
could do short of telling him everything, betraying
herself, and ruining her chances with Fitzroy. She
hated herself for her obsession with him, but like all
obsessions, in the end it won out.

They made love twice during the following few hours,
then dozed off for a while before making love once
again. Alix hadn't intended to start a love fest, but
because somewhere in the deep recesses of her mind
she feared she'd never see Jack again, it had happened nevertheless. Perhaps her fear was ridiculous,
perhaps not. All Alix knew was that everything connected with the Lafayette Institute had a way of changing . . . disappearing . . . being mutated. There was a
core of power there that eclipsed even her own dreams
and fears.

When it finally came time for Jack to begin getting

ready to leave, Alix couldn't bear the thought of letting him go. She wanted to keep him in her arms, his head cradled against her breasts, as he had been for the last half-hour. If only she could keep him with her, she could protect him. It was every mother's belief: by watching over her child, she could keep him from harm, even to the degree of coming between him and death. But Jack Campbell wasn't a child. And he'd made his decision to leave Washington—as an adult—and this was the point where Alix had to let him go.

"You're going to be a disaster at work today," Jack said groggily as he crawled from the bed in the cold predawn darkness.

"I'm calling in sick today, that's what I'm doing," she said, feeling the thrill of playing hooky from life. "The Lafayette can live without me for one day."

"I hope I can," he said somberly.

Alix smiled at him standing there naked in the half-light cast by the bedroom lamp. Jack Campbell was so much a man, yet the look on his face, the tiny twitch at the corners of his mouth, told the real story, a different story. Alix smiled bravely and resisted the urge to extend her arms to him, to entice him back down to the warmth of her body. This time she knew her power would fail, that he would go away as promised. And like so many other countless women throughout history, Alix would say one last farewell to the man who, for reasons known only to the male ego, had to leave everything in search of his goal, the one destination that would validate his existence.

"You'll do just fine without me, Mr. Campbell," Alix said airily. "God knows you did before you met me."

"Ah, but that was different." He headed toward the bathroom. "I'd never had the best before. And now that I have, I'm spoiled." He turned on the bathroom light and for a moment was nothing more than a silhouette in the doorway. Then the door shut and he was gone.

Alix cried for him—for them—while he showered and shaved. She hadn't planned it that way, but as the door to the bathroom shut out the light, she remembered how she would feel for the next days, weeks, months, maybe years. Jack believed that the assignment in South America was innocent, but Alix knew in her heart it wasn't. And because of that she felt like she was in a world at war, where saying good-bye became a daily chore, where every farewell carried with it the unspoken footnote that it might be for the last time. The pretenses between them, the smiles, the lies, the blurry edges of her fear, were meant to diffuse the truth, but Alix had once lost a man, and she needed to tear down the facade of the departure to spare herself any false hopes that this time it would be different.

Alix wanted to get angry again, to scream at Jack that he mustn't go, to brand herself a traitor, a liar, a cheat. She wanted to accuse him of pigheadedness in the face of the mounting evidence of the power of Preston March and Alan Fitzroy and God only knew how many others. Yet she couldn't bring herself to utter a single word of warning. And in light of that, her self-defense mechanisms had already begun to work. Part of Alix had tried to convince Jack how wrong he was to go, while another part, equally as strong, began automatically to absolve itself of any blame or guilt should the worst happen and Campbell not come home. Once she'd let a man walk out of her life with no more than a peck on the cheek, and the guilt of that parting had crippled her for the next decade. That once was enough.

But now that the real business of Campbell's leaving was at hand, Alix was more than willing to put aside these bitter memories. Now it *was* time to pretend, to pretend he'd be back soon. Now was the time to talk about the future, about what they would be doing in two months and two years. Now was the time to forget that she was in love with a ghost, and to act as if this relationship were the core of her life, for his sake.

By the time Jack returned from the bathroom, his skin still glistening from the humid heat, his hair slicked back and wet, Alix had finished her crying. She'd cleared her eyes, washed up a bit downstairs, gotten dressed, and made the bed. He stood in the doorway expecting to find her as he'd left her; the sight of her calmly sitting in a chair confused him. His eyes flicked from the bed to Alix, and the smile fell from his mouth. So, she thought, now he knows he's going away for real, too.

"Thanks for cleaning up," Campbell said with strained politeness.

"How about breakfast?" Alix had peeked into the refrigerator and found it stocked with enough food for days. It was obvious this trip had really caught Jack off guard.

"No, don't bother cooking. I'll get something at the airport."

"I want to bother," she insisted, "if there's anything special you want."

"You might as well cook everything you can think of. When I went grocery shopping, I didn't know I'd be going away."

When you went out shopping, Alix thought, I hadn't visited Preston March at the Annex yet. I hadn't seen him at his worst, so near death, so insistent he'd live. When you went out shopping, the decision hadn't been made somewhere deep inside the Lafayette that you had to be gotten out of the way because they had big plans for me and were afraid that you'd interfere. "I'll make the biggest breakfast for both of us you've ever seen," she said. "I hope you're hungry."

"After the past eight hours? Are you kidding? Babe, I could eat a horse." Jack stepped into his jockey shorts, snapped the waistband for punctuation, then began searching for his trousers.

"Good enough, then." Alix neatly sidestepped the reference to last night's sex. If he were going, he'd have to be gone for good, in all ways, particularly sexually. "I'll call you when the food's ready."

By the time she'd heated some biscuits, whipped up some eggs into fluffy omelets filled with cream cheese, chives, and mushrooms, then cooked up enough sausages for an army, Jack was downstairs. He'd always been dressed traditionally—sport coat with a tie or over a sweater, oxford-cloth shirts, slacks, penny loafers—but now he wore jeans, a lightweight cotton shirt, and a windbreaker tossed casually over his arm, his feet encased in lightweight tropical hiking boots. Jack Campbell looked like a different man.

"Remember, it's going to be hot down there," he said, anticipating a comment on his clothing from Alix. "I don't want to arrive in ninety-degree weather wearing an overcoat and wool slacks."

"But you'll freeze on your way to the airport."

He shrugged in reply and immediately sat down to the enormous breakfast. Fifteen minutes later they'd finished. During that time all communication had been silent because neither of them had to, or wanted to, speak. Occasionally they caught each other looking, then turned away, embarrassed, as if eating this meal together were more intimate than the past hours in bed. And perhaps it was. Perhaps it was a glimpse of the life they might have had together had things gone differently.

"I've got to go," he said, checking his watch. "Can I drop you?"

Alix shook her head. "I'll walk."

"But it's cold . . . and dark," he countered. "I'd really feel better if I dropped you off."

"Thank you, but I'd just as soon be on my own from the minute I walk out that door. Just give me five minutes to do the dishes."

"No time." He got up. "The car will be here in a minute. Just scrape them off, I'll do them when I get back."

While Jack assembled his gear in the front hall, Alix collected the dishes, dumped what refuse there was into the garbage disposal, then piled them up in the sink. Jack would do them when he came back. Alix pictured the future, the sink full of dishes covered with green and gray mold, lying in state, a grotesque memorial to Jack Campbell's optimism and to his naive belief he would return here alive. She pictured the real-estate agent showing prospective clients the house and coming upon the monstrous growth in the sink. It would have been funny were it not so sad.

Alix turned on the tap water, but when she felt tears welling up in her eyes, she left it and fled the kitchen to join Jack. With him she was safe from despair because she'd promised herself not to cry in his presence. "You'd better get back soon, or that sink is going to come to life," she joked.

"It won't have the chance. I'll be back before you know it."

Alix nodded and stepped into his waiting arms, determined not to let the intensity of her feelings come between them during this last embrace. "I'll miss you," she said, just now touching the truth of the matter.

"And I'll think of nothing else but you," he said softly.

"For God's sake, take care of yourself!" She held him with a sudden urgency they both felt. "Think of me . . . all the way home on the plane?"

"You got it!" He kissed her long and hard on the lips, then stepped back from her and just looked for a moment. "Would it sound corny for me to say I want to remember how you look right now?"

"No, of course not," Alix whispered.

"I love you, Alix," he said softly. "And I want you to take care of yourself while I'm gone. No more snooping around, okay?"

She nodded her head, unable to look him in the eyes.

"But just in case your curiosity gets the best of you," he said lightly now, intuiting that Alix would never be able just to sit still, "I want you to have this." He dug deep into the pocket of his jacket and removed a silver .38-caliber pistol.

Alix looked at it in horror. "I don't want that."

"Take it," he said, forcing it on her. "It might come in handy."

Alix slipped the gun into her purse without even looking at it. Until now even the danger she'd felt had had a nebulous quality, as if it were a movie. Now, with the coldness of the gun still tingling on her palm, that danger had taken on a very real, very hard-edged quality. This was no cops-and-robbers movie, this was playing for high stakes against something as merciless and faceless as the government.

Jack kissed Alix once more on the lips, and just as

he broke away, a car horn sounded in the street. "That's for me. You know how it is: Time nor tide waits for no man."

Alix smiled at the lame joke and allowed Jack to help her into her heavy winter coat. What a contrast they presented: he dressed for tropical heat, she for blustery winter. But now they were of two different worlds, and Alix feared that in the end her world was that of the living, while his was that of the dead.

Jack hustled them out of the house, locked the front door, then raced down the sidewalk to the car. He was shivering in the nearly subzero weather, yet once inside the warmth of the car, he rolled down the window to take Alix's hand. He pulled her close for one last kiss. When they parted, he whispered, "I love you, Alix. Always remember that."

"And . . . and I love you, too," she said firmly, wanting him to remember those words as the last thing she'd said that cold, wintry morning in Washington.

Campbell's face dissolved into a glorious smile; then he grinned and finally laughed out loud. "On, you huskies," he shouted at the driver, who gave him a queer look. "Dammit, let's get the hell out of here!" The car revved up, slid around a bit in the snowy ice, then pulled out into the street; within seconds it was out of sight.

Alix kept waving even though the car was long gone. She stood silently in the pitch dark, waving at nothing. But she couldn't stop herself. How many times must I say good-bye? she asked herself. How many times will someone else touch my life, then pass on? Suddenly feeling overwhelmed by self-pity, she turned and ran up the street to Washington Circle, then on to Pennsylvania Avenue. Several times she almost fell, but it hardly mattered whether she did or not. Alix had to run to save her own life. She had to stay ahead of the fear, the loss, the anger, if only for a few minutes.

She crossed the bridge that spanned Rock Creek Parkway and was soon marching up Twenty-sixth Street toward home. The anger. That's what was left now. Anger. Rage. Impotent rage that she was being

sucked down by the evil men who were behind the
decision to send Jack Campbell to South America,
who had stolen Richard from her. She knew where the
orders had come from. She knew where the center of
that rot was, where to find the core of the boil. Of
course she knew; she worked there five days a week,
churning out data for the very man she hated. For
Preston March.

Alix walked slowly across N Street, not realizing
that her coat had opened, exposing her to the cold, not
realizing that she'd already passed her apartment.
She needed to be outside, to be in the fresh air. She
needed to be away from confinement of any kind, even
if it were her own cozy home. The home supplied by
them. Now she needed to be cold and to stay angry
long enough to get to the heart of the matter, and to
take revenge if it came to that.

She circled the block three times before wearily
climbing the stairs. Alix knew more about the Lafayette Institute than almost anyone else knew. She
wasn't merely a cog in the great machine, an intelligent robot who acts but does not question. She was on
her way up at the Lafayette, which was good, because
when she reached the top, she intended to rescue
Richard, then pull it all down, stone by stone.

Alix took a long, hot bath that so enervated her she
was barely able to dry off before falling into bed.
Before drifting off to sleep, she called the Institute
answering service and left a message that she was
sick; then she took the phone off the hook. Seconds
before her anxiety was banished by a long, dreamless
sleep, Alix decided that the best and easiest way to
get to the Lafayette's inner circle was through Alan
Fitzroy. And that the easiest way to get to Fitzroy was
through his bed.

"Alix, this is a surprise," Alan said two days later.
But he didn't sound surprised at all. "How have you
been?"

"I was sick with the flu, but I seem to have recovered."

"Sorry to hear you were ill," he said noncommittally.
He'd had a full report not only on Alix's absence from

the Institute but also on that last night with Campbell, which, he concluded, was the real reason she'd been unable to return to work.

"I'm much better now, thank you. So why don't we have dinner . . . or something?"

Fitzroy laughed heartily. "You don't like to beat around the bush, do you, Dr. Kendall?"

"If I did that, by the time I got what I wanted, I'd be too old to care."

"And what exactly is it you want?" Fitzroy now sounded interested.

"Dinner is as good a place to start as any," she said seductively. "My apartment? Tomorrow night about eight? I'll cook."

"You are a woman of many talents," he said.

"*Many* talents," she cooed, wondering if she sounded as much like a whore as she felt. "You have the address?"

"Of course. I sent you an invitation once, remember? But this time, why don't you let me take you out for dinner? You've been sick, and—"

Alix now laughed. "I'm very tempted to say yes."

"Then what's stopping you?"

"*I* invited you out. I can't very well let you take me to dinner."

"Sounds like reverse sexism to me, Dr. Kendall. Let's compromise: I'll take us both out and put it on the Lafayette's tab. How's that?"

"That'll be lovely."

"So I'll pick you up at your place at eight?"

"Fine. And one more thing before you go, Alan. . . . How's Preston? I tried calling the Annex but was unable to get through to him."

"Preston's coming along nicely," he said evenly.

Coming along nicely, Alix thought. Sounds like someone's baking a cake! The Preston March she remembered was so near death she could feel its presence in the room. Yet he'd been totally confident that he'd recover. And now Alan echoed that optimism. "When do I get to see him?"

"He should be released in a matter of weeks. You won't recognize him . . . I promise."

"But Preston was so sick—" she began to protest, despite herself.

"Alix," Fitzroy interrupted, "I really must go now. But one parting word: don't ever underestimate the work the Lafayette is doing . . . and has done. Anything is possible, particularly since TRAUMA was established. And that includes saving the life of an old codger like Preston March." He chuckled. "See you tomorrow about eight." He hung up.

TRAUMA. How long would it be before she had the courage to use her TIM card? She'd carried it with her every day for weeks, yet she'd been unwilling to use it, to tap into the source that would answer all her questions. But every minute she hesitated was another minute she was kept suspended between suspicion and knowledge, between fear and relief. She'd sent Campbell off to South America without telling him about TIM, without finding the very facts that might have convinced him to stay in Washington.

Alix went back to work after her call to Fitzroy, knowing that she could not operate under the premise that ignorance was bliss for much longer. One day soon she'd have to conquer her own fear and find out about TRAUMA. And she only hoped that when she did, it wouldn't already be too late.

—9—

Three hours after Alan picked Alix up for their date, they returned to his house. He used his own key to let them into this palace on R Street, and after taking her coat himself, he led her into the living room and offered a cognac.

"Where are the servants?" Alix asked, still awed by the scale of the house.

"I only keep two, really. The others were hired for the party. If I'm not entertaining during the evening, I let them go home."

"They don't live in?" she asked with a seductive smile.

"Too expensive these days. Besides, being a servant has fallen into disrepute, no matter what the pay. Both the butler and the cook insisted from the start that they live elsewhere." He handed her a cognac, then toasted: "We always seem to be toasting each other."

"Better than throwing stones," Alix quipped.

Alan laughed. "I can't remember when I've enjoyed an evening more. Going out is usually such an ordeal. I have to keep up the front everyone wants to see, everyone expects to see. With you I can just relax." He sipped his drink.

"I'm glad you feel that way," she said, feeling something like the proverbial spider, although in this case it was Alan's parlor they were in, not hers. "This house is so beautiful; is it all like this?" she asked to take her mind off herself.

"The rest isn't quite this grand. I do so much business-oriented entertaining that the public rooms must be impressive. Personally, I think it's a little overdone."

"What about the private quarters?" she asked quietly.

"Judge for yourself." He put his glass down, stood up and held his hand out to her, then led her out of the living room to the art-deco study at the back of the house. Alix had seen part of the room the night of the cocktail party, but she hadn't seen the bay windows that overlooked a formal garden in the back of the house, nor had she seen the yard bathed in light from hidden fixtures that caught a rabbit, blithely unaware it was being observed, scampering through the snow-laden flowerbeds. It stopped to sniff the air, then vanished into the darkness at the end of the garden.

"It's so beautiful, so peaceful here," Alix said, feeling that playing Mata Hari was a tougher role than she'd expected. The tranquillity of the scene had touched her, and as she turned to face Alan, she realized that a great part of her determination to uncover the Lafayette's secrets was an attempt to absolve her Richard of any blame when he was finally returned to her. Alix wanted him without sin. She had planned this date to be a cool, calculated gesture to ingratiate herself with Alan, but as she observed his handsome features in the half-light of the study, Alix admitted the real reason: she was here to make love to him after ten long years.

"This study is my favorite room," Alan said, taking a step closer to the window. "When I need to get away, to forget everything that's happened, I come here," he said almost wistfully.

"But your life is so full, so active. What could you possibly want to forget?"

He turned and smiled at her. "Maybe one day I'll tell you, but not right now." He moved closer and put his hands on her waist. "You intrigued me from the start because I couldn't believe so beautiful a woman could be as distant as Preston said. But now . . ." He smiled.

"Now what?" Her whole being was focused on the pressure of his fingers on her.

"Now I see that Preston March has become an old man. If he were younger, he'd see what I meant when I told him that Alix Kendall's distance can be gotten over, like a minor cold." He pulled her closer still and kissed her lightly, gently on the mouth.

"Oh, Alan," Alix whispered between kisses, letting the weight of her body fall against him. She needed to be held, to be supported by him. She wanted so much to give herself to this man, this man who was so much of her past that at times being with him was excruciating. Not that Alan only reminded her of Richard. No, it was far more than that. Being with Fitzroy reminded her of how she used to be herself, how she used to think, how she used to attack the world anew each morning, facing the dawn as a challenge. Alan brought back sense memories of her life in Washington ten years before. It was as if he'd opened a door onto a past world, but one still close enough for her to smell the flowers in bloom those many springs ago. Alix wanted to be young again. Alan was older than she, but his spark of life was years younger, and she wanted a part of that, if only by proximity.

He showed her the rest of the house as if neither of them expected to end up in the bedroom. He prattled on about the paintings in the dining room, about the topiary expertise of the gardener who, during spring and summer, turned the backyard into a green zoo; then he talked about the Italian marble in the entrance hall as if it had been snatched from the Vatican itself. Alan told her about the collection of Renaissance paintings that lined the staircase to the second floor and described in detail his collection of Dickens in a private study off the bedroom. In his bedroom, words finally faltered and he fell silent.

"And what can you tell me about this room?" Alix asked evilly. "I'm sure there's plenty to say."

"Nothing you'd want to hear."

It was true. Alix wanted to know nothing about Alan Fitzroy's love life. She wanted to know nothing about the women who at one time or another had stood where she was standing, who had looked at him like she was looking at him, who had anticipated the feel of his body as she was anticipating it. For the moment Alix wanted to believe that their union would be sanctified by its newness. It was a romantic dream, a high-flown fancy that Alix had only allowed herself with one other person . . . and until recently he'd been dead for ten years.

Alan kissed her on the cheek, then started across the room. "Why don't you undress. I'll be back in a moment." He went into an adjacent dressing room and closed the door.

Alix was trembling with excitement as she slipped out of her clothes. This was not a desire based on just surface sensation, a thank-you for a wonderful evening. It sprang from a place so deep inside that, had she analyzed it, she might have discovered the very core of her womanhood, developed and expanded, added to and embellished since she was a little girl first noticing boys. But as it was, all Alix recognized was a

trembling in her knees and a passion for intimacy
that made her caress her own body under the bed-
clothes in anticipation of Alan's touch.

He appeared from the dressing room wearing a silk
robe. He was no more than a shadowy figure, and as
Alix watched him approach her, his face hidden in the
darkness, she felt that at that moment she didn't
know who would lie down next to her. But when Alan
was at last by her side, his face illuminated in a shaft
of light from the hallway, Alix admitted the truth of
her infatuation: she had never thought of this man as
anyone other than Richard Hailey. From that first
encounter on the Georgetown street until now, she
had always viewed him as her fiancé returned to her—
maybe only on loan, but returned nevertheless.

And with that admission, Alix's memory took over
as she prepared herself to fall into a familiar pattern
of lovemaking. And when Alan removed his robe and
threw it on the chair, revealing his naked body to Alix
for the first time, history indeed seemed to have come
full circle. Alix reached out to him, knowing how he
would respond, how he would treat her. But she was
so very wrong.

Alan climbed on top of her, kissing her. His body
covered hers so that only her arms escaped him. Alix
arched her head back against the pillows and accepted
his kisses on her face and neck with a purring ardor.
She'd flung her arms over his back and now ran them
lightly, featherlike, down his back, over his buttocks,
to the backs of his thighs. His weight kept her pinioned,
but his passion lifted her up like a kite caught in an
April wind. She soared into the blue sky of his touch
and dallied there, yearning to break free and sail
further into the sky, into space, to dance among the
stars.

Alan whispered and talked to her, describing what
he was going to do to her body, what he had planned
for her. He made love to her with his words, and his
talk snapped the string that tethered Alix to earth.
She'd never before been made love to this way, had
never had the mechanics of sex catalogued verbally. It
was all so new, so exciting. His rough words thrilled

her, and she wondered why Richard had never done this. In fact, Alix wondered why everything about her past with Richard had seemed so magic when it was growing clear that she'd glossed over the bad times in favor of the good. She remembered Richard's lovemaking as transcendant, but in the arms of Alan Fitzroy it began to seem pedestrian.

Alix closed her eyes and concentrated on the man thrusting himself into her. How naive she'd been to believe she could relive the past by popping into bed with Alan Fitzroy. Alan and Richard. Richard and Alan. Whose mind was whose? Whose body belonged to whom? Just as she feared she would scream from the terrible emotional pressure that was building up inside her, Alix began to catapult toward her climax, driven on by Alan's frenzied strokes. She held on until the last minute, until she saw his face twist into a mask of ecstasy; then she let herself go and exploded along with him in a shower of pleasure that erased her fears, her memories . . . everything.

Later, when the phone woke her, Alix realized she'd dozed off in Alan's arms. She opened her eyes to find him staring wonderingly at her, as if he were trying to pry into her brain to read her thoughts, or perhaps to sense her dreams. Before she had the chance to ask just why he was staring, Alan got up from bed. "Be right back," he said on the way into the study, where the phone continued to ring.

Alix watched him. It *was* Richard's body ten years later, ten years during which time they would have grown together and raised a family. If they'd been together during those years, the changes in his body wouldn't be quite so apparent. Being with someone on a daily basis usually precluded noticing major changes. Alix would not have seen so much the slight paunch that had enveloped Alan's waistline, nor would his graying hair have been quite such a shock. She wouldn't have dwelt on these things because she would have been so involved in the happiness of her life with him that she would have been too busy to be negative. Or, had she seen his aging process, it wouldn't have mattered, for she, in her own way, would have been a part of it. She shook her head, hardly believing the way she was thinking. Richard's body, Richard's mind, Richard's soul—they'd all been buried ten years ago; why couldn't she just believe that, as everyone else did?

Alan returned five minutes later. He sat on the edge of the bed, his hands in his lap, his head bent low. "That was the Annex calling."

Alix didn't have to be told. "It's about Preston, isn't it?"

"He died about half an hour ago."

"Oh, no" was all Alix could manage to say. She wanted to be detached from this death, but she couldn't. With Preston gone, the full responsibility for the Lafayette's actions lay with Alan Fitzroy. And also, with Preston gone, it was possible there would be a total staff change at the Lafayette, one that might affect her position in Washington. Alix immediately promised herself to get to TIM as soon as she could. "Preston was so sure he'd live," she finally said.

"We all make mistakes." Alan's voice was so cold that Alix looked at him askance. "I only wish his death weren't among them," he amended.

"What happens now?"

"We appoint a new director of the Lafayette. I've been preparing for something like this for some time, you know."

"No, I didn't know," she said as coldly as he had seconds before. Preston, at least, had a touch of humanity in dealing with people. Alan, more and more, was beginning to sound like a machine encased in flesh.

"Preston wanted to live on the way he was more than anything else in the world and I—we both—hoped that he could do it through the Lafayette's research," Fitzroy said. "But as you know, the human body is a machine that wears down at a certain point. And once that's done, death inevitably follows."

"I always suspected that his vehemence about our research into the aging process had something to do with his own advanced state." She shook her head. "If only he could have traded bodies with someone younger until we got some concrete answers," she said dreamily.

Alan swiveled his head around and confronted her. "What a bizarre suggestion!"

"It's a solution, though." She got out of bed now. "Too bad it's only a dream."

"Too bad," Alan repeated slowly. "But maybe some-day in the future . . ."

She smiled and slipped on his robe. "Did Preston have a family? I never heard him speak of anyone."

Alan shook his head. "He's always been a bachelor; what family there was is all dead."

"How will his passing affect the Lafayette in the short run?"

"Don't worry," Alan assured her, "Preston was a man of vision. He knew one day he'd be gone. We made arrangements to deal with that eventuality. Ev-erything is mapped out. The transition of power will be made smoothly, efficiently." He looked up at her and grinned. "I am now the head of the Lafayette Institute."

"You already know who'll replace you, don't you?"

"Yes," he said simply.

"Care to tell me about it?"

"No," he said as simply. "Not now, at least. It'll be a few weeks before he's available."

"And in the meantime?"

"In the meantime things will run very smoothly by themselves. You don't seem to realize, Alix, that the Lafayette is itself a machine designed to function no matter what. It is, if I may say so, invincible."

Alix smiled and walked into the bathroom, thinking: When I get through finding out about the Lafayette, you might have to come up with a new meaning for the word "invincible."

Twenty minutes later they stood at the door, Alan in his robe, Alix in her coat. "It's been wonderful, Alix." He leaned forward and kissed her.

"Let's get together again . . . soon?"

"After Preston's funeral; a day or so."

"You're arranging that, too?" He nodded. "And you

said Preston didn't have any family. Why, Alan, *you're* his family," she said sweetly.

"That's a nice thought, but it's just my job."

Preston March's funeral drew an enormous crowd of friends, celebrities, political figures, media representatives, scientists, and also a small select group of mourners headed by Dr. Philip Greenspan and his wife, Nancy. It was this last group Alix was most interested in as she stood in a pew in the Washington Cathederal waiting for the service to begin. There were four of them now—Nancy and Philip, of course, and the others. What would their names be now? Alix wondered. She recognized them as Linda Strong and Jack Finlay, but no one else knew that. To most people in the cathedral they were just two ordinary-looking nicely dressed young couples. To Alix they were one of the final pieces of the puzzle that, when fitted together, spelled TRAUMA.

The ceremony was properly dignified, but there was, beneath the solemn surface, an undercurrent of excitement that proclaimed the funeral a media event, a "big deal." The array of speakers who sang Preston March's praises ran the gamut from a famous television personality to the vice-president of the United States. March, it seemed, had touched a responsive chord in the American public. He'd become a father figure, the grand old wizard explaining to his eager, though somewhat backward children the mysteries of science. He could make anything sound palatable, it seemed. And Alix wondered if he'd used those very charms to convince the government that his program—the TRAUMA project—was worth any price that had to be paid.

Alan Fitzroy sat at the front of the church with the important guests. Alix's attention moved from him to the group that surrounded the Greenspans and the nameless couple. Five of them, if she included Alan. Five mutants. Five young bodies somehow emptied of all personality, then filled with another. She knew it had happened with Sarah Williams and Tim Donoghue, and so it was true that Alan was one of them, too.

Alix stared at him, and as if he could feel the intensity of her curiosity, he turned momentarily and immediately focused on her. When Alix nodded, Fitzroy gave her a grin, a tight-lipped smile, then turned away.

Philip Greenspan had seen Fitzroy's attention waver, and following his eyes, made contact with Alex. He stared at her blankly for a moment, and there seemed to be a flash of recognition. He stared a moment longer, then slowly turned away. Alix wondered if Greenspan remembered her from Fitzroy's cocktail party or if he'd been told about her in another context and shown her photograph. After all, she was now Ted Winner's replacement, and Greenspan, as a product of the Lafayette, would certainly be interested in that fact.

Like Alan Fitzroy, Philip Greenspan was another "wonder boy," Alix had discovered through some research. He was a mathematician in his mid-twenties and he'd already been media-blitzed. But unlike Preston March, Greenspan was young and seemed to epitomize the *zeitgeist;* he was as popular as a video game. He'd appeared on the cover of *People* magazine and had been a guest on the Carson show. In the years to come, he might attain the solid reputation Preston had enjoyed, but in the meantime Philip Greenspan was the darling of the electronic media and the popular press. And the significance of his work on advanced nuclear theory for the government was rarely if ever mentioned.

The croak of organ music brought Alix back to reality. A famous Broadway star walked to the altar to face the congregation and began singing "Climb Ev'ry Mountain." By the time the ceremony had concluded and March's casket had been returned to the hearse for the short ride to the cemetery, Alix was in cautious good spirits. Outside the church Alan momentarily broke away from his companions. His face was still a mask of grief, but when he maneuvered Alix off to the side, he broke into a grin. "You look radiant. Do funerals always make you look this way?"

"Only when I feel the person isn't really gone," she said.

There was a ripple of anxiety on Fitzroy's face; not enough to shatter the composure, but enough for Alix to see it. "Whatever do you mean?" he quickly asked.

"Admit it, Alan, it's not like Preston's *really* gone, is it? I mean, after all, the great work he's done in his lifetime will live after him. I guess that's what people mean when they talk about immortality, isn't it?"

"That's one kind of immortality, yes," he said, touching her lightly on the arm. "When do we see each other again?"

Alix managed to blush, then looked away. "How about later in the week? Thursday? Friday? I'll call your office. My work is in something of a shambles after all this." In fact, that day, for the first time in its history, the Lafayette was completely shut down.

"Okay. But don't wait too long. And remind me one of these days that we need to have a little talk."

"About . . . ?"

"You and the Lafayette." Alan squeezed her arm again. "Will I see you at the cemetery?"

The thought was macabre. Billing and cooing over an open grave was hardly Alix's idea of a third date. "I think not. I've got work to do."

"Then . . . *à bientôt,*" he said with such guileless charm that Alix was forced to smile. He was swept up into the crowd and disappeared like a small boat sucked down into a whirlpool that had suddenly appeared in the middle of the ocean. But Alix didn't have to watch to know that he'd rejoined the others. They were the magic five, and she shuddered to think how many more of the Lafayette's creations were living out other people's lives.

Alix walked slowly back to her car knowing that she'd reached the major turning point in her relationship with Alan Fitzroy. She now understood that from that first day when she'd seen him on the Georgetown street she'd confused her feelings toward Richard with her feelings toward Alan. But Alan Fitzroy was not Richard Hailey. He never had been. They shared the same body, that was all. Her Richard was suspended somewhere deep inside, his persona encapsulated by the process known as TRAUMA. Until now Alix had tried to protect Richard by protecting Alan. Now it was all too clear that this was a deadly mistake.

If she ever wanted to hold Richard Hailey in her arms again, Alix had to expose Alan Fitzroy and the Lafayette Institute. She could no longer excuse Fitzroy's complicity to protect her own selfish needs. Alan was a madman who performed his loathsome duties willingly, with malice aforethought. Alan is not Richard, she said to herself as she drove away from the church. He's not Richard, he's not!

It was important that Alix remember this, for one day soon she would have to kill Alan Fitzroy to get Richard back. And to do that she had to know every detail of TRAUMA.

Alix sat for a few minutes at the computer control panel wondering what to do. Under her fingers the typewriter keys of TIM waited expectantly. If she typed in the correct letters or figures, TIM's information about the Lafayette TRAUMA project would be hers. But which letters, which figures, were the right ones?

She slipped the shiny plastic TIM card into the proper slot in the upper-right-hand corner of the panel. TIM instantly lit up, and its metallic hum deepened into a throaty *whir*. Alix looked at the keyboard again, then typed in the word TRAUMA and waited. Microseconds later a monitor in the control panel sprang to life as a series of letters filled the screen. Alix leaned forward to read.

```
              TRAUMA/PREFIX: TRA
                  1st  Run - 00010
                  2nd  Run - 00020
                  3rd  Run - 00030

         BACKGROUND - 00040
         COSTS          - 00050
         FUNDING      - 00060
         MISCELL       - 00070
```

Alix stared at the screen. Here was the key to the information she needed. Now all she need do was type out the right code and that information was hers. She reached out to begin typing, but her hands were trembling so badly she had to stop. Alix was on the verge of committing herself to a path that, once followed, couldn't be strayed from. When she punched in the correct TRAUMA codes, her life would change forever. And for right now, right this second, she wasn't sure she was ready to take such a giant step.

Then she remembered Jack in the backseat of the car as it drove off into the cold winter dawn. And Richard ten years before. And Sarah Williams, whom she'd never even met. And the others. Alix was the only thing standing between the Lafayette and the rest of the world. And the responsibility she felt terrified her. But not enough to keep her from punching TRA 00040 in TIM.

The monitor was wiped clean and three short paragraphs headed TRAUMA PROJECT PROJECTION appeared.

With the approval of the President, the development of a scientific project coded TRAUMA has begun.

TRAUMA shall be directly funded through various government agencies and shall be terminated at the discretion of the President in office. Because TRAUMA is an Ultra-Top-Secret project, all coordination shall be managed through the Lafayette Institute, whose main function is to prevent knowledge of TRAUMA from being made available to the general public.

Because of the sensitive nature of TRAUMA research (the acquisition of suitable specimens for neurological reorganization), the government will disavow any knowledge of it, should the project ever come to light publicly. Any steps necessary to protect this claim will be taken immediately.

Alix read through the paragraphs several times. She'd hoped to find more, but the projection was purposely vague. Even Preston had told her more than this did. She reread the last paragraph several times,

becoming more aware of its ominous tone. It was a
threat, veiled, but a threat nonetheless: "Any steps
necessary to protect this claim will be taken immediately." That could only mean the elimination of the
sources of possible leaks—murder by executive order.
Alix had always heard rumors about political assassi-
nations being planned, but she'd always refused to
believe it was true. Yet here was the proof before her:
Be quiet or die!

But what was perhaps more disconcerting was the
phrase "acquisition of suitable specimens." Exactly
what did that mean? What made one specimen more
suitable than another? Nancy Greenspan's smiling face
flashed into Alix's mind, and she suddenly knew exactly what a suitable specimen was: a young person,
in good health, physically appealing; a young person
with no family and few friends, a "loner" in many
cases. That way, when they were "acquired," no one
caused a fuss about their disappearance.

That explanation, horrible though it was, was
simple enough. Now for the phrase "neurological
reorganization." It didn't make sense, though. From
what Alix could figure, implanting electrodes in the
brain certainly fell under the heading "neurological."
But "reorganization"? To Alix that meant reconstruction, surgery, and in its widest sense might even in-
clude transplants. Transplants! Winner had been doing
research on mice . . . cell transplants . . . neurological reconstruction. Could it be . . . ? Alix closed her
eyes and swallowed hard to digest her fear.

Brain transplants!

The idea was preposterous! But there were the words,
the proof still flickering on TIM's monitor. Transplanting organs was a difficult, sometimes impossible task;
transplanting the brain *had* to be impossible. There
were just too many ways to slip up, too many factors
to consider. If the brain were deprived of oxygen for
more than two minutes, irreparable damage occurred.
Surely it was impossible. Yet the words were still there.

Alix keyed in TRA 00030, the third run of TRAUMA,
and waited anxiously. The screen cleared, then filled
with a list of names. Alix knew intellectually she

should be shocked, but emotionally she felt nothing. She'd seen the same list before, seen the names, and could even now, in her memory, match faces with them. The additional information she hadn't possessed—physical type, age, blood type, medical history—was superfluous. She'd seen Sarah Williams, Jack Finlay, Tim Donoghue, and Linda Strong before. She was comfortable with their names, as if they'd become friends somehow. And maybe it was for that reason that when she saw next to each name the words PARENTS DEAD, NO LIVING RELATIVES, that Alix began quietly to sob. Four young people alone in the world with only a few friends to care about them; friends who, because of their own tough work schedules, were too involved to miss them if they were to leave. Four young people who might one day just vanish from the face of the earth and whose absence would soon be forgotten.

Alix wiped her eyes, then punched in TRA 00010, knowing what she would see. Even before the names appeared on the screen, her sobs had become a low moan. There was another list of four people that duplicated the later one. These four also were without parents or relatives, without anyone who legally could investigate what had become of them. Alix blotted her eyes and read the details of the first name. No one would miss him. Or so the monsters at the Lafayette had thought. But they'd been wrong! Someone had missed him, did still miss him terribly, and that someone was about to get her revenge for that loss.

The first name on the list was Richard Hailey.

She scanned the other names and recognized Randy Metcalf—Hawkins. So, he too had been in the first run of TRAUMA—before the techniques had been perfected probably. There'd been an accident and Metcalf was brain-damaged as well as physically disabled. Preston had said it was caused by an electric shock, but it was a lie. Just as everything else about her life in Washington had become a lie. Hawkins had tried to warn her, and for his trouble he'd been further mutilated. And when he'd tried to warn her again, Alan Fitzroy had seen him. Fitzroy. Richard. No, Rich-

ard was dead! That monster Fitzroy, whoever he was,
was behind all this. He was probably the one who
conceived of TRAUMA in the first place.

Alix wiped away the last of her tears and removed
Winner's card from TIM. The computer wound back
down to a hum, and she pushed her chair away and
headed for the door. In the last ten minutes she'd been
exposed to more horror than she ever would have
believed possible, but she hadn't crumbled. She no
longer questioned her own sanity. TRAUMA was a fact.
And people were dying because of it. And Alix, her
fear now galvanized into a silent rage, was going to do
something about it, even if it killed her.

Ten minutes after Alix walked out of the Lafayette
into a light drizzle, Alan Fitzroy sat at the control
panel of TIM talking on the telephone to the Annex.
His voice was jubilant. "Did you see her?"

"The monitoring system in the computer room is
very effective, Alan. So now Alix knows everything."

"Everything." He repeated the word. "This is the
turning point for her. She seemed quite upset about
all this."

"Give her time," the other man said. "It's a shock,
you know. We're used to it." His voice was thin and
sounded very far away.

Taking note of this, Fitzroy asked, "How's it going?"

The man laughed heartily. "The body's a good one,
Alan. It'll probably make you jealous." The laugh became a cough. "Guess I need some rest right now.
Carry on, and we'll talk in a week's time. Oh, one
more thing. Talk to her, and if during that time Alix
doesn't come around, take care of her, will you? We'll
need to find a replacement."

"Let's give her a little more time—until she gets a
chance to talk with *you* personally." Fitzroy's hesi-
tancy had more to do with the thought of Alix in bed
than with her potential to carry on with TRAUMA.

"Okay, but only until I'm back on my feet."

"We're having dinner in a couple of days. It'll be
okay," Fitzroy said confidently. "You take care, and
we'll talk soon."

Fitzroy hung up and went back upstairs to Preston

March's office. If Alix *didn't* come around, there'd be hell to pay trying to find someone to replace her. It would be a real administrative problem. But that wasn't what really was bothering Fitzroy. He liked Alix and truly hoped she had the sense to say yes to their offer. She was one fine-looking woman, and much as Fitzroy liked to kill, he hoped he wouldn't have to exercise that particular talent on Alix Kendall.

—10—

Alix spent the next morning at the Washington *Post* searching through its files. She'd thought of going to *The District Columbian*, but that might be risky. Someone at the newspaper—probably Flanagan, Jack Campbell's "friend"—was in touch with the Lafayette, and Alix couldn't risk being discovered—not just yet. After an arduous morning's work, a short lunch break during which she went for a walk to shake off her mental cobwebs, she returned to the newspaper. By five o'clock she'd found what she was looking for. She copied names and dates onto a legal pad, read and reread them, then caught a cab and went directly to the Lafayette.

All the way through Georgetown Alix looked at the grim winter streets, feeling like a thief in the night. She turned and looked out the back window, wondering if any of the cars following her was driven by a flunky of Alan Fitzroy's or of the late, great Preston March. It hardly mattered now. She no longer had anything to lose, and that, in a way, made her invulnerable.

Once back in her apartment, Alix fixed herself a stiff vodka, curled up on the couch in front of a cozy fire, and tried to relax. She felt a growing admiration for herself and for the way she was handling this situation. In the past she'd overcome her father's prejudices about women doctors when she'd become one. She'd gone ahead with her plans because she knew that to accept anything less than what she wanted from life was to be untrue to herself. And if that happened, she'd regret the decision all her life.

Now, in the midst of this trauma, Alix was able to depersonalize what was happening to her and to make it her duty as a human being to stop the Lafayette. It never for one minute occurred to her that she might fail. Despite the fact that the forces of the Institute were well organized and easily mobilized, Alix knew she could destroy it. Despite the fact that all odds were against her, that the federal government was without a doubt involved, she knew she had the power to succeed. She had discovered four names at the *Post* to fit Philip Greenspan and his friends, and she now knew whom she was dealing with. Theoretically TRAUMA was brilliant—in both its conception and realization—but it was loathsome in its execution if it were what she suspected.

Compiling the list of TRAUMA names had been easier than she'd expected. All it took was a little common sense. Alix knew from Jack's notes on Alan Fitzroy when Alan had made his appearance on the Washington scene; and—again, courtesy of Campbell's investigations—she knew approximately when Sarah Williams and the others had disappeared. Reading through several weeks' obituaries prior to those dates had produced five logical names, five suspects, five people whose expertise and knowledge would be sorely missed if buried along with their dead bodies.

Surely a case *could* be made for keeping those five people alive, no matter what the cost. Their mental gifts were invaluable. And that's what the Lafayette was all about, wasn't it? Keeping people alive longer? It was done slowly, painstakingly, at the main building through research, trial and error. But what about at the Annex? What about the members of TRAUMA? What if they'd discovered a faster way to speed up research, or if they'd actually *found* the answer to extending life? Surely out of that would come a priority system to perpetuate the brilliance of an elite corps so that they might use their special talents to deal with the inevitable world crises of the future. And how ironic that the very people who had created so many of these crises in the past could be kept alive indefinitely to untangle them in the future.

Alix looked at the names on the pad once again. Next to them she'd drawn lines connecting them to their present-day incarnations. This scribbling alone was as good as a death warrant, should the wrong people get hold of it. However, she had no intention of letting that happen. Ten names, five people. The idea was perfect! Her finger traced down the page until it came to the name Philip Greenspan. She paused, then traced a line across the page to the name Max Pomfrett; Nancy Greenspan and Gretal Heilbrunn; Linda Strong and Antonia Watson; Jack Finlay and George Alistair. And finally, Alan Fitzroy and Herbert Windom. Ten names, five people. She now knew why, and all she needed to know was *how?*

Alix scaled the pad away from her in disgust. It landed on the floor in front of the fireplace. What could she do about all this? She knew the names, knew who the people really were, yet what did that matter? If only there were help. But there was no one. Even a local police investigation would open wide an official channel leading straight to the FBI, CIA, maybe even the Oval Office itself. And when that happened, Alix Kendall, like so many others, would disappear. In that event, she was trapped, for there was no one to miss her, no one to ask where she'd gone. There'd only been Jack Campbell, and chances were that he was already dead—and if so, it was her fault.

She sat curled up in the corner of the couch in her living room like a frightened child. Even the fire crackling in the fireplace across the room didn't warm her. She felt nothing. She stared at the familiar objects in her apartment and was gradually filled with such hate and loathing that it almost made her physically sick. Ten years before, Richard Hailey had been a

"suitable specimen," and he'd died so that . . . so that
Alan Fitzroy—Herbert Windom—might continue living.

Alix closed her eyes as the vodka began to fight
against her rising panic. She knew that in a matter of
minutes the alcohol would help her not to care about
what she'd discovered. Unfortunately, once it wore off,
nothing would have changed. She'd still have to face
the knowledge that she was involved in work so monstrous that she couldn't bear thinking about it. Jack
Campbell's moral conundrum had finally come true!

What exactly her part in all this was—was to be—
was still a mystery. Alix's work had to do with research,
with working with animal thymus glands. There was
nothing out of line about that, nothing that could be
questioned. All it cost was the eventual deaths of a
few laboratory mice; not exactly murder. But what if
Ted Winner had agreed to do similar research, but on
human subjects? What if Alix were being groomed to
take part in experiments on people instead of white
mice? The thought made her gag, and she quickly
pushed it as far from her mind as she could.

As a sleety rain slapped against the windowpanes,
Alix's eyes fluttered open again; she needed to stay
awake and alert. From now on she couldn't trust anything in her life that wasn't planned. It was late
afternoon, and the grayish moon that earlier had been
the sun was almost set. The light in the apartment
seemed dirty, and were it not for the fireplace's glow,
indoors would have been as gloomy as outdoors. But
in the end, what did it matter, really? In a matter of
weeks her whole life had turned around. Her first
instincts to stay away from this cursed city had been
proved true. Now it was too late.

She struggled up from the couch to pour herself a
third vodka. She was getting very drunk, but what
the hell? She deserved the chance to let her hair
down. After all, anyone who'd been through what she
had deserved a little escape. Dammit! She was so
lonely. If only Jack were in Washington, she'd call
and insist he come over. For a moment Alix felt the
strength of his body as he took her in his arms. She
felt safe there, cherished. But Jack was gone. Suppos-

edly to South America. Dammit! Why didn't he listen
to her?

Impetuously Alix picked up the phone and called
information. She asked for the phone number of *The
District Columbian* and minutes later was talking to a
very confused Mike Flanagan. "I want to know where
Jack Campbell is," she demanded sloppily.

"Who is this?" was the very controlled response.

"That doesn't matter. Just tell me where he is."

There was a slight pause, then a little sigh. "Jack's
on an assignment for me in South America. If you'll
leave a message, I'd be—"

"You'd be a liar if you said he was coming back,"
Alix snapped. "In fact, you're a liar as it is, aren't you,
Mr. Good Friend Flanagan."

"Who *is* this?" His voice had grown strident.

"Nobody who counts, but somebody who wouldn't
send him off into the hands of the enemy just because
a little pressure was exerted . . . or was it money that
got you to betray him?"

"Go to hell!" was the short reply before the phone
went dead.

So it was true! Alix replaced the phone and began to
sob. Flanagan was surprised that she was onto him.
He'd probably been guaranteed that no one would
ever know of his treachery. But Alix knew. And in his
voice she'd heard his guilt, and she hated him for it.
Moments later the phone rang. Alix let it ring twelve
times before answering it.

"Alix? Alix? Are you there?" It was Alan.

His timing was perfect. Five minutes earlier, Mike
Flanagan receives an accusatory call from a drunken
woman, and now Alan Fitzroy calls her. Well, Alix
thought, I'm as good an actress as they are actors! She
pulled herself up straight, and when she spoke, her
voice was breathless but sober. "Alan? Is that you?"

"Yes, are you all right?"

She laughed and exhaled loudly. "I was just in the
bath. I almost broke my neck getting out here. How
are you?"

"Fine," he said, using his clipped business voice. "I
didn't mean to interrupt."

"No problem. I needed to get out anyway. On days like today, I like nothing better than soaking in a hot tub for hours. You should see me, Alan. I look like an albino prune." Her voice was perfectly modulated, with a tinge of sexual excitement she knew Fitzroy would appreciate.

"Sounds inviting," he said, falling into the trap. "I didn't expect to find you home."

"I usually like to go out and shop on Saturday, but I'm giving myself the day off. I hope you're not calling to cancel dinner tomorrow night."

"*That's* why I called," he said quickly. "Just to check on the time: eight sharp, wasn't it?"

"Eight sharp. Now, look, Alan, I'm standing here naked, dripping wet. We'll have plenty of time to talk tomorrow, okay?"

"See you then," he said, and hung up.

Alix dropped the phone in her lap and let her head slump forward. She was exhausted and scared. But her act had worked, she could tell. At first Alan was skeptical, but as she talked, as she laughed and bubbled and gushed, he'd begun to believe her. He'd probably thought that Jack Campbell had another girlfriend stashed somewhere that no one knew about. Well, whatever the case, it seemed Alix was off that particular hook . . . for the time being.

She left the phone off the hook as she stretched out on the couch to have a nap. Being drunk was no good. She needed her wits about her from now on, particularly now that she'd decided to fight these bastards. Well, here I am, she thought. Alone again. It was the way she'd spent most of her life, people dropping into it intermittently, touching her in one way or another, then leaving. It used to frighten her to think of herself living such a solitary existence, but no longer. She trusted herself, and that was what was important. And with what she had in mind for Alan Fitzroy and the Lafayette Institute, she'd need all the trust she could muster.

Alix felt herself begin to drift off, and she prayed that sleep would help her to escape the horror that was building up inside her. Preston March was dead—at least they said he was—and she should have been relieved, but she wasn't. Though she'd been to the funeral she wasn't convinced. Preston, of all people, would want to save himself. It wouldn't have been difficult finding a "suitable specimen" for him. She kept picturing his brain, alive somewhere outside his body, suspended in an aqueous solution, connected to the great god electricity. It was a vision that had haunted her since his burial.

What must it be like, she wondered, to be suspended without a body in a vat of fluid? What must it be like to exist as if the world were a sensory-deprivation tank? Did they connect sensors that allowed the brain to hear? And if so, how would the brain respond? How would the brain see?

There were so many questions that Alix's mind finally closed down on itself and she drifted off to sleep and almost at once began dreaming. In her dream Alix was being led blindfolded down a cold, damp hallway. She heard doors opening and closing, felt the extreme changes in temperature as they moved from one place in the darkness to another and finally stopped in the coldest room, where she sat down. In the distance a humming, a whirring sound grew louder, until, after a moment, it seemed to originate from within her own head. At first the sound was soothing; then it began to grate, like the insistent sound of a dentist's drill, and finally it hurt so much that she wanted to scream but couldn't.

Alix sat perfectly still in her chair, waiting for something to happen. She heard footsteps, and then the blindfold was pulled from her eyes with a sudden jerk. She found herself in a vast concrete room whose walls dripped rivulets of water. Written across one wall in blood was the single red word TRAUMA. In front of that stood a huge tank of clear chemicals in which, suspended by hundreds of tiny wires, was a brain, the largest human brain Alix had ever seen. It seemed to breathe, to beat as a heart beats, growing slightly larger, then contracting, expanding then contracting with a sound like a sigh—the very sound that filled her ears.

Alix covered her ears with her hands to block out the sound, but it was no use. The humming grew louder still, and when she could stand it no more, she leaped up from the chair and ran to the tank, where she began beating its wall, screaming, trying to get at the brain. But the brain remained passive, contracting and expanding. Alix knew that somehow it was watching her, reading her mind, trying to control her thoughts. She knew that if she didn't do something, it would take her over, like it had taken over Richard and the others. If she didn't act soon, she'd die!

Alix grabbed a metal chair and crashed it through the side of the tank. The glass shattered into hundreds of deadly shards that, catapulted by the force of the outpouring of chemicals, lacerated her face and body. The force of the flood threw Alix backward, and she fell to the floor in a pool of her own blood and chemicals. When she finally opened her eyes, she realized that the brain had been dislodged and had escaped through the hole in the tank. It rolled toward her on the floor, slowly, inexorably contracting and expanding.

Alix raised her hands to stop it, but she was powerless. And when the slimy brain rolled onto her, completely covering her, shutting off her air supply, Alix woke up screaming. She turned on the light and looked around the room, for a moment unsure of where she was. Gradually, as the coffee table and the bowl of flowers she'd placed there that afternoon came into focus, she realized she was safe and her fears began to dissipate. She turned on her side and forced herself to stay awake. The whole thing had been a dream. If only that were true for the rest of her life. . . .

The next night, Alan arrived with flowers and candy, and gushed over Alix like she was his first date. Alix was tense at first, but when she remembered that Alan Fitzroy and everything he stood for was no longer an unknown quantity, and therefore the worst kind of threat, she began to relax. Alix knew the best way to handle men of his kind, and that put her at ease further.

"How about a brandy?" she asked after dinner. "They say it loosens you up." She poured them both a drink. "I'm sorry we haven't seen more of each other, Alan." She handed him an enormous snifter containing a dainty amount of the amber liquid. "To be truthful, I was seeing someone at the time, and ..." She shrugged.

"I'd already guessed as much." He sipped his drink approvingly. "I didn't think a woman as beautiful as you would be holed up alone in her apartment every night."

"Or holed up at work?" she teased.

"Work's different, somehow. Isn't it?"

"Somehow," she said dreamily, "but let's not talk about work or ex-boyfriends, okay?"

"Ex-boyfriends? I thought Campbell was ..." Fitzroy realized his gaffe too late.

But Alix continued on as if she hadn't noticed him calling Campbell by name when she'd said nothing. "Jack and I were close once, I guess ... at least as close as you can get with a newspaperman." She shook her head. "That isn't very close, I'm afraid."

"So that's over with?"

"Finito! Kaput!" She hoped she sounded convincing.

Alan smiled grandly. "I'll drink to that." He touched his glass to hers, finished his drink, then put it down. Now that Campbell was out of the way and Alix was once again on her own, she had a very appealing air of vulnerability about her.

"Alan, why are you staring at me?" Alix asked with mock horror. "Just exactly what is going on in that oversized brain of yours?"

"You really want to know?"

"Of course."

He moved closer to her. "You excite me, Alix. You excite me in a way no other woman ever has." He insinuated his arm behind her, letting it touch her shoulder gently.

"That's very flattering, Alan. And I find you exciting, too." Alix wished it weren't the truth, but it was. Of course she'd find him exciting—she'd loved his body ten years before, and for ten years in her mind, and now, being united with it was an experience that bordered on the profound.

Fitzroy pulled her into his arms and kissed her gently, lovingly. "We'd make a good team, you know that?"

"Team?" she mumbled through his kisses.

"Sure, we're both part of the Lafayette in one way or another—I on the business end, you on the research side. We both have a common cause."

"And what's that?"

"Achieving goals in science that have never been thought of before," he said after a moment's deliberation.

Alix pulled away from him. "Prolonging life, you mean? I guess it has always been one of man's main fantasies, but never a reality."

"That's changing." He pulled her back into his arms. "One day soon the secrets of the Lafayette will be yours." Fitzroy wanted to give Alix every opportunity to tell him what she'd learned from TIM; she remained close mouthed about using her computer card, however.

"And what happens when all the secrets are mine?"

"Then I hope we'll be drawn closer together." He kissed her lightly on the tip of her nose. "That's up to you."

Though Alix smiled, she felt a shiver of fear tighten her body. Alan thought he was being cryptic, but Alix knew all about TRAUMA now, and his words carried a special meaning, a meaning that sounded like a threat. Without having said as much, he'd told her that her compliance was an either/or situation—either she joined forces with him or . . . or she followed in Ted Winner's footsteps into whatever darkness they'd thrown him.

"If getting closer to you is *my* decision, then here's my answer." Alix locked her hands behind his head and pulled him to her, kissing him with a passion that wasn't totally insincere. Alan Fitzroy didn't know it, but tonight was one of their last times together, and Alix wanted to make it memorable. Tonight, having sex with Fitzroy would begin to close and lock the door to the past that had stood open for so many lonely, angry years.

So caught up were they with each other that they undressed in the living room and made love on the couch in front of the fire. Alix kept her eyes open throughout. She wanted to remember Alan's body in every detail. She wanted to be able to reconstruct it in the future when this satanic farce was over. And she wanted to remember that even though she'd miss this body, there was no choice but to destroy it—she had to stop the TRAUMA project before anyone else died.

Alan's mouth caressed every part of her body, and for a few frightening moments Alix began to doubt her sanity once again, despite what TIM had told her. The very idea of brain transplants seemed more bizarre than ever. Did she really believe that this man, who now suckled her breast like an infant, had actually died ten years before—an old man? Organ transplants in smaller mammals had proved that indeed it was possible to perpetuate life by implantation in a series of hosts, but it had never happened with man. Then she remembered Winner's work.

At that moment Alan entered her with such force that Alix gasped and tugged at his hair in a paroxysm of overwhelming sensation. And as her fingers danced over his scalp, the real horror of the TRAUMA project was revealed. When Alix stiffened, Alan took it to mean she was approaching fulfillment and he began pounding into her deeper, trying to push her over the edge. But sex was over for Alix. She feigned excitement and continued to run her fingers through his hair, across his head, feeling the unmistakable trace, the footnote to Alan Fitzroy's biography that also included mention of the name Richard Hailey. Concealed under Fitzroy's hair was a small suture line that circled his head like an unholy tonsure. As Alix touched it lightly, she could almost see the laser beam grinding through the skull to expose the brain. Then the change took place, and Richard Hailey became Alan Fitzroy.

Somehow Alix made it through the next hour without breaking down completely. She kept her mind roaming, kept focusing on anything that would maintain a distance between her and the memory of that suture line, which, in her mind's eye, she envisioned as a roadmap of both her past and her future. Alan was apparently unaware of Alix's distance, and as he walked out the door later, he again said that they were made for each other, emotionally as well as physically.

When he'd gone, Alix collapsed onto the couch, which still smelled of their animal lust. She cried as she had never before cried in her life, the years of tears exploding into the dead stillness of the apartment. And when the phone rang, its harsh tones sounded like a death knell, like a bell tolling for her youth, her innocence. Alix considered not answering it, but she knew she had to; to give up now was to admit defeat, and that was the last thing she'd allow.

When she picked up the phone, she heard nothing but static at first. Then a man's voice broke through. "Alix? Alix, is that you?"

Whoever it was sounded like he was thousands of miles away . . . in South America? It couldn't be possible. That would be too good to be true! "Jack, is that really you?"

"Who did you expect, Che Guevara?" Campbell laughed. "How are you, darling?"

Alix couldn't speak. She was so sure Campbell had been gotten out of the way, killed. In her mind, to have him back was nothing short of a miracle. "I'm wonderful . . . now. Simply wonderful."

"Any news?"

"News?" She laughed until she began crying again— this time for joy. "More news than you'd ever believe."

"Tell me," he said so softly that the static almost drowned him out again.

"Where *are* you? We can talk about me anytime."

"Still in South America," he said, louder this time. "What's this news?"

"No, not on the phone," she said quickly. "When are you coming home?" Home. The word rung in her ears. She meant "home to me!"

"In a couple of weeks. Have you been reading my stories?"

"Stories?"

"In the newspaper. Alix, are you sure you're all right?" Concern filled Campbell's voice.

"No, no . . . I'm not sure . . ." She began to sob again. "Oh, Jack, I miss you. I don't want to go through this alone. Get home as fast as you can."

"Is there anyone you can call?"

"No one but you. Preston died," she said, realizing she'd unconsciously categorized March as someone she could have turned to.

"March dead?" Campbell sounded incredulous. "What happened?"

Alix told him briefly, not daring to tell him she suspected he might have been put through the TRAUMA process. "It was at his funeral that I made the discovery that led me to find out everything."

There was a slight pause; then the line crackled like an open fire. "Discovery? What discovery? Alix, what's going on?" Jack's voice was strident.

"I really can't tell you now." She wondered if the very people she didn't trust were listening in. "I'll explain everything when you get back. Just hurry." As if it were up to Campbell to plan his return. She was so grateful he was still alive that anything seemed possible now.

"It'll be ten days to two weeks. I really don't know yet. Things are pretty rocky down here. You can be with me—in a way—by reading my newspaper reports. Now I've got to go."

"Will I hear from you again before you come back?"

"I'll try to call, but I can't promise anything. We're going back into the jungle soon. There's no telling what'll be going on then."

Alix inhaled a great sob. "Be careful . . . and I love you."

"I love you, too, Alix. And you be careful too." The static suddenly ended and the line went dead.

Alix stared into the phone like she could see Campbell at the other end, somewhere in South America. It had been so good to talk to him, so good to hear his voice. It was like hearing a voice from the grave. Moments before, she'd been bereft because she was all alone in the world; and now she wasn't . . . nor ever would be again.

She searched through her collection of past issues of *The District Columbian* she'd been too lazy to throw out and found several articles with Campbell's byline. She had to have been daydreaming to miss them. How ironic that the very proof that he was alive had been in her possession all along and she'd been too worried, too distraught to see it. Now she read every word, hearing Jack's voice as she did. The contents didn't matter, but being with him again did. It wasn't like him having his arm around her, but it was close enough for the time being.

Two weeks, he'd said. She wondered how she was going to last that long.

The two weeks went by like seconds. In the aftermath of March's death, things changed at the Lafayette. March was replaced—at least temporarily—by a phalanx of men, some of whom Alix recognized as the original founders of the Lafayette Annex whose photographs she'd seen earlier. So one man had died and five had replaced him, in administrative matters only; for whereas March had been affable and friendly, these men, when encountered singly or in a group, were solemn to the point of misanthropy. March always had time to stop by, even if it were only to say "I don't have time to talk," but the committee was so impersonal that, more than once, they totally ignored Alix when they ran into her in the hallways. In the presence of these men, Alix felt she was finally confronting the true heartlessness of the Lafayette.

Once again Alix decided to look further into TRAUMA. And one night she stayed late again, and again gained access to TIM. Using the same technique as

before, she punched in TRA 00010 to continue her
investigation, but nothing happened. She tried every
possible combination, but the screen remained blank.
She finally gave up. TRAUMA was gone for her.
And on her way home Alix began to wonder if
she hadn't been set up by Alan Fitzroy or Preston.
Maybe they'd hoped she'd use the TIM card all along
and had made it so easy to get the information that a
child could have done it. But why?

What possible reason could there have been for letting her see the whole picture? Suddenly a possible
answer câme to her, and unpleasant though it was, it
certainly fitted the modus operandi of the Lafayette.
All along, there had been hints from March that one
day she would be drawn into the Lafayette's inner
circle; they loved her work, respected her, wanted her
to be a part of the team. Winner was out and Alix
Kendall was in, but in name only. The essential thing
she was missing was knowledge—knowledge of what
TRAUMA really meant. To assume Winner's place fully,
she'd have to know everything, and because of the
deadly sensitive nature of that, she'd have to be trusted.
What better way to guarantee that trust than to let
her "discover" the truth of TRAUMA and then monitor
her reactions!

Alix's anger erupted at the thought. She'd been
allowed to think she was stealing TIM's information,
while all the time they'd been watching her. If she'd
made one move toward the police, toward any government agency, she would be dead right now. But she
hadn't made a move because she'd been stymied by
her own fear and the need for revenge. And because of
that, she hadn't betrayed them, and in turn, she'd
been saved. How ironic that she was still alive!

Campbell called two weeks later from Dulles Airport before he'd even collected his luggage. He wanted
to see Alix but he needed a day to talk to his editor
and to find his footing once again. Did Alix want to
have dinner with him at his house tomorrow night,
just the two of them? She admitted that wild horses
couldn't keep her away.

The thirty-six hours before her date with Jack were the longest of her life. But she made the effort; she went to work knowing there was no way she'd ever get anything done. She presided over her work, reread her notes a thousand times, but all the while her mind was on her date with Campbell naked in bed, his arms encircling her, a warm cocoon.

But when Jack opened the front door of his house that night, Alix immediately felt let down. It seemed he'd changed. He was deeply tanned, his hair was cut very short and had been bleached almost white from the sun. And, not surprisingly, he'd lost a considerable amount of weight. The weight loss suited him, but it still came as a shock to see this metamorphosis; Alix still remembered—and cherished—him that freezing, snowy morning as he'd proclaimed his love, then driven away. Now she was confronted by a tanned stranger.

"Do I look so different?" He laughed as she slid by him into the hallway.

"You must be a mindreader." She giggled nervously. She'd missed Jack, but until she saw his smile, she hadn't realized just how much she'd missed him. "You've lost weight."

"You look the same . . . which is to say 'Perfect.' " And without another word he pulled her to him and kissed her roughly on the mouth even as his hands insinuated themselves through her open coat to her waist.

After a moment Alix pulled back breathlessly. "My God, is this what happens to men when they go into the jungle?"

"It's what happens when they go into the jungle and leave *you* behind." He winked, took her coat, and hung it in the closet. And the moment the closet door shut, he again ensnared Alix and pulled her so tightly to him that it hurt.

"Jack," she complained, pushing him back more forcefully this time, "there's plenty of time for that, okay?"

A blaze of anger crossed Campbell's face, but it vanished almost immediately. "I've just been thinking of you all this time," he said softly. "Forgive me?"

"Of course, but . . ." She walked into the living room. "How about offering me a drink before we hop into bed?" Campbell's advance had been crude, and it made her angry.

"Two drinks coming right up. What'll it be?" He stationed himself by the bar.

"The usual," Alix said as she flopped down on the couch. "God, it's good to be back here. I really love this house." She turned her attention back to him; he was at the bar, motionless. "Anything wrong?"

"I think the jungle heat must have fried my brain. I've forgotten what your 'usual' is."

She laughed and shook her head. "You have been out in the sun too long—a white wine, of course." She had a momentary feeling that something was wrong, but it quickly passed. "How was it down there?"

"Hot, dangerous . . . lonely." He poured two white wines and sat down next to her. "Cheers!"

Alix touched glasses with him, but the uneasiness returned. Jack hated white wine. More than once he'd said he'd rather not drink than put up with that muck. "Muck"—that was exactly the word he'd used. Yet here he was sipping it as if it were Scotch. What am I thinking? she immediately chided herself. I've waited for someone like Jack Campbell for so long, and now I have to ruin it. And suddenly, without warning, she began to cry.

"Hey! What's the matter?" Jack asked, putting his arms around her. Alix looked at him but couldn't say anything. "It's been rough on you, hasn't it?" He kissed her lightly on the forehead. "It's as much my fault as it is yours. If I hadn't started all that mumbo jumbo about the Lafayette, your life would have been a lot simpler."

Alix shook her head. "It all started even before I met you. In fact, the only reason I took the job at the Lafayette was because of something terrible I'd seen." She wiped her eyes and tried out a smile; it wavered, then crumbled. "I'm not sure I want to tell even you."

Jack pulled her closer. "I want to know everything, no matter how impossible it may sound to you."

"Don't ever let me forget how wonderful you are.

Promise?" She looked deeply into his eyes, then gave
him a peck on the lips.

"Promise. Now, tell me what's bothering you."

Alix began talking. It was as if she'd waited all her
life to unburden herself. She began with her personal
history—growing up in Chicago, going to school at
Georgetown, her love of medicine, her love of studying,
of acquiring knowledge. Academic work was like a
drug during those first two years, and her life was
tied to her books and to nothing else. Alix Kendall
was a free agent living in a garret apartment on N
Street near the Georgetown campus. Her life looked
like it would run a straight and true course . . . until
she met Richard Hailey.

Alix spared Jack no details of her life with Richard.
She lingered on the sexuality of their relationship
without feeling embarrassed, without feeling that Jack
might be jealous of a man who'd once been so important to her. She dug deeply into her past, deeply into
the dark recesses of her heart and mind, and dragged
forth everything she remembered about those days
with Richard.

"You must think I'm crazy," she interrupted herself
at one point, "giving you all these sordid details of my
life, but you also must believe me when I tell you it's
very important to me. You must know why I ran away
from Washington and why I returned. And most
important, you must understand what holds me here
now. As a prisoner. Perhaps you'll be able to help me
break the spell, drive out the demons of the past."

She recounted Richard's death without shedding one
tear. What was the point? Her loss was so old, so
familiar, that it would be like breaking into a sob at
seeing her own face in a mirror. The sadness was
gone, but the anger was still there, the injustice that
he'd been taken from her right when their happiness
together seemed assured. As she talked, Alix dug her
fingernails into her palms, not to quell the pain, but
to increase it. She wanted—needed—the anger, the
pain, the hurt, for they were the fuel with which she
would start the fire of her revenge.

In the end, Alix told Jack everything, including

bedding Fitzroy while he was away. She pronounced him, Herbert Windom, the secret head of the Lafayette Institute and probable founder of the entire TRAUMA project. As Preston March's superior he was also linked to the disappearance of Sarah Williams and the others. She told Jack she'd met the "Philip Greenspans," then told him exactly who they were and how they were "created." And lastly she told him she wouldn't rest until she stopped them all.

"They took Richard from me and turned him into some kind of a monster," she finally sobbed when she was finished. "Jack, I was holding my dead fiancé in my arms again, knowing that for ten years I'd missed out on every imaginable happiness because he was being . . . reprocessed or whatever they'd done to him. Jesus, it's not fair."

Jack took her in his arms and cradled her while she cried. "You're going to be okay. Do you believe that?"

"No," she sobbed. "I don't believe anything anymore."

"Hey, that's no attitude to take. You've been through a few shocks, that's all."

Alix pulled back and looked at him. *A few shocks?* Her whole life had come unhinged. "I don't think you believe what I've just told you."

"But I do," he insisted.

"Then why aren't you surprised? Why aren't you yelling or something? After all, you are the one who was suspicious of the Lafayette Institute in the first place."

He shrugged. "Maybe it was being in the jungle down in South America. Maybe it was dealing with a real crisis."

Now Alix's anger flared. "And you think this isn't a 'real' crisis? You think I'm just a hysterical woman, don't you?"

"I think you need another drink." He took her glass and got up.

Alix didn't like the way things were going. Jack was too cool, too accepting of her story. The Jack Campbell who had gone off to South America would have been calling out the army by now. But the Jack Campbell who'd returned from South America was so

. . . so passive. Alix watched him pour the two white wines, and once again her uneasiness came back. Something was wrong here. Something was dreadfully wrong.

"Did you really miss me?" Alix asked, turning the conversation around one hundred and eighty degrees.

"More than I could tell you," he said, sitting beside her.

She snuggled up next to him and asked dreamily, "Remember what you said to me the morning you left?"

He paused for a moment. "Sure I remember. I remember everything about that day—the cold, the snow, you standing on the street as the car pulled away."

His description of the scene relieved her anxiety, but not fully. Alix decided right then to keep her eyes open tonight and not let her heart carry her away.

They ate a candlelight dinner that was only a detour before making love. Dinner was unceremonious, quiet; each of them was absorbed in his own thoughts, but now and again their eyes met for a moment and Jack's sexual anticipation became more and more obvious. Even in the dim light Alix saw the line of tenseness that ran along his jawline. She suspected that if he had his way, he would leap across the table at her and take her right there on the floor.

Alix had to admit to herself that Jack had never looked better. She'd never considered him overweight, but without the pounds he'd lost—ten?—he looked trim and hard, and she guessed this new musuclar definition was the product of the hardships of the South American trip. He'd left Washington a man on the edge of comfortable middle age and had returned rejuvenated, at least outwardly. But there was something else about him, something jarring about his whole demeanor that Alix couldn't quite put her finger on. This feeling wasn't enough to disrupt her meal, but it was enough to put her on her guard.

Coffee and brandy after dinner by the fireplace did nothing to alleviate that unsettling feeling, particularly when Jack seemed unable to keep his hands off her even for a minute. Shortly after leaving the dinner table, he had her blouse open to expose her full, soft breasts to his anxious mouth and hands. Yet, despite the pleasure Alix felt, she was more wary than ever. Jack's caresses made her feel more like an object than a person, a stranger more than a lover. Not for one moment was Jack affectionate with her; that was something new and totally undesirable. One of the things about him that had first attracted her was his almost adolescent hand-holding, his tentative approach to sex. Even when they'd become accustomed to each other in bed, Jack always seemed uneasy when it came to being aggressive physically. He actually seemed afraid that Alix would turn him down with a sharp "Not tonight, honey, I've got a headache." But tonight was all different. And that made the sex between them all wrong.

Finally Jack had half-undressed both of them on the living-room floor, and Alix had had enough. When she suggested they repair to the bedroom, he readily agreed. As Jack led the way upstairs, Alix noted how slowly he mounted each step, how they seemed to be two feet away from each other instead of eight inches. Alix watched him, amazed at the apparent strain of the journey. He's walking like an old man, she thought as she trailed along behind him.

Walking like an old man! That was the discrepancy between how he looked and how he acted! That was exactly the description that fit Jack Campbell tonight. Everything he did, every motion he made, proclaimed him twice as old as he appeared. How ironic, how terrible to see this healthy, strapping, tanned man climbing the stairs with his left hand tightly gripped on the banister for support. Alix's mind skittered backward through the entire evening, and it all followed the same pattern.

Jack stopped at the head of the stairs and looked back at Alix. "Anything wrong?"

She looked up at him, only then realizing that she'd stopped dead in her tracks at the bottom of the stairs. Yes, there's something wrong, she thought. You're not Jack Campbell!

"Alix?" Jack took two steps back down toward her. "What is it?"

"Nothing, really. I just felt a little queasy . . . all the excitement, I guess." She couldn't go upstairs with him, couldn't go to bed with a stranger while pretending she didn't know that Jack—*her* Jack—was dead.

"I've got something that will settle your stomach," Jack said with a leer. "Come on." He took her by the hand and pulled her upward.

"I don't think—"

"Don't think!" Jack commanded, his grip on her tightening. "You always think too much for your own good. Now, come on." Despite the aura of age, this Jack was strong, and Alix was powerless to stop him.

Minutes later she and Jack were in bed, naked. He held her roughly, pulled her closer still, and whispered a string of obscenities into her ear just before biting her so hard she moaned with pain. His voice was low and insinuating, his breathing labored, his touch despicable. Alix wanted to pull away from him, to get dressed and leave without explanation. But somewhere deep inside she knew that he would never allow that.

"Something wrong?" he asked moments later as she shrank from another painful bite on the neck.

"Nothing," she lied. "It's just been so long."

"Too long. Much, much too long," he agreed as he kissed his way down her breasts.

Alix decided that unless she pretended to be enjoying herself, this man would suspect something was wrong. So she focused her mind on the love bites to her nipple, concentrating on the sensation only, not on the person giving them. Still her mind drifted. She pictured Richard instead. And then Richard became Alan. And finally Alan became Jack Campbell, the man she had once begun to love, whose physical body was bent over hers in the soft shadows of the night. He nibbled and bit her and moaned, and she moaned in return. Her arms flailed out in pain toward his recumbent form, and she grabbed his bobbing head, entwining her fingers in his hair.

And then she felt it!

Her body stiffened like a corpse finally in the grips of rigor mortis. Jack paused to look up at her. "Did I hurt you?"

"No. It just felt so good," Alix said weakly. She attempted a little laugh, wondering if he too heard its hollowness as clearly as she did. When Jack returned to his former position, she felt safe, momentarily.

Alix peered into the darkness, her hands poised just above his head, about to touch it, about to find out if the horror of the TRAUMA project had finally eclipsed everything in her life . . . future as well as past. She lowered her hands, then stopped. She couldn't do it! She had to be wrong. Oh, dear God, please let me be wrong! she thought as she allowed her fingers to descend.

"Love me more," she groaned, pulling his head closer, slipping her fingers into his hair. "Please, more, Jack, please," she said, using her apparent sexual voraciousness as a cover for her real intent.

Jack obliged and Alix dug her fingers into his hair. The suture line on Jack's skull was much finer than the one on Alan Fitzroy's. But then, ten years had elapsed between these operations, and the Lafayette TRAUMA team had obviously perfected its procedures.

So Alix had been right all along. Jack Campbell was dead. Not killed in South America by a stray bullet, but murdered twenty minutes away from here in Langley, Virginia. His newspaper reports were all written by someone else in the field and were then filed under his name. Chances were, even Flanagan at *The District Columbian* didn't know he'd sent his friend to his death. But none of that mattered now. That was all detail work, blanks to be filled in someday in the future. All that Alix needed to know was that Jack Campbell was gone. Dead. Only his body remained, and the question: Who was the man she was having sex with?

"Jack," driven by his own lust, suddenly changed positions and again entered Alix with one long, hard thrust. She moaned in existential pain, which he mistook for pleasure, then threw her arms over his back, not to pull him deeper, but to keep her self from clawing her way through his face to get at his brain. She closed her eyes and turned her head to one side so he couldn't kiss her lips anymore. But "Jack Campbell" was far beyond kissing. He enveloped her, surrounded her with his arms and legs, pinioned her in the middle, thrusting into her with increasing urgency.

To Alix each stroke felt like a knife blow. She felt herself falling out of control emotionally, falling into a darkness edged with so sharp a fear that it was like razors flaying her soul. And some deep instinctive part of her knew that unless she fought the fear, she ultimately would be lost. She had to concentrate on something other than his sweaty body; it was her only hope of escape. It was the only way she could keep from revealing that she'd guessed this man really wasn't Jack Campbell.

Alix's mind spiraled back over the past weeks, over Jack's departure and her own sadness at seeing him leave. She remembered the emptiness she'd felt after he left, remembered how she'd tried to reinvolve herself with work and then how she'd failed. She remembered Alan Fitzroy and Preston's funeral and the Greenspans at the cocktail party. And most of all she remembered the names she'd found in the newspaper files—four people with eight names. Four young men and women who had died so four more important old men and women might live. *More important!* What made them more important? By whose standards were they chosen?

But the pattern had been set: an old person dies, a young person dies. One person with two identities. The old and the new. Know the time of death for the old person and you can calculate the time of death and rebirth for the new. Jack was taken from her five weeks ago. Five weeks. Five weeks. Alix's mind wanted to stop. She'd already gone far enough, so far in fact that her brain recognized that it was perilously close to being overloaded. But Alix couldn't stop herself from unraveling this last bit of information.

And then she knew.

"Jack" shuddered with an agony of released pleasure, then fell on Alix with his full weight. She tried to

push him off to one side, anything, but she was trapped.
Minutes later he finally lifted himself off and looked
her straight in the eyes. "You're so beautiful, Alix.
I've always thought so," he said softly as he kissed her
mouth.

Alix closed her eyes and quietly began to plan what
she'd do next. She'd told everything she knew, including the fact that she was a traitor to the Lafayette
and to TRAUMA. She was a marked woman now, and
that meant her time alive was limited. She'd have to
act fast or be killed, and then this horror would go on
undiscovered. There was no doubt in her mind anymore what course she had to take. She wanted revenge.
She wanted blood on her hands. She wanted the smell
of it, the slick feel of it between her palms as she
rubbed them together while savoring her triumph.
For ten years Alix had lived in a cage *they* had forged
for her. And now it was time to escape, killing her
captors as she did.

And the greatest humiliation had just occurred. It
had become clear, the moment she looked deeply into
this man's eyes moments before, who he was. The eyes
might have been Jack Campbell's, but the intelligence
behind them that flickered through like a candle at
the entrance to hell could belong to only one man:
Preston March!

—11—

For the next two days Alix trembled whenever anyone
spoke to her. Her fear had combined with her anger to
produce a rage so intense that at times she feared it
would overwhelm her. Every shadow in the street
became a threat, every stranger in Georgetown became a potential enemy, every moment spent at the

Lafayette became part of an uncommutable death
sentence. The whole TRAUMA project had come full
circle. She'd lost Richard ten years before to its first
run, and she'd lost Jack to its latest. This stampeding
merry-go-round had to be stopped before it went any
further.

After she left "Jack" that night, Alix took a long hot
bath, submerging herself in acres of bubble bath and
refilling the tub each time the suds began to dwindle.
After that she'd finished her ablutions with a hot
shower, vigorously scrubbing her body in an attempt
to eradicate March's touch. And when she felt a little
cleaner, she went to bed and began thinking of ways
to stop them.

But what *could* she do? How could one person expect to overthrow the machinery of a conspiracy so
complex that it rose through the ranks all the way to
the front door of 1600 Pennsylvania Avenue? The idea
was preposterous. But then Alix remembered the vast
number of scientific miracles that had once been considered preposterous—brain transplants among them.
She had to start believing in herself right now. If she
took the attitude that she was going to fail, she would
fail. But taking the attitude that she would succeed,
though it might not absolutely guarantee success, would
certainly guarantee partial success, and right now
that was about all she could hope for. If Alix could
destroy just one part of the TRAUMA project, she would
feel vindicated.

For the next days Alix kept pretty much to herself.
"Jack" called several times; she talked with him but,
claiming a cold, put off getting together with him. He
said he understood, but there was a coldness to his
voice that worried Alix. She'd told him so much that
night together—too much, really—and she wondered
when he would spring the trap to ensnare her further.
Knowing Preston as she did, she figured he would give
her one last chance to come over to their side before
doing away with her. And that, for the moment, was
her trump card.

Alan also called several times, and she readily agreed
to a date with him. She wanted to pretend that she

was actively coming over to the Lafayette's side, and talking disparagingly of "Jack" to Fitzroy should do the trick. And just to be sure she was convincing, Alix made sure she and Alan ended up in bed after having dinner. Her passionate lovemaking was to be the proof, the thing that would convince both Fitzroy and March that her infatuation with Campbell was at an end. And to further that impression, she talked of nothing but the love of her work all night.

"I really believe when Preston asked me to join the Lafayette it was the luckiest day of my life," she said as they lay in bed entwined in each other's arms. "I don't know if I ever thanked him for that."

"I'm sure he knew," Alan said lazily.

"I hope so. It's strange, but once someone's gone and you know you'll never have the opportunity to talk to him again, all sorts of things pop into your mind, things you wanted to say but forgot, or just didn't think of at the time."

"Maybe in the future that will no longer be a problem," he said after a moment's hesitation. "That's one of the fruits of your research, isn't it? Prolonging that final good-bye."

"I hadn't thought of it that way," she agreed. "Keeping someone going on and on forever . . . what a thought!" This was the closest Alan had come to revealing that he knew she'd tapped into TIM, and she wondered how far he would go with it.

"But keeping someone alive forever wouldn't be available to everyone, obviously. There are grave psychological implications to this kind of operation, you know."

"Oh?"

He nodded in the semidark. "Imagine watching all your friends growing older, then dying, while you don't. It would be very difficult emotionally."

"I can see that," she said.

"And then, of course, if a chemical treatment failed to provide the desired longevity, an operation might do it—but that in itself would have its own set of special problems."

Alix tensed. She could feel Alan's mood shift down, grow more serious. "What special problems?"

There was a long silence before he spoke again. "What if there were an operation that made it possible to transfer human intelligence from one body to another ... from an older to a younger one? Imagine going to sleep in one body and waking up in another. Imagine the shock of looking in the mirror and seeing someone else's face."

"I thought TRAUMA dealt with prolonging cell life. Why all this talk about changing bodies? It sounds like science fiction."

"It's just a logical extension of the same idea, just more sophisticated. Actually, it's my dream."

"Sounds more like a nightmare."

"Why so?"

"Just where do you intend to get new bodies into which you'd put the old intelligence?"

"There'd have to be some way to acquire them." He paused, uncertain whether to continue the thought. "Perhaps society would sacrifice some of its young men and women to keep others—more important—lives going."

"What young men and women are you talking about, Alan? Do you believe there's a group of benevolent young people who are willing to die to help future generations? Look again, my friend!"

"I suppose you're right." He sighed. "This country's spirit of self-sacrifice has been lost for good, I'm afraid. No, we'd have to use involuntary enlistment."

"But you're talking about murder," Alix gasped, not at the thought but at the coldness with which Fitzroy related it.

"Maybe I am," he said as blandly as if he were discussing the weather. "But science mustn't be judged. Science is impartial."

"But it's tainted by the intentions of those who use it—you know that. What you're preaching, Alan, is totally immoral."

"I prefer to think of it as amoral," he shot back automatically.

"That's a cop-out," she said angrily.

"Maybe if you'd had your life returned to you even as you stood on the brink of death, you wouldn't be so quick to judge," he said hotly. "You don't understand, Alix. You don't understand anything, and I'd so hoped you would."

Alix felt a rush of fear. She'd pushed him too far, had been too outspoken. She'd forgotten that he was once Herbert Windom and that his first body had died of cancer ten years before. She'd forgotten that Windom was living proof of the very thesis he espoused. She'd forgotten that he couldn't feel guilt because that would condemn himself to a second lifetime of anguish. And most important, she'd forgotten that every minute they let her live was a test—and that she'd just failed the most important part.

"Maybe you can *make* me understand, Alan." She snuggled up to him and rested her hand on his thigh. "I'm willing to listen." And desperate to stay alive just long enough to stop you and the others, she thought.

He looked at her a moment, then smiled. "Later, baby. Right now let's just concentrate on one thing at a time." He rolled over on top of her, kicked back the sheets, and began covering her with kisses.

Alix submitted readily because her part in this sexual farce was far more complex that Fitzroy would have imagined. Alan must have been briefed by March about Richard Hailey's body, and he probably thought that that made his presence much more attractive to Alix, despite the anger she'd displayed. After all, she did have Richard back—one way or another. But in this case he was wrong: he mistook Alix's hate for love, her anger for lust. He embraced her believing she wanted only to love him, when actually she wanted only to kill him.

When "Jack" wouldn't take no for an answer, Alix agreed to see him. She'd have to confront him sometime, have to begin and end her plan once and for all. She'd hoped to have a few more days, a few weeks perhaps, to arrange for all the fine details of what she had planned. But time wasn't on her side, as it hadn't been all her life. So she invited "Jack" over for drinks at her apartment the very next night. And in doing

so, she set the timetable for the end of her part in the
Lafayette Institute and all its horrors.

She then called Alan and invited him, too. When he
declined, saying he'd been given a ticket to the opera,
Alix insisted very prettily, promising a good time, and
Fitzroy agreed to stop by for a nightcap after the
performance. Now, all she had to do was gather up
her courage and begin what surely would prove to be
the longest night of her life.

The next morning Alix had the man at the service
station fill three one-gallon plastic jugs with gasoline.
He warned her that it was very dangerous carrying
gas that way and that should a spark set them off, the
three containers would be detonated like bombs. Alix
blithely said she was aware of that, then promised to
be careful. And she would. She didn't want the gasoline to explode until she was ready to have it do so.
But that was later. That night.

Alix had the service attendant put the gasoline in
the trunk of her rented car, and she then drove directly to the Lafayette's delivery entrance, where she
had the canisters unloaded and taken directly to her
lab. She warned the maintenance man to be extra
careful because he was dealing with very potent and
very lethal chemicals needed for a series of experiments.
It gave Alix a great deal of pleasure to know that the
Lafayette itself was taking an active part in its own
demise. It was poetic justice, to be sure.

Alix hid the gasoline in her lab and spent the rest of
the day trying to work. She'd planned her day on a
very tight schedule because it was important that,
once she set off the chain of events designed to destroy
this part of the TRAUMA, she knew exactly where both
"Jack Campbell" and Alan Fitzroy were. She needed
to keep them incommunicado until she finished with
them.

Half an hour before "Jack" was due to arrive, Alix
carried the gasoline containers down to the computer
room, stopping en route to disconnect the sprinkler
system for the basement of the Lafayette. Using her
own TIM card, she gained admittance to the computer

room, placed one canister of gasoline in front of each
of the two main computers against the wall, and after
opening the third container, she covered the floor with
the gasoline, backing her way down the hallway as
she did. Her nerves were on edge, her teeth were
clamped tight with fear; if one guard saw her before
she had the chance to ignite the trail of gasoline, she'd
be shot and killed ... and then the terror would
continue.

Alix poured out most of the gasoline in front of the
basement's elevator doors, then continued down the
hallway, leaving a trail that led to the stairwell far-
thest from TIM. She stopped here just as the gasoline
ran out. The entire lower floor of the Lafayette now
stank from gasoline and Alix's fear. Unconsciously
she took in a deep breath, then gagged, momentarily
feeling dizzy from the fumes. But she'd gone too far
now to faint; there was no turning back.

She checked her watch. In fifteen minutes "Jack"
would arrive at her apartment. He'd be leaving his
house in five minutes, walking as he always did. Alix
felt a sudden flash of fear. Timing was of the essence,
and the new Jack might *not* walk, he might take a
taxi and get there before she did. Alix panicked for a
moment, then relaxed. He'd wait for her, she knew.
He'd hope to get her into bed again, but for that he'd
wait forever. And even if he did take a taxi, he was
almost sure to be out of the house when the news of
the explosion broke.

When she opened the fire door into the stairwell, a
rush of cold air gushed past her, upsetting the gasoline fumes in the hallway like heat dancing over a
summer pavement. Alix quickly removed a butane
lighter from her pocket, spun its ragged wheel across
the flint, and when the flame burst forth, she touched
it to the shore of the gasoline lake at her feet. The
flames leaped upward, then forward, burning her hand,
flaring right into her face. She jumped back, releasing
the door as she did. But for a moment the heavy door
stood open, and Alix watched as a wall of flames
licked its way down the hall toward the room where

TIM lay sleeping, blissfully unaware that it—and all
the details of the TRAUMA project—were about to die.

Alix took the stairs up two at a time. She had just
reached the second landing when the explosion from
the two cans of gasoline rocked the building. The
thundering sound reverberated up the stairwell like a
cannon shot. Then there was nothing. Nothing but
Alix's labored breathing while she waited for the inevitable reaction from the security guards. Moments later
the shouts and cries of the guards as they made their
way to the elevators filled the deadly silence.

There were two sets of stairs at the Lafayette, one
near the elevators and another farther away, where
Alix stood. She'd counted on the guards taking the
other stairs to investigate the explosion, and as the
voices grew dimmer, she knew they had. Alix cautiously opened the door onto the main corridor. It was
empty. Quickly, but without panic, she escaped down
the hall to the front lobby.

Just as she reached the front door, a guard appeared,
running in the direction of the explosions. He took one
look at Alix and stopped. "What the hell is going on
here?" he challenged.

This was no time to panic. She was too close to her
final goal, too close to eliminating the most important
part of the TRAUMA project. Her burned hand throbbed
painfully, and she was terribly frightened but she had
to say something. "My hand," Alix said weakly,
proffering it. "I was doing some work downstairs
when . . ." She closed her eyes and rocked forward.

The guard immediately came to her side and put his
arms around her. "You okay?" he asked, but his attention was being drawn to the shouts from the other end
of the corridor.

"Yes," she said bravely. "But there are others who
need your help. It was awful. I don't know what
happened. I was downstairs when suddenly there was
this terrible explosion." She allowed the guard to as-
sist her to a seat near the front door. "I'll be all right,
really."

For a moment the guard looked torn between his
duty to stay with Alix and his curiosity to see what

was happening in the Lafayette's lower level. Curiosity got the better of him. "I'll be right back. If you need help, use the phone in the office." He ran down the hall and disappeared into the stairwell Alix had used for her escape.

The second he was gone, Alix left. She walked briskly along the road by the Potomac. A full moon outlined the low, ugly shape of the Lafayette against the jagged landscape of rocky cliffs and ragged trees. She looked at it one last time, then turned away. The first part of her mission was done. Now for the second, hardest part.

Alix walked quickly along M Street to Wisconsin Avenue, barely feeling the wind as it whipped against her body; it was as if the heat of the fire had been stored up in her heart. She felt she'd never be cold again, never have to worry about being left alone at the mercy of fate. She turned up Wisconsin and moved into the crowds of people who, despite the weather, thronged the street searching for a restaurant or doing some last-minute shopping. Alix was tempted to join them for a last look, because this was her farewell to Washington, the city that had meant nothing but pain to her. But she had other, more important things to do.

In the few minutes before "Jack" arrived, Alix washed her face, then cleaned the burn on her hand before bandaging it. She changed from her somber business outfit to a colorful skirt and soft, clinging angora sweater—after removing her bra so her full breasts pushed seductively against the soft material. Tonight she needed "Jack" to be distracted long enough so her plan would work.

He arrived on time, still tanned, still grinning like a kid on his first visit to a brothel. He pulled her immediately into his arms, letting his hands roam over her breasts. Alix clenched her teeth at his touch and pulled away as soon as possible. Before she even had time to make them a drink, the doorbell rang. It could only be Alan Fitzroy. But it was too early; the opera couldn't have let out this soon. Alix went to the door. Her hand was already on the doorknob when the panic struck. Alan always carried a beeper with him that told him he had an important phone call. If he'd been called away from the opera because of the explosion at the Institute, he'd know immediately who caused it and he'd know exactly where to come.

Alix's hand faltered for a moment as the bell rang again. She swallowed hard and opened the door. Alan stood there, dressed formally in black tie and dinner jacket. He broke into a wide grin. He didn't know. Alix's heart began beating once again. "I kept thinking of you during the performance and I couldn't stay away a minute longer." He strode into the entrance hall and swept her into his arms. "God, you're beautiful," he said.

"Exactly my thoughts," Jack Campbell said from inside.

Fitzroy released Alix and stepped back. "What the hell is going on?" he asked angrily. "Who *is* this?"

So the cat was out of the bag; earlier than she'd expected, but out, nevertheless. "Don't look so surprised, Alan. You two know each other."

"I don't believe we do," Campbell said, rising stiffly from the couch.

"Alan Fitzroy," Alan said, walking awkwardly across the room to shake Campbell's hand.

"Jack Campbell," he said equally as stiffly.

Alix took Alan's topcoat. "Now, how about a drink, boys?" Alan asked for his usual Scotch, Jack for a white wine. "The Jack Campbell I know detests white wine," Alix said as she sailed out into the kitchen. She was gone only two minutes, but during the entire time she heard low whispers from the two men in the living room.

"For two strangers, you seem to have a great deal to talk about," she said cheerfully as she handed them the drinks. "But then, I suppose you know why you're here." They looked blankly at her. "No? Then I'll tell you . . . but first I want to propose a toast: To the three of us . . . and to the Lafayette Institute . . . and to the TRAUMA project." She lifted her glass and sipped. The two men looked at each other cautiously, then drank, too.

In the distance, fire trucks whined and screeched through the night. As Alix listened, a bemused smile spread across her face. Surely the engines were heading for the Institute right now. She wondered how much real damage she'd inflicted on TIM. It hardly mattered, for the fire was nothing more than a gesture, really, a warning that *someone* was on to TRAUMA.

"What's all this about a trauma?" Jack asked.

"Yeah, what the hell are you talking about?" Alan also asked from his chair.

Alix shook her head and took a seat opposite the men. "Both of you must really take me for a fool. You've been dangling bits of information, crumbs, insinuations in front of me for months. Did you think I hadn't noticed? Or did you think that what you wanted me to know was *all* that I knew?" Now both men looked extremely interested. "Jack knows exactly how much I know about TRAUMA, so you must too, Alan." She sipped her drink thoughtfully. This was turning out to be more fun than she'd expected. Macabre fun— but fun, still.

"Why do you insist that I know Campbell?" Alan asked in all innocence.

"Because you and Jack are one of a kind. You are the wave of the future, the never-dead, the immortal, the products of TRAUMA." Her anger flared and she flushed.

"So you do know," Alan marveled.

"I know everything," she agreed.

"When did you find out about him?" Alan turned toward Campbell, who now was looking sheepishly down at his feet.

"The same night we went to bed," she admitted softly. "In exactly the same way I found out about you—I ran my fingers through his hair."

Fitzroy glared at Campbell. "Jesus, Preston, I warned you. I told you not to touch her. The plan was to have the 'new' Campbell cool off and leave town. She wasn't supposed to know anything." Alan talked as if Alix weren't there. "Leaving town" meant that he'd go into the hospital for a series of minor plastic-surgery operations that would change his appearance enough to keep his true identity a secret when he resumed his duties as head of the Lafayette.

"I tried to stay away from her, but I couldn't," March admitted slowly.

"You blew it, Preston. All because of her, you blew it," Fitzroy spat out. "Now we're going to have to change our plans."

"You'll have to change your plans, all right," Alix said, "but I guarantee they'll be different from what you expected. It's so ironic to see you both here, you know that. The two men in my life who meant something to me are now only shells, housing for someone else." She shook her head sadly. "I left Washington promising never to come back because you, Richard, had died." She stared directly into Fitzroy's eyes. "And until Preston offered me the job, I kept that promise; until I saw you on the Georgetown street. Imagine how I felt, Richard, after ten years."

"Alix, please," Fitzroy said with a real touch of sadness in his voice. "We had no idea."

"Of course you didn't. Just like you had no idea that I was involved with Jack Campbell. Either way, it makes no difference. Science is amoral, Alan, remember? And therefore people's feelings don't count, do they?" She went to her desk, opened the drawer, and removed the .38-caliber pistol the real Campbell had given her. She returned to her chair, gun in hand.

"Do you really think you're going to shoot us?" Campbell asked incredulously.

"I *know* I'm going to shoot you," Alix rejoindered.

"I doubt that." Fitzroy shook his head.

"You can't stop me," she said confidently. "Try."

Both men simultaneously attempted to pull themselves up from their chairs ... and were unable to stand. They tried again, but their muscles had gone slack. Automatically they both looked at their drinks and knew the truth: Alix had drugged them.

"You've killed the only men I ever loved in my life—one ten years ago, the other ... What were you going to tell people about Jack Campbell? He'd be missed, you know."

"He got lost in South America. After a while there

would have been a report of his death. It was very simple," Alan said.

"Very simple," Alix repeated. She picked up the gun and released the safety.

"This won't solve anything, Alix. We're only two people. There are more of us," Alan said defiantly.

"Like poor Hawkins? How many more mistakes were there in your TRAUMA project?"

"You can't stop us," Jack repeated. "Trying is like trying to pick up quicksilver between your fingers."

Alix ignored him completely. It was getting late, and she had to pack and attend to four more executions before leaving Washington for the last time. "How ironic; here I am with the two men who at one time meant most to me . . . and now . . ." She raised her gun and aimed it first at Alan Fitzroy. "I lost you once, Richard. Now I'm about to lose you again."

She pulled the trigger. There was a flash of light and a *bang* that shook the room. The space between Fitzroy's eyes caved in and a fountain of blood poured out. His head snapped back and he fell sideways in the chair.

March looked at him, then at Alix, terror in his eyes. "Don't," he pleaded. "Our work is too important."

"Your work is finished." She pulled the trigger a second time, but March feinted to the right. The bullet blew his left ear off. He reached up in pain and covered the bloody stump with his hands. His eyes were wild with fear. Alix pumped the third bullet into his stomach, and when he bent over to clutch at it, she sent a fourth bullet through the top of his skull.

Because Alix knew that the occupants of the other two apartments in the building were out of town, she took her time cleaning up. She showered, then had something to eat, and finally went to bed. She lay in the dark for a long time. The two dead men in the living room didn't bother her at all. She'd been living with dead men all her life, it seemed. What were two more?

Alix set her clock, then slept two hours before getting up. She left the apartment with her suitcase without bothering to take a final look at the dead men. Once in her rented car she rechecked the addresses of the Philip Greenspans and the Harry Taylors—the former Jack Finlay and Linda Strong. She put the gun in her purse and started the car. The night was far from over. There would be more blood and pain, more hate and revenge. And sadness. And when it was over, Alix knew there'd be a void in her life that could never be filled. But that was the price she'd have to pay for keeping her soul. She started the car and drove slowly off into the cold early morning.

—EPILOGUE—

The Palm Springs sun burned down on the desert with a fury. Everything glistened and shimmered in slick waves of heat that rose from the sand, the pavement, even the dirt of gardens kept moist by hundreds of underground sprinklers. At seven A.M. it was nearly ninety. By noon it would be well over one hundred.

Janet Pullman made her way along the cool corridor of the convalescent home to the nurses' station. Her rubber-soled feet made no noise as she walked, and an old woman near the station, seeing Janet through a partially open door, confused her with the Blessed Virgin Mary and silently prayed that the agony of her prolonged life might soon be ended.

Janet was cool and efficient, the perfect hospital administrator. She greeted the nurses with restrained politeness. Everyone liked Janet, but they all agreed behind her back that there was something a little *too* reserved about her. She seemed to have wound her emotions very tightly, as if to keep them under control at all times. Still, she was charming and very beautiful—the nurses also didn't understand why she never dated, or at least never talked about it.

After giving Janet the morning report, the night nurses left and Janet sent a subordinate to the cafeteria for fresh coffee. Out in the hallway, breakfasts were being served from tall chromium carts, and there was a lull now between night and morning. Janet dispatched the nurses' aides to the patients who needed to be fed, and for a moment she was left alone.

Someone had tucked a copy of yesterday's newspaper under a chart, and after putting the chart away, Janet strolled into the treatment room and casually flipped through its pages. She'd given up reading newspapers months before, right after she arrived in Palm Springs from the East. There was nothing new Janet needed to know about people, nothing she hadn't already learned from the old people in her charge and their children who did—and didn't—visit.

Janet was about to throw the paper out when a small item on the back page caught her eyes:

MYSTERIOUS EXPLOSION DESTROYS FACILITY

The Lafayette Institute Annex in Langley, Virginia, was torn apart late this morning by a series of explosions of unknown cause that destroyed the facility completely.

The explosion marks the end of a series of tragedies surrounding the Lafayette. Six months ago the Institute's head, Dr. Preston March, died, and several weeks later, one of the members of its board, Mr. Alan Fitzroy, the noted founder of the Roth Corporation, was found murdered along with Jack Campbell, a newspaper reporter on *The District Columbian*. Both were found in the apartment of Dr. Alixandra Kendall. The police, who have been unable to locate Dr. Kendall for questioning, suspect a love triangle.

A government-official spokesman said there are no plans at present to rebuild the Annex, and he further stated that the main building in Washington, which was closed after a recent fire, also will not be reopened.

Janet reread the article twice before crumpling up the newspaper and throwing it away. What did she care about the Lafayette Institute? Those days were over. Someone in government had gotten her message loud and clear. There was nothing more to do, nothing more to say. The past was truly dead and buried now.

She left the treatment room just as her assistant returned with a cup of steaming hot coffee. Janet gratefully took it and drank its warmth. She liked being here at this hospital in the desert. Like so many other facilities around the country, they were short-staffed and hadn't bothered to check the references that proclaimed her a professional administrator. She'd taken a job as assistant and, five months later, when her boss quit, Janet was promoted. The first thing she did in her new job was to check everyone else's references and begin to get the hospital in shape, because the patients deserved it.

Janet liked working with old people. They didn't fight beyond a certain point to hang on to life. They accepted death as the inevitable end, and most of them, while they could, valued their lives—and the lives of others.

If only Preston March and Alan Fitzroy had felt the same way, Janet thought as she walked into the room to greet her favorite patient. If only they hadn't believed they deserved to live and others deserved to die.

Medical Thrillers from SIGNET

Buy them at your local
bookstore or use coupon
on next page for ordering.

∅

SIGNET Titles by Stephen King You'll Want to Read

Great Reading from SIGNET

Buy them at your local

bookstore or use coupon

on next page for ordering.

The Best in Fiction from SIGNET